The Lake

The Lake

JØRN LIER HORST

Translated by Anne Bruce

MICHAEL JOSEPH

MICHAEL JOSEPH

UK | USA | Canada | Ireland | Australia
India | New Zealand | South Africa

Michael Joseph is part of the Penguin Random House group of companies
whose addresses can be found at global.penguinrandomhouse.com

Penguin Random House UK,
One Embassy Gardens, 8 Viaduct Gardens, London SW11 7BW

penguin.co.uk

Penguin
Random House
UK

Published in Great Britain by Penguin Michael Joseph 2025
First published in Norway by Bonnier Norsk Forlag as *Tørt land* 2024
001

Copyright © Jørn Lier Horst, 2025
English translation copyright © Anne Bruce, 2025

The moral right of the author has been asserted

Set in 13.5/16pt Garamond MT
Typeset by Falcon Oast Graphic Art Ltd
Printed and bound in Great Britain by Clays Ltd, Elcograf S.p.A.

The authorized representative in the EEA is Penguin Random House Ireland,
Morrison Chambers, 32 Nassau Street, Dublin D02 YH68

A CIP catalogue record for this book is available from the British Library

HARDBACK ISBN: 978-0-241-53385-7
TRADE PAPERBACK ISBN: 978-0-241-53386-4

Penguin Random House is committed to a sustainable
future for our business, our readers and our planet. This book is
made from Forest Stewardship Council® certified paper.

MIX
Paper | Supporting
responsible forestry
FSC
www.fsc.org   FSC® C018179

The Lake

I

The water level had dropped by more than a metre since he had last been here and an old rowing boat had surfaced. It lay on its side, the hull peppered with holes, partially submerged in silt, the stern trapped in the murky lake.

Evert Harting perched on the car tailgate, pulling on his boots. The air was still. He straightened the brim of his baseball cap and sat looking out over Lake Farris. The surface was almost flat, undisturbed by ripples. The reflection of the sun's rays was so strong that he had to avert his eyes.

Along the shore, the retreating water had left a broad, colourless strip, a smooth and placid stretch of dry land.

Fastening his utility belt, he lifted the metal detector from the car boot and swept it across the rear wheel to test it out. A high-pitched beep sounded when the sensing probe closed in on the metal rim, letting him know that the onscreen signals were working exactly as they should.

A long-billed bird took flight as he strode towards the search area. The dried-up clay lake-bed had split open, and a network of cracks now zigzagged across the entire expanse of foreshore. Here and there, rocks and stones protruded from the surface, dotted in some places with clumps of dried, withered rushes.

The thin crust of earth broke, flaking off under his feet.

Once he had located the boulder where he had last stopped, he began his methodical work. The footprints from his previous visit were still visible. He walked parallel to these as far as the cliff edge, where he turned around and retraced his steps. In the background, he could hear the distant hum of traffic crossing the motorway bridge to the south.

The detector registered a find – the high-frequency tone told him something made of light metal was buried in the ground. He had some idea of what it would be and used his foot to scrape back the earth, uncovering an empty beer can. The whipped-up dust irritated the back of his throat. Walking on a little, he adjusted the sensitivity and continued his search.

What he was hoping to find was some trace of the ancient Fresjeborgen, a fortress said to have been situated somewhere here along the shoreline, destroyed by a flood at some point in the seventeenth century. It had apparently been endowed with both maidens' bowers and iron spires, but he would be happy to find as little as an old hand-forged nail.

He took a few mouthfuls from the water bottle attached to his belt before trudging on.

Several broken planks of wood, stained with deep-rooted green algae and partly rotted, criss-crossed the parched lake-bed.

He swung the sensing probe over them but heard no beep in response.

Beside the rock face that bounded the search area, he saw some sunken driftwood. He manoeuvred the probe in between a grey timber post and a gnarled tree root. There was an immediate beep, an oscillating tone, and the onscreen signal indicated copper or some similar low-conducting metal.

Laying down the detector, he moved the root aside. A fishing lure, coated in verdigris, was caught in one of the twisted tree roots.

He was equally excited each time the detector produced a strong signal, but mostly it turned out to be nothing but junk.

Once he had found a Danish silver coin from 1642, from the reign of Christian IV, lying at the edge of a field beside a ravine in Stokke. Another time he had come across a silver finger bowl that had been dated to the late 1800s.

He left the lure hanging there and walked back alongside his footprints, making sure to swing the sensing probe in such a way that it overlapped his previous route. The sun was burning his neck, and perspiration made the back of his shirt feel sticky.

With each lap he came closer to the lake. He reckoned he had three lengths left when he heard another beep from the sensor. The indicator pointed to gold.

Evert Harting felt his pulse race. He turned the sensing probe round in circles to home in on his find. The fluctuating signal was unmistakable. According to the onscreen information, the object was located relatively deep, between twenty and thirty centimetres beneath the surface.

He could hear the loudest beep above a narrow crack in the dry lake-bed. Marking the spot with the edge of the probe, he laid aside the detector and pushed his cap back, wiping sweat from his brow with his shirtsleeve.

He unhooked the trowel he kept tucked into his belt before kneeling and digging up a couple of scoops and then starting to filter the crumbly earth, filled with small pebbles and plant residues, through his fingers.

He knew he would have to delve deeper and continued to work his way painstakingly downwards. Eventually the clay grew damp and lumpy and at this stage he laid the trowel aside and took out his pinpointer. It beeped and vibrated in the palm of his hand when he moved it towards the base of the hole. Whatever he'd found seemed to be buried at the far edge of the pit he had excavated.

Drops of perspiration stung his eyes. Blinking them away, he grabbed a fistful of earth and crumbled it in his hand. Nothing there. He tried again and this time felt his fingers snag on something. When he raised his hand, he brought with it an object that looked like thread. A gold chain.

Coiling it in his palm, he flipped it over into his other hand and then back again to remove the grains of earth.

A delicate necklace, maybe forty centimetres in length. A pendant dangled from the middle of the chain. The letter A. The link closest to the catch was damaged, as if the chain had snapped.

A cool breeze stirred up dust as Evert Harting clenched his fist around the gold chain and got to his feet. He spotted a kayaker making his way across the lake. On the opposite side, the sun reflected off moving vehicles and he thought he could make out figures below the steep mountainside facing the lake.

He stood there for a long time, impassively watching, before swallowing hard and gazing down at his hand again. He carefully uncurled his fingers.

He had only seen a necklace like this once before, in newspaper photographs – and that must have been a few years ago now.

At the top of the A, a tiny hole had been drilled to attach it to the chain. The same process had been followed again on the right, at the base of the letter, allowing it to hang at a slight angle on the wearer's neck.

With his thumb, he rubbed the letter clean and used his nail to pick off some soil from the link where it was attached to the chain. Then he tucked the necklace into his breast pocket and tamped down the earth with his foot, back into the hole he had dug.

2

Following the directions he'd been given over the phone, Wisting found the right turn-off. Dense growth of deciduous trees lined both sides of the road, with sunlight slanting through the branches and casting dappled shadow on the rough gravel track ahead.

He did not have to drive far before he spotted the others. The vehicles were parked in a wide semicircle in a clearing beside Lake Farris.

Clouds of dust whirled around his car as he braked and drew to a halt. Nils Hammer stood at the verge alongside two young, uniformed officers.

Wisting pushed the car door open and stepped out. The overheated engine was making a ticking noise at his back.

Hammer drank deeply from a bottle of water. 'I thought you'd want to see it for yourself before any action was taken,' he said.

The police officers moved aside and Wisting walked forward to the low wooden fence to look over the edge. A third officer stood five metres below them on the shore. Everything previously hidden by the water was now exposed and clearly visible. He caught sight of an old fridge, a cooker, a lawnmower, several coils of rusty barbed wire, old roof tiles, an assortment of unidentifiable pieces of scrap metal and, the focus of their attention, a motorbike.

'You were the one who registered the missing vehicle,' Hammer said. 'LU 4813. Yamaha DT, 100 cc.'

He could make out footprints on the dry sludge of the lake-bed, surrounding the heap of junk. Someone had gone right up to the motorbike and wiped the number plate, but apart from that, everything appeared to have been left undisturbed.

Wisting turned around and gazed back along the track he had left behind him. The motorbike was about six metres from shore. Its speed must have been so excessive that the rider had been unable to clear the bend.

'The landowner built the fence seven years ago,' Hammer explained, 'to prevent people from dumping rubbish here. He was the one who reported it.'

The sun glinted on the chrome-plated exhaust pipe.

'Locals call this place the Yeller,' Hammer went on. 'The folk who lived nearby stood here and shouted for the ferry whenever they wanted to travel up to Siljan or down into town.'

He pointed at the remains of a few mooring posts on the mountainside.

'How do I get down there?' Wisting asked.

One of the police officers pointed out the route they had taken, via a dried-up stream on the right-hand side of the small plateau. Wisting pushed branches aside as he embarked on the rugged descent, with Hammer following close on his heels.

The hillside was steep and Wisting had to catch hold of a pliable branch for the first few metres before scrabbling for footholds on the final stretch.

The officer who had already scrambled down came forward to greet them. He was one of the young temporary recruits employed during the summer months.

'There's a safe here too,' he said, pointing to it.

Wisting lifted his hand to shade his eyes from the blinding

sunlight. Half-buried in the heap of debris, he could make out a grey steel safe, partly concealed by twigs hooked on to the coils of barbed wire. A dented car bumper protruded halfway up beside it, as well as other discarded car parts and something that looked like an electric heater.

'Well spotted,' Wisting said, taking note of the raw recruit's response to the compliment.

'Must have been stolen and dumped here after being ransacked,' he said.

Wisting agreed. 'We'll take a look at it later.'

They navigated their way towards the motorbike. The grey clay of the lake-bed, baked hard by the sun, crunched under their feet.

All of a sudden, Wisting's feet broke through the brittle crust of earth and he sank up to mid-calf. He was forced to use a rusty washing machine for support. Water trickled in and filled the hole as he pulled his feet out, but he managed to avoid getting soaked.

The motorbike, and still-seated rider, lay on its side with the front wheel completely buried. A black leather jacket partially covered the fuel tank and handlebars. A pair of disintegrating blue denim jeans and a collection of grey bones poked out of a boot.

Wisting skirted round before taking up position in front of the motorbike. The rider's helmet had fallen half a metre away with the visor down, and he could see pale vertebrae spilling from the neck opening.

'It's almost eight years to the day since he disappeared,' Hammer commented.

Wisting nodded as he spoke the name to himself. *Morten Wendel.* Sixteen years old. His life destroyed in one fatal summer.

'What are your thoughts?' Hammer asked. 'An accident, or did he do this deliberately?'

'I don't know,' Wisting answered. 'Everything about the case points to the latter.'

Taking a few steps towards the motorbike, he crouched down and moved the left sleeve of the stiff leather jacket to one side. On the handlebar grips, fragments of bone were entangled in what looked like the remains of black rubber gloves.

Hammer gave a loud sigh and swore under his breath.

'What is it?' asked the young officer beside him.

'Tape,' was Hammer's terse reply.

The young officer still didn't understand.

'He'd taped his hand to the handlebar to make sure he couldn't change his mind,' Hammer explained. 'When he started to ride out, there was no way back. He had to stay with the bike all the way to the bottom of the lake.'

The young officer looked queasy at the idea.

'I've alerted the forensics team,' Hammer said. 'They're on their way.'

Standing up again, Wisting turned aside and stared out across the water. A kayak was approaching from the southern shore of the lake, the kayaker propelling himself forward with precise movements and rhythmic strokes of the oars.

It was 13:48 exactly, on Monday 13 July, scarcely halfway through summer.

3

Evert Harting caught sight of the two empty plastic containers when he opened the car boot and took out the metal detector. Damn, he should have filled them while he was on the road, but it had slipped his mind entirely.

He left them where they were. They had enough water to last until tomorrow. This was the first time the well had gone dry and the pipes were making only a hollow sound. At first, he'd thought the electric pump had let them down, but he was relieved to avoid the cost of repairing that when he realized the well had quite simply dried up.

Ella was sitting in the shade on the covered verandah with one of her crosswords.

'I forgot the water,' he said before she had time to ask. 'I'll get some if I go out again.'

'Were you thinking of going out again?' she asked.

'I can always do it tomorrow,' he said.

She smiled at him. 'That's fine,' she said. 'Did you find anything?'

Evert Harting shook his head. He had stowed the gold chain in the car's glove compartment. 'Nothing but junk,' he said. He placed the detector under the bench and plugged in the charger cable.

'The pork chops have to be barbecued today,' Ella told him. 'They've been in the fridge since Thursday.'

'Are you hungry?'

'No, not yet.'

'I can grill them later.'

Glancing at his watch, he checked the thermometer on the shady side of the verandah pillar. Half past two and twenty-seven degrees Celsius.

'There's some cold squash in the fridge,' Ella said.

With a nod, Evert Harting went inside and filled a tumbler. Beads of condensation formed on the glass as he poured. When he brought it outside, he noticed that Ella's glass was empty.

'In the house, eight letters,' Ella said, scratching her chin with her pen. 'Starts with I-N-T.'

Evert Harting took a mouthful of squash as he stood gazing out over the bay where roe deer came regularly in the evenings to lap up the water.

They had been married for thirty-eight years and now every day was the same, even out here at their cabin. Most things had already been said. From time to time, it struck him that crosswords were an attempt on Ella's side to initiate some conversation. Sometimes she really knew the answer but asked him anyway because the solution might prompt something she wanted to talk about.

'Inside,' he suggested, without counting the letters.

'That's not in the *house*, though,' Ella corrected him. 'I first thought of *interior*, but that doesn't fit.'

They had met at work. He was an administrator, and she had been in accounts. It was strange that crosswords were what she spent her time on after she retired, since she had worked with numbers all her life. Or maybe that was exactly why.

'Did you speak to Kjell-Tore about the toilet?' he asked.

'Yes, he'll take a look at it when he comes,' Ella replied.

They had bought the cabin beside Lake Farris following

the distribution of the estate after her parents had died, but it was still her brother who took care of the maintenance.

'It's no problem just using the outside toilet,' Ella said. 'After all, we had nothing but that before.'

Evert Harting took another mouthful of squash. Kjell-Tore had also installed the incinerating toilet unit. It was only a couple of years old and had worked well until recently, but now the burner refused to ignite.

'He was in Flensburg, on his way up,' Ella added. 'I asked him to buy some Jägermeister for you and those sausages that were so tasty. He's got the fridge in the van, of course.'

'Great.'

Kjell-Tore usually turned up in the middle of July. They spent a few days together before he and Ella borrowed his motorhome and drove north for a few days while Kjell-Tore was left alone at the cabin.

A bird with a wide wingspan flew over the treetops on the northern bank of the lake and soared out across the water. The wings flapped a couple of times before it disappeared behind the trees on the opposite side of the bay.

'*Internal*,' Evert suggested, downing the rest of the squash.

It seemed as if Ella did not know what he meant.

'In-house,' he clarified. '*Internal*.'

She looked down at the crossword, running the pen tentatively across the squares. 'That fits,' she said, a note of triumph in her voice.

This was the sort of thing he was good at. The ability to avoid getting locked into a particular mindset was something that had proved useful in his career. Always searching out alternative solutions and answers. Maybe that was one of the reasons why his thoughts had wandered far and wide when it came to the gold chain.

'I'm going to sit inside for a while,' he said.

'In this heat?'

Without answering, Evert simply headed indoors to sit at the kitchen table where the laptop was kept. Ella followed him inside to fill her glass with squash from the fridge and opened a window to air the room.

He waited until he was alone before typing in two search words. *Annika* and *missing*.

The top results were from Norwegian online newspapers. Scrolling down, he selected instead an article from the Swedish *Aftonbladet*. A photograph of the missing fourteen-year-old Annika Bengt filled the right-hand side of the screen. His suspicions were immediately confirmed. She was wearing the same kind of necklace as the one he had found. The A for Annika lay on her suntanned skin, just below the hollow of her throat.

The article was almost four years old, and Annika had been missing for five days when it was published. The organized search had ended, and the police were left with no clues whatsoever.

The leader of the Swedish police investigation was pictured at Bovikstrand Campsite outside Gothenburg, where Annika had been staying with her parents when she disappeared. The picture was one of the last photos taken of her and had been used in every single report about the case, in Norwegian and Danish media outlets as well as Swedish ones. She looked a bit like the Annika in the Pippi Longstocking films, with a mop of dark hair and dark eyes that narrowed when she smiled.

There were also other photographs of her, which friends had published and that had spread even further. Several of these were from her schooldays in Vetlanda, but mostly they were of that last summer at Bovikstrand. In one of these she was buried up to her neck in sand, so that only her head was visible. That was one of the very few in which the gold chain was nowhere to be seen.

He clicked away from the images and located a more recent article, from the previous summer. The missing person case remained a mystery. Every trace ended when she left her group of friends on the beach just before midnight. A misunderstanding had led to her not being missed until the next morning. She had been supposed to spend the night in a caravan with two of her friends but had gone to her parents' van to fetch something. Her friends thought she had changed her mind and stayed there, while her parents thought she was fast asleep, safe and sound, at the opposite end of the campsite. In the article written three years later, no reservations were expressed about her disappearance being due to anything other than a criminal act.

Out on the verandah, Ella switched on the radio, choosing a station that broadcast music and traffic reports.

Evert returned to the search page and combined *Annika Bengt* with the words *gold necklace*. The only results were articles in which the chain with the letter A was mentioned in descriptions of her, nothing about where the piece of jewellery had been bought or where it came from.

The initial necklace was what they called it. There were various types to be had. The one he had found was what seemed to be styled *a chain with side-hanging letter in yellow gold*. He found a Norwegian online store that sold an identical type of chain to the one Annika had owned. There it was described as *an asymmetrical design of personal jewellery* and cost less than he had anticipated. Just under 3,000 kroner for the chain and pendant.

Thousands of satisfied customers bragged the online store. He tried to make an estimate of how many necklaces they might be talking about. Half the Norwegian population were female. He could not envisage Ella with a necklace like that – she was too old for it. He rounded the number down to exclude both the oldest and very youngest prospective customers. And there were twenty-nine letters in the Norwegian alphabet, but not all of these were equally widespread in use. If he divided two million by twenty, he ended up with a hundred thousand potential purchasers. However, he could not imagine that more than one in a hundred had bought the very same necklace. It was a bit like walking through the streets – you would probably pass more than a hundred women before you would come across someone wearing identical clothes to any of the previous passers-by.

One in a hundred.

A thousand initial necklaces sold in Norway. Maybe double that in Sweden.

How many could have lost their chains?

The likelihood began to shrink.

Slowly, he closed the laptop lid. It was mere speculation, going nowhere. Anyway, he wasn't sure this was something he should try to pursue any further.

All of a sudden Ella was there in the room. Time had passed quickly while he had been busy in front of the laptop. Nearly two hours had gone by.

'I think there's some potato salad left, isn't there?' she said, opening the fridge door.

He rose to his feet. 'I'll go and light the barbecue,' he said, but he lingered for a moment, lost in thought.

What he should really do was throw the necklace back where it came from, into even deeper waters.

4

There was no shade down on the crazed lake-bed. Wisting
had scrambled back up to Hammer to follow the crime scene
technicians' work from above. A huddle of crows bickered
in the background.

Wisting leaned against the low wooden fence. The case of
the young man who had vanished with his motorbike had certainly crossed his mind from time to time. It had hung over
him as an unsolved mystery. He no longer spent time dwelling
on what might have happened, but it had become an enduring
blank. Nevertheless, the boy's discovery now brought him no
satisfaction. Quite the opposite, in fact, since Morten Wendel
could no longer be held accountable for what he had done.

The technicians worked methodically on the site below.
Before they started on anything else, they had taken overview photographs and measured distances. The rear wheel
of the motorbike was six metres and thirteen centimetres
from shore, on what would be a depth of around five metres
at normal water levels.

The young summer recruit who had greeted Wisting earlier
at the pile of debris was watching carefully.

'Could I ask you something?' he ventured tentatively after
they had been standing in silence for a while.

Wisting responded with a nod of the head.

'How do you actually go about becoming a detective?' he
asked.

The man by Wisting's side was somewhere in his early

twenties. He appeared to have a family background from Pakistan or somewhere near there. His hair was thick and dark and his beard neatly trimmed, making him look older than he really was.

'What's your name?' Wisting asked.

'Daniyal.'

When he held out his hand and introduced himself, Wisting shook it warmly.

'Daniyal Rana,' the young officer elaborated. Wisting recognized the name from reports he had read.

'So that's who you are,' Wisting said, nodding. 'You were out at the break-in at the warehouse in Hegdal last week, weren't you?'

'That's right. Have you made any progress on that?'

Wisting shook his head. 'Were you thinking of becoming a detective, then?' he asked.

'I think it seems an interesting prospect,' Rana admitted.

A call came in over the police radio and one of the other officers answered. The controller at HQ wanted them out on the E18 to assist a motorcycle patrol in following an unsteady vehicle that was refusing to stop. The two other officers rushed to their car, but Daniyal Rana remained behind.

'There are a number of routes leading to a job as an investigator,' Wisting said, responding to his earlier question. 'But the most important one is probably to show a keen interest.'

That was how he himself had ended up as a detective. The first few years after Police College he had spent on patrol duty but while many of his other colleagues had simply written reports about what they'd experienced at a crime scene or on an assignment, Wisting had also enjoyed following these cases up. He had made his own enquiries and provided extra information in various instances, above and beyond what was expected of him. This had been noticed and meant that the doors to the criminal investigation department had opened wide for him. Nowadays the situation was different. Formal qualifications counted for more than personal qualities.

'What do you look for when you take someone on?'

'Several things,' Wisting said. 'Wide experience as a general basis, of course, but also qualifications that are difficult to measure. Aspects such as the ability to cooperate and the skill to spot connections between different pieces of information.'

They continued to stand in silence, watching the painstaking work of the crime scene technicians. All the fragments of bone were collected in a large cardboard box, while clothing was sorted, marked and packed in paper bags.

'Did he simply disappear?' Daniyal Rana asked.

'It's a mystery, to be honest,' Hammer confirmed.

'He was supposed to have been alone at home for a few hours that evening,' Wisting explained. 'When his parents returned, he and his motorbike were gone. They assumed he'd just decided to drive around, but when he didn't turn up, they feared he'd had an accident. First of all, they phoned the emergency doctor and the hospital, then they called the police. No one knew anything.'

'Was there no trace of him at all?' the summer recruit asked.

'Nothing,' Hammer concluded, lifting the bottle of water to his mouth.

'But surely he was reported missing?' the young man continued. 'Someone must have seen him?'

Nils Hammer screwed the lid back on the bottle.

'We publicized pictures, both of him and the motorbike, but that didn't lead to anything specific,' he replied.

'What about CCTV at petrol stations and suchlike?' Daniyal Rana insisted.

'We checked everything like that,' Wisting explained. 'It yielded nothing.'

'What about neighbours, then? Did nobody see or hear him start up and drive off?'

'It seemed as if he'd sneaked out and away,' Hammer replied. 'Now we know why.'

He pointed in the direction of the discovery site where the technicians were finishing off. One of them was wiping his forehead with a rag.

'Why did he take his own life?' Rana asked.

Wisting glanced across at Hammer to see if he wanted to tell the story. Before either of them managed to say anything, however, they heard the loud approach of a heavy vehicle. A recovery truck crawled towards them along the narrow gravel track, pushing twigs and branches aside as it travelled. The driver leaned out when he reached them. A young man in a grey T-shirt with patches of dried sweat along the neckband. Wisting stepped forward and explained what kind of assistance they required. The driver jumped out and looked down at the scene on the shore before reversing to the wooden fence and taking up position.

The technicians gathered their evidence containers at the foot of the rock face and transferred them into a lifting bag. The man from the recovery truck manoeuvred the crane arm out over the edge and fired out a wire with a hook on the end down to them. In no time, it had all been hauled up.

The helmet, seemingly still with human tissue and hair inside, was dropped into a large plastic bag.

Wisting opened the package containing the leather jacket and lifted it out. When he felt the material, he realized there was something tucked into the inside pocket, so he handed it to Daniyal Rana.

'See what you can find out,' he said.

Following Wisting's example, Daniyal Rana checked the jacket pocket and took out a wallet. Stiff and brittle, the seams had frayed in a few places and the leather cracked when he unfolded it.

There were sections for banknotes and cards as well as a coin purse with a zip. In the top card pocket, he found a pink plastic driving licence. Rana fished it out and glanced at it before handing it to Wisting.

The text and image were still clearly visible. Morten Wendel, driving licence class A1.

The very same day he had obtained his licence, he had bought a light motorbike. Only three months later, he had disappeared along with the bike.

Daniyal Rana checked the rest of the wallet. It contained a plastic bankcard and a library card, both filled out in the same name. In the section for banknotes, he found a 50-kroner note folded with some papers that had crumbled away. The coin purse contained 12 kroner and a small key.

Wisting kept the driving licence while Daniyal Rana returned the wallet to the paper bag with the jacket.

'Have you been in touch with his parents recently?' Hammer asked.

'Not since last summer,' Wisting told him.

The revs on the recovery truck increased as the crane arm shot out towards the motorbike. The technicians had attached lifting straps, and it was slowly hauled out of the bed of solidified sludge. The front mudguard hung crookedly, and clumps of earth loosened and dropped off. One of the technicians had tied a rope to the rear wheel and steered it towards the recovery truck. There was a screech of scraping metal when it was laid flat on the truck bed.

'Cover it with a tarpaulin,' Wisting instructed. 'I haven't informed the next of kin yet.'

He turned to go back to his car.

'What about the safe?' Daniyal Rana asked.

Wisting retraced his footsteps to the rocky edge and peered down at the grey metal cabinet, jammed beneath barbed wire and other scrap metal with the door turned down.

'Take it with you,' he said. 'See if you can find out where it came from.'

5

The entrance was located on the shady side of the modest house. Boisterous children in the neighbouring garden were playing on a trampoline, their gleeful shrieks carrying on the still air.

Wisting pressed the doorbell but could not hear any sound from inside.

To the left of the door, three tubs were overflowing with lilac flowers. A wet patch beside them suggested they had just been watered.

No one arrived to open the door. He tried the bell again and knocked on the door a couple of times. Still no reaction. It occurred to him that the occupants might be out in the garden on the other side of the house.

The gravel crunched under his feet after he descended the steps. Before he rounded the corner of the gable wall, a small delivery truck drew to a halt out in the street. The engine rumbled and idled for a few seconds before falling silent.

Wisting turned and headed in that direction instead. Allan Broch-Hansen was now standing beside the vehicle, leafing through a sheaf of papers. He was still employed in goods transportation and the company name was printed on both his T-shirt and the side panel of the truck. The vehicle looked new, but Broch-Hansen had grown older in the time since they had last talked. Gaunt and grey-haired. Clearly startled to see Wisting, he dropped a sheet of paper when he caught sight of him.

'Anything wrong?' he asked.

Wisting shook his head. 'Nothing to worry about,' he replied.

Allan Broch-Hansen shot a glance in the direction of the house. 'Have you been speaking to Irene?' he asked.

'I tried the doorbell,' Wisting explained.

The high jinks in the neighbouring garden seemed to have developed into a squabble. Broch-Hansen bent down and picked up the paper he had dropped.

'The doorbell's disconnected.' He studied Wisting's face as he said this. 'Are you here because of Adine?'

'Partly,' Wisting answered. 'It's to do with Morten Wendel.'

Broch-Hansen blinked, and his face contorted. 'Have you found him?' he asked.

'We think so,' Wisting replied, waving his hand in the direction of the house. 'Let's do this inside, unless you'd prefer to tell Irene yourself.'

'No,' Broch-Hansen was quick to demur. 'Come on in.'

He strode ahead to the front door, his back stooped. Halfway to the house, he stopped and turned to face Wisting.

'Adine's coming home on Wednesday,' he said. 'One week's leave of absence. She's at a centre in Hurum that treats both drug dependency and psychological problems.'

'Is it going well?'

Broch-Hansen shrugged. 'It's too early to tell,' he answered.

Unlocking the door, he called out his wife's name. She appeared at the end of the hallway, looking past her husband to meet Wisting's eye.

'Everything's fine with Adine,' her husband assured her. 'They've found the Wendel lad.'

Irene Broch-Hansen touched her chest nervously. 'He's not alive, is he?' she asked.

Her husband looked at Wisting. 'He's come to tell us,' he replied, taking off his shoes.

Wisting did the same. His shoes were grey with dust from the parched lake-bed and his trousers were badly stained.

They moved into the living room, where sheer curtains fluttered in the doorway that led out to the terrace. Irene Broch-Hansen shut the patio door.

'We can sit here,' she said, settling on the settee.

Her husband sat down beside her and Wisting chose an armchair on the opposite side of the coffee table.

'He's dead,' he said. 'He has been ever since that time.'

The couple on the settee briefly exchanged looks. A photo of their daughter from her high-school days was displayed on the wall behind them. She had been seventeen that summer, in the class above Morten Wendel. They had been neighbours at that time, and both had been left alone at home for a few days while their parents were absent. Adine Broch-Hansen had been sunbathing out on the terrace when Morten Wendel had slipped through a gap in the hedge and asked her for help. The family's pet dog had started breathing oddly and he was afraid it was choking.

Adine raced with him back to his house.

'He's upstairs in my room,' he had told her, running up the staircase to the first floor.

When they came across the dog, it had seemed perfectly healthy – just glad not to be shut inside any longer. They concluded that something must have got stuck in its throat and had dislodged by itself. Later, Adine felt it must all have been pre-planned.

'Don't go,' Morten Wendel had pleaded, blocking the bedroom door. 'You're so gorgeous.'

She had laughed at him and wriggled away when he started

23

touching her. She had managed to escape from the bedroom, but at the foot of the stairs he had caught up with her. He hadn't succeeded in dragging her upstairs again but had attacked and raped her in the living room. He had held her captive for an hour, gagged and taped tightly to the furniture. She broke free when he went to the bathroom, and had darted out into the street, stark naked.

'Where did you find him?' Allan Broch-Hansen asked.

Wisting explained about the motorbike and the spot where it and the body had been found out at Lake Farris.

When Irene Broch-Hansen began to sob, Wisting appreciated it was from sheer relief.

'Sorry,' she said. 'It's been difficult, not knowing what had become of him.' She wiped her eyes with her fingers. 'Mostly for Adine, of course, who didn't know if he would come back and try it again.'

'He took his own life, then?' Allan Broch-Hansen asked.

'It all points to that,' Wisting said, nodding.

Morten Wendel had been arrested a few hours after Adine had escaped. He had his own version of what had occurred, claiming that Adine had approached him, dressed in only a bikini, and had been the one to take the initiative. Everything had been consensual. The evidence at the crime scene told a different story. After a fortnight in custody, he had nevertheless been released, partly because he was so young. Six days later, he had vanished.

Wisting looked across at Allan. 'You said Adine's coming home in two days' time?' he asked.

'On Wednesday, yes,' Allan Broch-Hansen confirmed.

'She should probably be told before that,' Wisting said. 'The discovery's bound to be a major news story.'

'Maybe she could come home a day early?' There was a

hopeful note in Irene's voice as she suggested this. 'We can't tell her about this over the phone, but if I speak to the person in charge there, we could probably pick her up tomorrow. They know what she's been through and what she's struggling with.'

'I'm driving all day tomorrow, though,' Allan said.

'That could wait till the next day, couldn't it?' Irene said. 'We were planning to go on Wednesday, after all.'

Allan Broch-Hansen nodded. 'That's what we'll do, then,' he agreed.

An uneasy silence lingered around the table. Wisting had been prepared for an angrier reaction. Irene Broch-Hansen in particular had placed all the blame for Adine's problems on the sexual assault eight years earlier. That Morten Wendel had simply disappeared and never been held to account made everything even more difficult. Prior to the rape, Adine had been a lively girl, but afterwards she had withdrawn from social contact. Suffering from anxiety and depression, there were concerns about potential suicide risk and eventually abuse of alcohol and other narcotics. Now that the perpetrator had been found dead, the situation had changed. The uncertainty was gone, and the attack would be easier to cope with.

Wisting prepared to leave. 'I can call in again once she's here,' he said. 'She's sure to have a lot of questions.'

'We'd welcome that.' It was Irene who had answered.

Wisting got to his feet, as did Allan Broch-Hansen.

'Have Reidar and Gunn Hilde been told?' he asked.

Irene frowned, as if it were unreasonable to spare a thought for Morten Wendel's parents.

'Not yet,' Wisting replied. 'I'm driving over to see them next.'

'You don't need to tell them you've been here,' Irene said.

With a brief nod of the head, Wisting allowed Allan Broch-Hansen to accompany him to the door.

6

The first time Wisting had been tasked with conveying bad news, it had affected him more than he had anticipated. It concerned a mother who had lost her son in a drowning accident. Unable to stay on her feet, she had collapsed on the floor, completely distraught. She had lain there, twisting and turning in her anguish over the loss, and there was nothing Wisting could do to ease her distress.

There was no easy way of breaking the news of a death. Words were useless, no matter how compassionately expressed. But exactly because this was a difficult assignment, it was something Wisting was never willing to delegate to others.

Gunn Hilde Wendel stood with the garden hose in her hands, watering a flower bed. Barefoot, she was wearing a skirt and camisole and had a straw hat on her head. It took a few minutes for her to realize she was no longer alone. Wisting had to walk out on to the brown, scorched grass and move right up beside her. The jet of water swung out across the dry lawn when she spotted him.

Wisting nodded and gave her a reassuring look. The water collected in a small puddle before she managed to turn off the tap.

'It's been a long time,' she said, wiping her hands on her skirt. 'I thought you'd have retired by now.'

'They changed the pension rules,' Wisting replied with a smile. 'But I've come with bad news, I'm afraid.'

'About Morten?'

'Yes.' Wisting looked around. 'Is Reidar at home too?'

Gunn Hilde pointed at the door.

'Inside,' she said, and walked on ahead of him.

The temperature indoors was pleasant. Reidar Wendel was seated at a circular coffee table, a brown mongrel dog at his feet. He put down his mobile phone and stood up when he noticed them. On the wall behind him, an air-conditioning unit purred as it lowered the room temperature.

'It's about Morten,' his wife said.

'Have you found him?'

'A few hours ago,' Wisting answered.

They stood for a minute or two, gazing at one another, before Reidar Wendel indicated they should sit down. The dog sprang up when Wisting drew out a chair. It padded off and lay down further across the floor, close to the spot where Adine Broch-Hansen had been raped.

Wisting surveyed the room again. The fixtures and fittings were more or less the same as in the crime scene photographs. The massive dining table was in the same place, where the girl who had lived next door had been taped tightly to the table-legs.

He returned to the business at hand and took out his note-book to support the timings and other essential facts.

'He was found with his motorbike at the bottom of Lake Farris,' he began, before correcting himself: 'What used to be the bottom. The water has pulled back almost five metres because of the drought.'

The couple both nodded.

'It looks as if he went awry at the bend somehow,' Wisting added. 'A track on the western side, near Vassvik, very little used. A spot called the Yeller.'

'Didn't you look there?' Gunn Hilde asked, her voice hoarse.

'I'd need to go back to the case paperwork to check, but there's nothing to suggest we did,' Wisting replied.

'Why not?'

'We searched along all the roads and in the ditches, but we would have to have used divers to find him there.'

He left a momentary pause, forming the next sentence in his head before he went on to break the news.

'It does look as if he launched himself out into the water deliberately.'

The words sounded heartless, no matter how carefully and considerately he expressed himself.

Gunn Hilde Wendel's voice was trembling. 'How can you say anything of the kind?' she asked.

'There are certain details I've seen before, in similar cases,' Wisting answered calmly. 'One hand was firmly fixed to the handlebar, as if he had made up his mind. As if he had come to a decision.'

The woman facing him swallowed hard, her eyes shining with tears. Her husband put his hand on hers, but she pulled away.

'You drove him to it,' she said. 'Accusing him of all sorts of things. Trying to put him in prison.'

The dog lifted its head but remained sprawled on the floor.

'It was that girl you should've arrested, coming out with all those false accusations,' Gunn Hilde went on. 'She was already using drugs at that time. She was mad, without a doubt. Look at her now – in and out of psychiatric care. She even tried to set fire to our house before she burned down theirs.'

Wisting had heard this spiel before and was prepared for this reaction. He had spared the parents certain aspects of the case. The crime scene technicians had examined their son's room and found semen stains on the wall at the window overlooking the neighbours' garden. They had concluded that he had stood there masturbating while watching Adine. On his phone, they had found photos of her, going back almost a year in time, some of them taken through the windows. In one of these, she had been indoors, walking naked between the bathroom and her bedroom. Telling Gunn Hilde Wendel about this evidence of obsession would probably not persuade her to think any differently about her son, but all the same it was not something Wisting was keen to bring up.

'I'm sorry,' he said.

Gunn Hilde Wendel sat back firmly in her seat, in a clear demonstration of her rejection of his sentiment. Her husband put his hand on her arm.

Wisting was aware that doubt and uncertainty would surface in them both and he was unwilling to leave them in such a situation, so he set out the facts he had in his possession.

'The body is being sent for forensic examination,' he told them. 'We already have his DNA profile. In the course of the next forty-eight hours, we'll have final confirmation.'

'So you're not entirely sure it is him?' Reidar Wendel asked.

'It is his motorbike, his helmet and his clothing,' Wisting replied, anxious not to leave any doubt about it. 'We found his wallet with his driving licence. The examination at the National University Hospital is really just a formality.'

Reidar Wendel nodded.

'I can contact an undertaker to take care of the practical details afterwards,' Wisting continued.

'Gabrielsen,' Gunn Hilde interjected. 'We used them when Mum died. Fortunately she was spared all this.'

Wisting was familiar with the firm but wrote it down all the same. Mostly for the sake of appearances.

'If you like, I can take you out to the discovery site,' he said. 'Not today, but any other time that suits you.'

Reidar Wendel leaned forward slightly. 'Where did you say it was?' he asked.

'Near Vassvik,' Wisting said, launching into further clarification.

'I know where that is,' Reidar Wendel interrupted him. 'I just don't understand how Morten ended up getting lost in that neck of the woods, away on the other side of town.'

'He wasn't himself, though,' his wife pointed out.

Wisting did not have any better answer to offer.

'There are a few things you should prepare yourselves for,' he said. 'The media are certain to show interest in all this.'

Gunn Hilde Wendel's lips tightened. 'Do they have to know about it?' she asked.

The dog struggled up from its spot on the floor and stared across the room at them. Wisting shifted in his seat. It was difficult to find a humane way of explaining why the discovery of a body on the bed of a dried-up lake would spark interest in both journalists and readers.

'Many people are already involved,' he said. 'We can't prevent the farmer who alerted us from passing on the information to other folk. It's an unusual case. It's bound to get out.'

Gunn Hilde's tense lip began to tremble. 'They wrote so much nasty stuff at the time it happened,' she said.

'They're going to write much of the same stuff again, I'm afraid,' Wisting told her.

'But he was never found guilty of anything,' Gunn Hilde said. 'He's innocent. Can't they write that?'

Wisting composed his face into sympathetic lines. Naïve questions from close relatives were always difficult to answer.

'It's not up to me or you,' was his response. 'I don't think journalists will contact you, but you should prepare yourselves for them reporting on it. Maybe they won't mention Morten by name, but they'll certainly write about what took place.'

Tears began to trickle down the face of the woman opposite. The dog came padding across and sat down, curling up underneath the chairs, between Gunn Hilde and Reidar Wendel.

Wisting tucked his notebook into his pocket to demonstrate that his visit was over.

7

The chair unbalanced, tipping over on one leg, when Evert Harting leaned forward for the jug of fruit squash. The surface of the barbecue area was uneven, and the concrete had cracked. Kjell-Tore had promised to lay paving stones on top, but nothing had come of that as yet and it had been left as a large, rough platform.

Taking his plate, Ella moved the remains of the chop on to hers and stacked the two plates, one on top of the other.

'Thanks for the lovely meal,' he said, refilling his glass.

'It was delicious,' she replied as she carried the plates inside to wash up.

Evert Harting stayed where he was, sipping his drink. He heard the noise of a plane overhead, flying from the mountain slopes in the east. He ducked his head and peered out from under the parasol. The chair tipped up again.

He saw that it was one of the single-engine propeller-driven planes used by the forest fire surveillance service. It approached at high altitude and veered north.

Ella returned with a magazine tucked under her arm. 'Isabell has sent a message,' she said, holding up her phone. 'She's arriving by train at noon tomorrow.'

She sat down to write a reply. 'We can do some shopping before we pick her up,' she added.

Evert Harting took another sip from his glass. 'She knows Kjell-Tore is coming?' he asked.

'He can sleep in his motorhome while she's here,' Ella

answered. 'She doesn't usually stay for more than a couple of days, anyway.'

Their daughter was thirty-two. She had followed her mother's example and studied economics. Now she taught at the Business School in Nydalen. Although she had two months' summer holiday, she seldom spared time to spend more than a day or two at the cabin with them.

She had been a late baby, but didn't seem in any hurry to establish a family of her own. There had been a few boyfriends when she was in her early twenties, but no romance since then.

He had thought she might prefer girls but had never mentioned that to Ella. It would be fine if that were the case. There was nothing either they or Isabell could do about that, but she was the only one who could carry their family line forward. Both his and Ella's. He himself had no siblings and Kjell-Tore had no children either.

Ella's brother was her junior by fifteen years and different from her in every way. He had no education and chopped and changed between various trades. In the past few years, he had worked for a landscape gardener during the summer months, laying paving stones and building retaining walls. One of his most recent jobs had been to pave the area around the new national museum in Oslo. Some winters he had worked on a factory trawler off the South American coast, but in the last few years he had remained at home.

'We should buy some fresh salmon,' Ella said. 'She likes chargrilled fish. Maybe you could row out one evening and try to catch something, the way you used to do.'

'The boat's stranded on dry land, though,' Evert pointed out. 'We won't be able to use it until the water comes back.'

'Oh, of course,' Ella said.

She opened her magazine at the double-page spread of crosswords and sat down, pen in hand.

Evert gazed out across the arid stretch of shoreline in the bay where the lake had previously been. A few empty oil drums and bundled logs lay close to the water's edge. He and Ella had surmised that they must be what was left of a raft built by scouts on the other side of the peninsula a few years earlier.

'No,' he said, finishing off his drink. 'I'll take the car and fill those water containers, then that'll be done.'

'Don't you want to wait until tomorrow?'

He got to his feet. 'And I can use the toilet facilities while I'm there,' he said.

They were in the habit of filling the water containers at the new petrol station on the E18 and usually made use of the opportunity while they were there. Ella had been to the outside toilet before they had dinner. He didn't think she would want to come with him.

'Would you like me to get anything?' he asked.

She had a think but finally shook her head. 'Are you going to take the rubbish too?'

Nodding, he pushed his chair towards the table and picked up the bag from the bin below the bench. They did not have a refuse collection contract, but occasionally threw some bags into the large container beside the dog owners' club.

The car was parked with all the windows left open. He waited until the air conditioner had kicked in before closing them.

The narrow gravel track leading down from the cabin snaked through an area of beech forest before emerging beside Lake Farris. On the straight stretch before the dog club premises, he drove out to the edge and pulled to a halt.

A cloud of dust from the track engulfed him, blanketing the front windscreen.

Evert Harting sat still for a while before reaching forward, opening the glove compartment and fishing out the gold initial necklace.

It looked mass-produced, with no craft marks or detailing to differentiate one chain from another. Even the initial was dull rather than shiny and marred by tiny scratches.

He ran his thumb over it. It felt almost as if it had been rubbed with sandpaper. The images on the internet were too grainy to make out whether the chain belonging to the missing girl was similarly the worse for wear. The beach photo in which she was buried in sand up to her neck came to mind, but he could also think of other explanations. The most likely was that the abrading was a result of the time spent submerged in the lake, with waves and underwater currents moving it back and forth along the sludge.

The first time he had heard of Annika Bengt had been in the radio news, when Ella had passed comment on it. Bovikstrand had been the last place Kjell-Tore had spent the night before arriving in his motorhome. He had been there when the girl had disappeared.

A young woman, slim and shapely in close-fitting clothes, came jogging towards him along the track. He hid the chain in his fist and the woman glanced at him indifferently as she passed. Perspiration had gathered around her neckline.

Evert Harting shifted his gaze to the rear-view mirror and watched as she ran into the shadows cast by the nearby trees before opening the car door and stepping out.

Lake Farris shimmered in the bright sunshine. He walked on to the hillside, to a popular spot used by teenagers for swimming. No one there now. The ground below was dry and hard-packed, but the slope was steep. An underwater shelf was what they called it. The water lay only three metres from shore.

Opening his hand, he let the chain slide between his fingers and used his thumb to lace it over his ring finger, under his middle finger and across his forefinger.

His suspicions would not evaporate if he got rid of it. On the contrary. This was not something he could simply dispose of. He was determined to find out where this initial neck-lace came from, no matter how uncomfortable the answer might be.

8

Insects were buzzing around the outdoor ceiling lamp. Wisting sat in the pale evening light out on the terrace, reading an article about the quietest room in the world. It had featured in a magazine supplement that accompanied his newspaper. According to the headline, this room was quieter than the grave. Inside it, you could quite literally hear your own heartbeat.

The radio in the living room behind him was switched on and the newsreader's monotonous voice reached out to him. It was 10 p.m. and none of the news reports were of any interest.

He tried to go on reading, but his thoughts returned to Morten Wendel, Adine Broch-Hansen and the two sets of parents he had met a few hours earlier. The two couples had entirely different stories about what had happened eight years earlier. The investigation supported the Broch-Hansen family's version, but Wisting felt sympathy for both sides. What they had in common was that they had been on opposite ends of an extreme situation. All of a sudden, unpredictably and unexpectedly, they had found themselves part of something much bigger than themselves. Something they were unable to control, and which robbed them of both security and dignity.

Wisting had met countless people in similar situations. Had stood face to face with anger, anguish, despair and dread. The only thing he knew for certain was that it would pass. He had experienced this for himself when he lost his wife, Ingrid, almost fourteen years ago. The loss had been heavy to bear, but it faded in time. Missing her was something that never really ceased, but it grew easier to endure. Life was like that. It moved on. This was no consolation for those who were affected in the here and now, but nothing lasted for ever. A young person would eventually grow old. Someone sleeping would wake. Everything was in a state of flux, like a law of nature. Night became day and after the sun came the rain.

Love had returned to his life but had slipped back out again. When Ingrid died, he had thought he could never love anyone else, right up until he met Suzanne. Their relationship had lasted a few years, at which point she had made up her mind to move on without a police detective by her side.

He reached out his hand for the glass of water on the table. The loss still weighed him down. Not as much as the loss of Ingrid, the mother of his children, Line and Thomas. Ingrid was gone for ever. Suzanne, on the other hand, lived not far away. She ran a combined art gallery and coffee bar in Stavern, and he could drop in there any time for a coffee.

What he was really waiting up for was a phone call from Line. She and Amalie, his granddaughter, were in the USA, staying with Amalie's father in Washington, where they were six hours behind Norwegian time.

This was the first occasion since Amalie's birth almost eight years ago that they had paid a visit to her father. John Bantam had been in Norway on an assignment for the FBI. Wisting had worked alongside him and his partner during the weeks they had spent here. Line and John had met by chance. Despite the pregnancy, they had both agreed that what had taken place between them would not be enough to build a relationship upon. Two years ago, John had surprised them by returning to Norway. Since then, they had kept in close contact, but Line claimed there was nothing more to it than friendship and sharing a child.

A water sprinkler started up in the next-door neighbours' garden. Wisting heard water dripping on the leaves of the bushes that lined the adjoining fence. This practice went on for half an hour every evening, despite the local council having introduced a total ban on watering gardens. Probably he should point that out, but precisely because he was a police officer, he had dropped the idea. He was not keen on mixing his role as a policeman with his private life.

The Broch-Hansen family and the Wendel family had been neighbours since before their children were born. For a time, Allan Broch-Hansen and Reidar Wendel had worked for the same transport company and took turns driving regular routes to Denmark and Sweden. Their wives had spent much of the time they were absent in and out of each other's houses. They worked in different clothes shops in the town centre and had talked about starting up their own boutique, though nothing came of that.

Wisting tried to focus on the magazine article and read the last paragraph again.

The room with no echo was situated in Minneapolis and was described as 99.99 per cent soundproof. No one had succeeded in spending more than forty-five minutes at a time inside it. The silence made them begin to hallucinate.

He turned the page. Detailed building instructions were given. The walls consisted of thick glass-fibre panels overlaid with double layers of steel and concrete.

The phone rang before he had finished reading. A video call from Line.

Wisting answered and smiled at the screen. Little Amalie was sitting on her mother's lap, waving at him.

'I saw a cowboy!' she exclaimed.

'A cowboy?' Wisting asked.

'With one of those hats,' Amalie said, touching her head.

Wisting laughed. 'I know what you mean.'

'We went to the park for a while,' Line explained, swivelling round in her seat.

They were sitting out on a verandah. Wisting recognized the view towards the Potomac River. The weather looked bright and sunny.

'Amalie met a few children of her own age,' Line went on. 'She does understand some English of course, so it was a great success.'

'How are things going otherwise?' Wisting asked.

'Amalie's a bit bored,' Line replied. 'There's not very much to find for her to do hereabouts. Tomorrow we'll drive to the coast so that we can have a dip in the sea. There are some amusement parks out there too.'

Amalie slid down from her mother's knee.

'Then we're planning to travel up to New York at the end of the week,' Line continued. 'It's no more than four hours' drive. John has friends there and we'll stay with them. They have a daughter around Amalie's age.'

'She's not missing home?' Wisting asked.

'Not yet,' Line answered. 'Is it still as hot over there?'

'Hot and dry.'

'Have you remembered to water my house plants?'

'I was there this morning.'

'Any news apart from that?'

Wisting hesitated. In his first few years in the police force, he had refused to discuss his experiences. However, Ingrid noticed when something was worrying him, and she had begun to ask questions. In time they had found a way of talking about his work, in which Wisting felt he could express himself freely, without expending too much energy on weighing his words out of consideration for his duty of confidentiality. It had also been good for Ingrid. She had felt included, and she no longer had to worry that his behaviour had anything to do with her. That was something he had never really achieved with Suzanne, but once Line had stopped working as a news reporter, he had been able to continue the habit in his conversations with her.

'Has something happened?' Line asked when he did not answer.

'Do you remember Morten Wendel?' he asked. 'He disappeared on his motorbike and was reported missing the summer you were pregnant with Amalie.'

'The rapist?'

Wisting had to agree with her description.

'He and his motorbike turned up today,' he said, and went on to tell her about the unexpected discovery.

'There's been nothing about it online,' Line pointed out.

'Not yet,' Wisting replied.

'The media are going to have a field day,' Line said. 'That's the kind of story they love. You should really give a statement to make sure you're on the front foot. Then you'll avoid any fuss when the rumours begin to circulate.'

Wisting had not regarded the situation from this point of view, simply believing that, out of respect for the families involved, the discovery of the body was not something the police should announce on their own initiative.

'Why didn't you find him at the time?' Line asked.

'We had no idea where to search for him,' Wisting replied.

'Wrong answer,' Line said. 'You're going to be questioned about it, so you ought to prepare something better than that.'

'There was nothing to suggest that as a possible search area,' Wisting told her.

'Why wasn't it considered possible?' Line pressed him.

'There were no witness sightings,' Wisting answered. 'No information on which route he had taken.'

'But that was where he was actually found,' Line went on. 'Wasn't it a place you should have searched? After all, you had divers in the harbour basin.'

He realized she was teasing him now. The dive activity in the harbour had been initiated after someone had spotted oil on the surface of the water, but this was not the answer to her question.

'You should assign someone to deal with the case, someone who was not involved at the time,' Line advised him. 'Then it will be easier to avoid critical questions. Someone who can rattle off the answer that they're not familiar with the decisions made at the time.'

Wisting thanked her for her input. They sat chatting about other topics for a while before Line brought Amalie back to the screen to say goodbye.

The sound of the water sprinkler in the next-door garden abruptly stopped. Wisting folded his magazine, picked up his glass and headed inside. He had not told Line any more than would soon emerge in the media. But there was certainly more to tell.

9

The dew still speckled the grass when Evert Harting rose from bed and went out. He padded across to the outside toilet and attended to his morning duties. The cavity facing him stank to high heaven and he avoided looking at where his jet of urine landed – he could hear just a trickle from down below.

Back at the cabin he took his spade from the shed and placed it in the car. Then he washed his hands in the bowl set out on the verandah and headed indoors to brew some coffee.

Ella, emerging from the bedroom, said good morning.

'Are you sure Isabell knows we don't have any water?' he asked.

'Yes, of course,' Ella replied. 'And she's been used to the outside toilet since she was little.'

She disappeared outside. On her return, she toasted a couple of slices of bread and took out the pot of orange marmalade.

'I'm going out with the detector,' Evert told her. 'I'll do it now, this morning, before it gets too hot.'

Ella nodded as she finished chewing. 'I'll write a brief shopping list while you're at it,' she answered. 'You'll be back in good time before twelve, won't you? We should buy some ingredients for a salad too. Isabell made one with mango for us last summer. That might be a good idea.'

Evert grabbed a napkin and wiped his mouth. 'I won't be long,' he promised.

Twenty minutes later he was back at the spot where he had searched the previous day. The water, shining in the bright sunlight, had pulled a few more centimetres further back and reflected the drab surroundings.

Changing into his boots, he walked down to the original water's edge. He could see the location where he had dug up the gold initial necklace, maybe twenty metres away. A mere stone's throw.

He bent down and picked up a pebble. It weighed slightly more than the chain, but its round shape would mean that it would behave differently in the air. Instead, he broke off a twig from a low-growing bush and peeled off some of the side shoots until he felt the weight was about right and then took aim, throwing the twig as far as he could. It whirled through the air and landed a couple of metres further out than the spot where he had found the necklace.

The metal detector was still in the car. He had brought only the spade and the pinpointer. Compacted, parched earth crunched under his boots as he walked.

The first few turns of the spade scooped up the soil he had filled in the day before. Slowly and methodically, he extended the circumference and depth of the hole. With each turn of the spade, he shook the soil carefully off the spade to check if he had brought up anything that hadn't shown a result with the metal detector.

The porous earth was easy to work with. Soon the hole was one metre in diameter and almost half a metre deep, big enough for him to step into it and dig down further.

He was not quite sure what he was looking for. If the necklace had been thrown from shore, it was unlikely that anything else would be found in the same place, but if it had been dumped from a boat, then he might well find something.

Loose earth drizzled down from the edge into the hole. Something round and oblong-shaped came with it. Evert Harting felt his heart begin to race. Laying aside the spade, he crouched down and picked up the item. It was smooth and grey, and his initial hunch was that it must be a bone.

Scraping it with his nail, he turned it this way and that and lifted it up to his nose to sniff it. Most likely a fragment from a tree, he decided. He held it in both hands, at first bending it cautiously, then with more force until it snapped in the middle. Splinters of pale wood projected from either side.

He tossed the two sticks away and continued his efforts with the spade. The base of the hole became damp, with the consistency of sticky, smelly slime. His boots sank into it and produced gurgling noises when he tramped around.

It was now harder to dig. Perspiration crept from his neck down towards his shoulder blades. Eventually his lower back began to ache. Using the spade for support, he stood up straight and tilted his head back. A few streaks of white cloud had appeared in the western sky. They were drifting away from him and, in any case, would not bring rain.

It was now almost 10 a.m. He gave himself another quarter of an hour, but it began to dawn on him that he was not going to find anything here. He should really just be glad of that, he told himself, as he forced the spade into the ground again.

Instead of throwing earth up out of the hole, he turned halfway around to pile it behind him. He wrenched the spade from side to side and kept his eye on what dribbled down. An object appeared in the dry earth, making a faint clinking noise against the metal spade.

Blinking sweat away from his eyes, Evert picked it up.

It was a nail. Blackened with age and its outline uneven, slightly wavy in shape. The head was thick and angled.

He used his thumb to rub it clean, revealing tiny marks, traces from a blacksmith's hammer.

It had lain close to the transition to the moist part of the hole, further down than the metal detector had managed to reach.

A hand-forged nail. Machine production had taken over completely by the mid-nineteenth century. The find he held in his hand could be several hundred years old, from the time of the Fresjeborgen fortress, but despite this, he felt neither enthusiasm nor any real flicker of interest.

Stuffing it into his back pocket, he clambered out of the hole and returned to his car. Before he settled behind the wheel, he dried his hands and face on a rag he kept stashed in the boot. It was soon grey from sweat and dust.

The car shook on the uneven ground. He kept his speed low and steered around the largest heaps of junk.

The water in the bottle held between the two front seats was now warm. He took a few gulps all the same, spilling a little before he screwed the lid back on again.

Ella had hoisted the flag on the rise behind the cabin. She may have found out that a member of the royal family had a birthday today. Several of them were in the summer months, he knew, but it was probably mostly intended to honour Isabell's arrival.

He drove all the way up to the cabin wall and parked the car where it would be in the shade until they left again.

Ella glanced up from her crossword. 'What a sight you are,' she commented. 'Did you find anything?'

'Yes . . .' He thrust his hand into his pocket. The gold chain was there, along with the nail.

'First this,' he said, placing the nail before her.

Leaning forward, Ella studied it and picked at it with her

index finger, as if it was something that had to be handled with care.

'It looks very old,' she said.

'Hand-forged,' he agreed. 'Wouldn't be surprised if it's from the 1600s.'

Ella sat in silence, as if letting this information sink in.

'What else did you find?' she asked.

Now Evert Harting took out the necklace. He had to share his thoughts with someone, or at least lay the groundwork for them to talk about it.

'This,' he replied, setting it down in front of her.

Ella scrutinized it in the same way that she had the nail. Nothing to suggest it had any kind of association for her.

'Someone must have lost it while they were in swimming,' she suggested.

'I think it's gold,' he said.

Ella picked it up, felt the weight in her hand and agreed with him. Then she lifted her crossword pencil again.

'Are you going like that?' She indicated his clothes.

'No, I'll get changed. Have a swim first.'

The nail and the necklace were left lying on the table as Evert went inside to fetch a towel.

'You'll have to add some length to the planks,' Ella said when he came out again.

When the well had run dry, he had laid a broad stretch of planking down to the water's edge so that they could walk up and down to the lake without getting their feet dirty. Now it was lying on dry land.

'Do you need help to carry anything?' Ella offered.

Evert glanced down at the gold chain that lay undisturbed on the table.

'It'll be OK,' he said.

There was a stack of shuttering timber behind the cabin from the time when Kjell-Tore had built the barbecue area. Nettles were growing in profusion around them now. He pulled out one plank that was almost loose from the left-over pieces of concrete, heaved it on to his shoulder on top of the towel, and then strode to the lake and set it down to extend the length of the wooden walkway. The last metre or so jutted into the water.

He stripped off and waded out, shampoo bottle in hand. Nobody could see him, and he liked to swim naked.

The water was warm, most likely around twenty-five degrees Celsius.

He swam out a few metres, ducked under and popped up again.

With nothing to stand on, his feet sank into the sludge on the lake-bed. It was cold and he struggled a little to find his balance before opening the shampoo bottle. As he worked up some lather, he gazed at the remains of what he and Ella had decided must be the raft that scouts had sailed around on the previous year. Now he was not so sure that this was what it was. He couldn't see any ropes, and the logs were rough, as though they had sunk and lain there from the time when timber float-ing was common practice. The barrels were of different sizes. Two oil drums and a blue barrel made of hard plastic with a taut string holding the lid in place. It looked more like rubbish pieced together by the waves and strong underwater currents.

Plunging in again, he rinsed off the soapsuds and walked back up to the cabin with his towel tied around his waist. Ella had now changed her clothes and placed her handbag on the table.

'We should take that gold necklace with us and hand it in,' she said.

Evert Harting lifted a corner of the towel to dry his ear. 'Hand it in?' he queried.

'Aren't you duty bound to do that when you're a member of the metal detecting association?' Ella retorted. 'Anyway, neither of us has a name that begins with A. It's no use to us.'

The initial necklace was no longer on the table. Ella must already have put it into her bag. 'We can call in at the police station since we're going into town anyway,' she said. 'That way, we'll be rid of it.'

10

The air between the basement walls in the archives section was fresh and cool. Wisting picked his way among the shelves to cases from the summer of eight years ago. Two of these pertained to Morten Wendel. A thick folder for the rape and false imprisonment and another much slimmer folder from the missing person case. Both had been shelved prior to the start of full digitization of police records and contained external documents that could not be viewed on his computer screen.

In addition, there were two other case folders that involved Morten Wendel and Adine Broch-Hansen. One was an arson attempt on the Wendel family home and the second from the time when the Broch-Hansen's house had burned down.

Wisting left the fire cases but took the first two with him.

The door in the corridor that led out to the forensics garage lay wide open. Wisting called in to take a look. Morten Wendel's motorbike had been placed on a tarpaulin. A note with a case number was attached to the handlebars. Beside it was the safe that had been found among the other scrap metal. The back was facing out and Wisting moved in to examine it more closely.

The door showed obvious signs of having been forced open and was hanging from one hinge. The marks looked as though they had been made by both a cutting torch and an angle grinder, and the steel was clearly distorted. The storage space inside was empty and all that could be seen was the remains of dried mud from the sludgy bed of Lake Farris. A metal plate on one side of the safe had been wiped clean to reveal the model and maker's name. *Euro Si, model DS2121* from Christian Rasmussen & Son in Denmark. Manufactured in 1988.

The flickering fluorescent light on the ceiling above him buzzed and died. Wisting took the stairs up to the criminal investigation department and his own office. At the very back of the folder dealing with the search for Morten Wendel, he found a sealed envelope marked with a minus sign and his own name. Laying it to one side, he took the rest of the papers to Maren Dokken's office.

Slanting sunshine shone through the venetian blinds and lit up her desk. She had not been here the summer Morten Wendel disappeared. That same autumn, she had arrived at the police station as one of eight police students embarking on the practical part of their training course. Even then she had distinguished herself as a competent investigator. Thoughtful and independent, she wrote concise but comprehensive reports. When Wisting was her age, her grandfather had been his boss. Maren Dokken possessed many of the old man's qualities. A singular ability for analytical thinking combined with critical common sense. In addition, she had a rare capacity for concentration that allowed her to wade through huge quantities of information. Now she had been given responsibility for the investigation of the previous day's discovery of the corpse on the lake-bed.

'You found them?' she asked, her eyes fixed on the case files.

'Yes,' Wisting replied, setting them down before her.

The sun was in Maren's eyes when she leaned forward. A few crinkles were visible around her eyes, but apart from that she had not changed much since the day she had sat for the first time in the front row of the briefing room. On that occasion, her blonde hair had been pulled back in a ponytail, whereas now it was loose around her face, mostly to hide a scar on her left cheek, beneath her ear, Wisting imagined. She had been seriously injured in an explosion while working in the patrol service. Subsequently, she had been transferred to Wisting's department. That had been almost five years ago now.

Maren glanced at the clock on the wall above the door. In conjunction with one of the police lawyers, they had drawn up a brief press release. In addition to the facts about the missing person case they had obtained data about the water level and amount of rainfall. Two photographs were also attached. The statement was currently on the desk of the communications adviser at the administrative headquarters in Tønsberg and would be sent out at half past ten. It was now quarter to.

'I read through some of the online news coverage from the time when the lad disappeared,' Maren said. 'The press were fairly kind to him then. In the rape case it simply states that an acquaintance around the same age as the victim had been charged. When he was reported missing in the media, you really have to read between the lines to find any connection.'

'His mother wouldn't agree with you,' Wisting replied. 'She believes the reports were part of what drove him to it.'

'Of course, it would feel different on the inside,' Maren admitted. 'When they know who is under discussion.'

Her mobile rang. She held up the screen to Wisting – it was the communications adviser on the line.

Answering, she switched to loudspeaker and said that Wisting could also hear what he was saying.

'Just one last thing before I send out this press release,' the adviser said. 'Shouldn't it be made clearer that there is no suspicion of any criminal act in connection with his death?'

Maren deferred to Wisting.

'I mean, it doesn't say that it's being investigated as an accident, either,' the adviser continued, 'just that an investigation has been launched.'

The text was printed on Maren's screen. She pushed her chair back as Wisting leaned forward to read it through one more time.

'Strictly speaking, there's nothing criminal behind it,' he said. 'Morten Wendel was charged with rape and false imprisonment, but it would be difficult to include that.'

He gave this some thought as he read.

'You can add one more sentence,' he said, drafting it in his head before dictating: 'The discovery does not provide evidence to support suspicion of criminal intent.'

They heard the rattle of a keyboard. 'I've got it,' said the communications adviser. 'I'll get that out.'

When the conversation ended, Maren peered up at Wisting. 'Is there anything suspicious here?' she asked him.

Wisting looked at her. 'You're the one who's investigating,' he said, tapping his finger on one of the cold case files. 'See if you can find anything.'

Maren grabbed hold of the file. 'Does it say anything about the fires in here?' she queried.

'No,' Wisting replied, sitting down on the vacant chair. 'There were three in total,' he said. 'The first happened a few days after Adine Broch-Hansen was raped. Morten Wendel was in custody, the forensics technicians had released the crime scene, and his parents were planning to move back in the next day. Something had been burning on a corner of the verandah. They didn't discover it until after a couple of days. Apparently lighter fuel from the barbecue had been used but the fire had died out by itself without doing much damage.'

Maren Dokken scribbled down some notes.

'The second fire occurred two days after Morten Wendel was released,' Wisting went on. 'No one was at home – the family had moved away to get some peace and quiet. Two windows were smashed, and the curtains were set ablaze, but the fire didn't take hold.'

'Did anyone come under suspicion?' Maren asked.

'Not officially, but Gunn Hilde Wendel was convinced that Adine was behind it,' Wisting explained. 'No evidence was collected, but it was also our hypothesis that Adine, or someone else in her family, couldn't bear the thought of her rapist continuing to live in the house next door.'

'But the third time it was the Broch-Hansens' house that went on fire?' Maren said.

'It was totally destroyed,' Wisting replied, nodding. 'They lost everything, but it also made it possible for them to start all over again. They bought a new house in another location, a different neighbourhood altogether.'

'What was the cause of the fire?'

'The conclusion inclined towards the idea that it was arson, but it proved impossible to establish anything definite.'

'When was that fire?'

'The day after Morten Wendel disappeared,' Wisting told her. 'We searched for him in the ruins of the fire and kept at it for three days before we could say with any certainty that he wasn't present. Some people felt he was the one who had started the fire, whereas others thought that Adine Broch-Hansen was behind it, that she had set fire to her own house to avoid having to go on living there.'

Maren Dokken nibbled the end of her pen and leaned back in her seat. 'So there are still some unanswered questions,' she said.

Wisting got to his feet. 'There always are,' he replied.

I I

The journalist from the local newspaper was urging her to hold up a rusty bicycle for the photo. Kicki Dalberg lodged her chewing gum on the roof of her mouth, took hold of the frame with both hands and adopted a sombre expression. This was only one of eight bikes they had hauled out of the shallows in front of the dam, as well as four electric scooters. In the pile of junk, they had also found car tyres, shopping trolleys, camping equipment and other rubbish that had been tossed over the edge or else carried with the water to the outlet pipe. A lot of refuse was still left down there beside the dam gates.

Jonas and Mia stood by her side with their arms folded. They had agreed in advance that they should all wear black clothing. *There is no planet B* was emblazoned on Kicki's long-sleeved T-shirt. The close-fitting cotton clung to her body in the heat.

The camera clicked. Beads of perspiration glistened on the overweight, balding journalist's forehead. He had interviewed Mia and Kicki a couple of years earlier in connection with a theatre production at the Art and Music College. Now Jonas was the one who spoke up. He had been in charge of the local organization for the past ten years and had plenty of experience of doing so.

'Thanks, that's fine,' the journalist said, slinging the camera over his shoulder again and taking out his notepad.

'The climate has already changed,' Jonas said. 'There hasn't been a drop of rain since May. The temperature is five degrees above normal. The results are obvious to anyone who cares to look.'

He flung out his arm and pointed behind him. 'At the same time, other crimes against the environment are being exposed. They're quite literally coming to the surface.'

The journalist wiped the sweat from his forehead with the back of his hand. Jonas waited for a moment before continuing: 'In the course of two days, we've brought up more than a tonne of rubbish, and we're nowhere near finished yet.'

'Where are you putting it all?' the journalist asked.

It seemed this question caught Jonas off guard. 'We've alerted the local council and assume they'll take matters further,' he replied.

Kicki was unsure whether anyone had in fact been in touch with the council yet.

'Why are you doing this, anyway?' the journalist continued his line of questioning.

'Both to tidy up and to publicize the problem,' Jonas answered. 'A lot of what we've dug up so far has been consumer-related plastic waste. Through slow decomposition, environmental poisons and micro-plastics are dispersed throughout nature.'

It sounded as if he was rattling off something from a brochure.

'Picture it for yourself – the bath will overflow if the sink is clogged and the tap keeps on running,' he added. 'Would you simply mop up the water and let it continue, or would you turn off the tap? That's how we also need to think about pollution. We must turn off the tap and prevent any more contaminants from spreading throughout the natural world and the oceans.'

Kicki glanced at the journalist. It looked as if he was taking it all down, but she was afraid he was going to confuse the environment with the climate. Many folk believed they could do something about the climate by picking up litter.

'The use of fossil fuels destroys the climate, while plastic is the greatest danger for the environment,' Jonas went on, as if he had read her thoughts. 'Unless we change the way we consume, produce and dispose of plastic waste, researchers believe that within a few decades, the amount of plastics will exceed the number of fish we have in the sea.'

Jonas turned to face Lake Farris again. 'It looks idyllic on the surface, but it's very different on the lake-bed.'

The journalist folded up his notepad as if he wanted to indicate that he had heard enough. 'I've got what I need, thanks,' he said, looking across at Kicki and Mia. 'Great to have such passion for your subject.'

He wiped the sweat from his brow once again. 'I expect it'll be published sometime this evening,' he said, thanking them before he headed to his car.

'That went pretty well, I think,' Jonas said once the journalist had left.

Kicki picked up some bashed beer cans and tossed them into a shopping basket. 'All the same, people don't understand,' she said. 'We should really do something to trigger dramatic headlines.'

'Such as what, then?'

Kicki shrugged. She had lost any faith she'd had that demonstrations with slogans and banners or minor newspaper articles were what was needed to create a more sustainable route into the future. The belief in change had been replaced by fear that time was running out. That it would soon be too late.

'I don't know,' she replied. 'Blow up the water company,

maybe. If people had no water in their taps, they might under-stand what's going on.'

Mia looked at her as if wondering whether she really meant it. The idea had also been far from her mind when it was first mooted. But, measured against the melting glaciers, the rising sea levels, the disappearing forests, and the animal species that were dying out, this was a modest proposal. Something to shake people out of their complacency and highlight the crisis threatening them all.

'We're a non-violent organization,' Jonas reminded her.

'Something else, then,' Kicki said. 'Scatter nails over the roads so that motor traffic grinds to a halt, for example.' She sighed loudly. 'I'm just so fucking fed up with nobody listening.'

Jonas did not appear willing to discuss other types of action. 'Let's finish up here,' he said, moving towards the ladder beside the dam.

Mia climbed down after him. Kicki was left standing on her own for a while before she took her turn to descend.

'We could each buy a cheap ticket to the Med and chain ourselves to the nose wheel of the plane, instead of board-ing,' she suggested.

'That's not how to persuade people to give us a hearing,' Jonas insisted. 'If we're going to be taken seriously and take part in the debate within society, we can't afford to make our-selves unpopular.'

Kicki shrugged again and distanced herself slightly from her two companions. A corner of a black plastic bin bag was sticking out of the mud, almost at the very edge of the water. They had pulled out several of the same type already. Rubbish bags that people had simply hurled into the water.

She tugged at the bag, but it proved very resistant, as if it had been sucked right into the ground.

'How long are we going to keep on with awareness-raising and attitude-changing?' she asked.

The other two had no answer for her.

'It's urgent,' she added, using both hands to catch hold of the bag. 'We have to do something to force politicians to take action.'

The plastic bag tore but she found another, bigger corner to pull. It came unstuck from the sludge and she managed to hoist it up.

The bag was half-full. She dragged it across to the ladder. Brown murky water poured out when she lifted it. It smelled foul and she had to turn away to avoid breathing in the rank odour.

Halfway up, the bag snagged on the joint of the extending ladder and ripped again. A large pebble slid out, struck one of the rungs and bounced down to the ground.

Mia screamed and pointed at the bag.

Kicki had no idea what she meant, but the scream caused her to jettison the bag, and it landed at Jonas's feet. The head of a dead animal was poking out, the remains of scrawny grey fur around pointed, mottled teeth.

'Yuck!' Kicki groaned. 'Somebody's drowned their cat.'

Empty-handed, she clambered on up the ladder.

'Now I really can't be bothered with any more of this crap,' she said, casting a glance behind her. 'Who knows what else might be lying here.'

1 2

They were early, nearly a quarter of an hour before the train was due. Evert Harting unfastened his safety belt.

'I'm going to stretch my legs,' he said, pushing the door open.

'Leave the engine running so it doesn't get too hot,' Ella said. 'The butcher meat mustn't sit too long until we can put it into the fridge.'

The car ran silently, so it was unlikely anyone would hear it idling.

Evert Harting strolled to the end of the station platform, before turning and gazing in the direction he had come from. The heat haze shimmered on the railway tracks.

It amazed him that Ella had not recognized the gold chain. The fact that Kjell-Tore had been at the same campsite, the one from which Annika Bengt had gone missing, meant that the case had been a hot topic of conversation at the time. They had followed the news avidly and examined the missing person photograph together. Bovikstrand had several thousand visitors and Kjell-Tore had not recognized her or her parents, who were also depicted.

He strode back along the platform into the shade of the covered waiting area.

But maybe it wasn't common to go around remembering such things, he mused. Ella had never been particularly interested in crime stories. She found other things to do when that sort of documentary was shown on TV. As for himself, he wouldn't mind being a detective – he thought he would have had a talent for it. He had good observational skills and at work had received regular feedback that he was patient and painstaking. He had always been a problem solver and was used to getting to grips with the minutiae of the legal system.

Travellers began to gather on the platform. Evert Harting cast his mind back to the summer days of four years ago. He could clearly recall the main events. Kjell-Tore had arrived at the start of the week. They had spent a few days together before he and Ella had borrowed the motorhome and driven north. They had been gone for almost ten days while Kjell-Tore had stayed at the cabin. That was more or less the drill every year.

Ella kept a diary in the kitchen drawer, where she made various notes. A bit here and there about the weather, anyone who had paid a visit, and whether anything unusual had happened. She held on to them and by now they went back several years. Occasionally she might look them up to see what the weather or the bathing temperature had been compared to this year. She had most certainly jotted down the days when Kjell-Tore arrived and left.

He had reached the opposite end of the platform when an idea struck him. Four years ago – that must have been the summer Kjell-Tore had brought a kitten with him. It had accompanied him from a campsite on the east coast of Sweden. The owners had simply left it behind, he had told them. Kjell-Tore had given it some food and hadn't had the heart to leave it when he moved on.

Ella had not liked it. She thought the cat could have all sorts of diseases and that there were regulations about taking animals across country borders. It had been that same summer. He remembered it now. On the journey to Norway, the kitten had made a mess in the motorhome and Kjell-Tore had had to scrub it down twice when he arrived at the cabin. The smell of ammonia and chlorine had still hung in the air when he and Ella had driven off a few days later.

He walked once again up and down the platform, weaving his way through the waiting passengers, and looked up at the information boards. The train would be here in three minutes.

Ella had stepped out of the car and was standing behind the boot with her mobile phone in hand. He strolled up to her to keep an eye on the vehicle while she moved forward to greet Isabell.

'They've found a dead man in Lake Farris,' she said, waving the mobile to show that this was where she had picked up the news. 'The body appeared after the water level went down.'

He looked at her. 'A man?'

'He vanished eight years ago,' Ella told him. 'Lost control when he drove round a bend on his motorbike.'

Evert Harting took out his own phone.

'It's on the *VG* site,' Ella said.

He located the story on his phone. The blazing sunshine made it difficult to see the screen, but he read enough of it to understand that the news had nothing to do with his own discovery.

He kept the phone in his hand. Although it was fairly new, photographs had been transferred from his old phone. It was usually Ella who took photos but sometimes he used his camera too.

He opened the image collection, navigated four years back in time and found two of Kjell-Tore. One from the first evening after he'd arrived from Sweden. They were barbecuing meat he had brought with him. It was raining. Kjell-Tore had dragged the barbecue under the parasol. He was standing in sandals, shorts and a high-neck sweater with the barbecue tongs in his hand. He looked pleased with himself as he stood there, with little streaks of laughter lines on his suntanned face. His sleeves were rolled up. Veins and sinews ran across the backs of his hands and snaked up over his arms.

The other photo was from a sunny day. Kjell-Tore stood bare-chested with his hands by his side and his back half-turned. Lake Farris was visible in the background. The kitten had also been caught in the picture, curled up on the grass with its head down.

This photo had been taken immediately before he and Ella had left to drive north and before Kjell-Tore had started building the new barbecue area.

A screech of metal sounded as the train arrived at the station and braked.

'Will you look after the car?' Ella asked. 'And I'll go and meet her.'

Looking up, Evert returned his phone to his pocket as the train jolted to a halt. Ella disappeared and left him standing there on his own.

13

Someone had spilled coffee on the stairs, a large puddle that was fast drying up. Wisting stepped around it and walked down to the basement car park.

He had assigned a patrol to head out in advance to make sure that no journalists or onlookers were present when Gunn Hilde and Reidar Wendel visited the discovery site.

They were waiting in their car just within the cordoned area when he arrived. Wisting got out, spoke to them through the side window of their vehicle and asked them to follow him.

A few small birds flew up from the gravel on the narrow track. Wisting drove slowly forward. Heavy branches bowed above their heads and strips of sunlight glinted through gaps in the foliage.

He stopped the car in approximately the same spot as before. Reidar Wendel drove up behind him. Together they walked forward to the wooden fence.

Gunn Hilde's face was ashen, as if she had not slept for a long time.

'Was it here, then?' she asked, placing one hand on the fence.

Wisting confirmed that it was. 'The fence was erected only a few years ago,' he explained.

He clambered over the lowest part of the fence and held out his hand to assist Gunn Hilde. She didn't seem to notice and instead used the fence for support. Reidar Wendel followed her. Wisting let them walk ahead, across to the edge. Gunn Hilde was moaning softly, and her shoulders began to shake. Her husband put his arm around her.

It was easy to make out where their son had been found. Footprints led to and from the pit where the motorbike had been dragged out of the dry earth. Nevertheless, Wisting pointed out the exact location and explained that it was normally submerged under five metres of water.

Leaves rustled in the surrounding silence.

'Have you spoken to the undertakers yet?' Wisting asked after a lengthy pause.

Gunn Hilde nodded. 'Gabrielsen phoned this morning,' she said. 'But we don't know anything more.'

Wisting reciprocated her nod.

'I spoke to an investigator from the ID group at Kripos before I came here,' he said. 'They've completed their examinations, but we won't receive the final formal confirmation until tomorrow. Gabrielsen won't be able to collect him before that.'

Prior to the undertakers assuming responsibility, the police were the official link between the next of kin and the deceased. All that Wisting could contribute was factual detail. He explained how the work was organized at the discovery site and told them that a recovery truck equipped with a crane had hauled out the motorbike.

'There's nothing left of him down there,' he assured them, in case they had any lingering doubts.

'What about all the other stuff lying there?' Reidar Wendel asked, waving his arm to indicate the pile of rubbish below.

'People have been disposing of refuse here for years,' Wisting said. 'That's why the fence was built. The landowner was anxious to put a stop to it.'

Reidar Wendel moved his hand away from his wife and walked forward a little.

'I want to go down and see for myself,' he said.

'It's rough terrain,' Wisting warned him.

Wendel moved further forward. Wisting pointed out the route but remained standing there beside Gunn Hilde.

A turboprop plane flew in from the north, approaching slowly and quietly. Gunn Hilde took no notice of it. Her husband had managed to find his way down. He manoeuvred between the odds and ends of scrap metal to the hollow where the motorbike had been located. For a while he simply stood there with his hands clasped in front of him, then he looked around, found a small metal plate and began to scrape the hard-baked earth until he had filled the hole.

Gunn Hilde raised her head heavenwards. The turboprop aircraft had veered to the east. Reidar Wendel completed his task.

'What have they done here?' he shouted up to them, pointing to the spot where the safe had been situated.

Coils of barbed wire had been hauled out to remove it.

Wisting waited until Reidar Wendel returned before explaining what else they had found.

'Do you know where it came from?' Wendel asked.

'No,' Wisting answered. 'It looked as if it had lain there for years.'

Gunn Hilde touched her throat, fiddling with her necklace.

'Would you like some time here alone?' Wisting asked them.

She shook her head. 'I want to go home,' she said.

Wisting followed them back to their car and watched it turn on the narrow track before they drove back. He cast a glance behind him at the steep precipice down to Lake Farris before he too got into his car and checked his phone.

Allan Broch-Hansen had not replied to his message. Wisting decided to drive there anyway to hear how things were going.

Once out on the main road, he issued instructions to the police patrol to remove the crime scene tape and open up the cordoned area. He drove on with his window open, turning on to the Helgeroa road.

An estate car was parked outside Allan and Irene Broch-Hansen's house, in the shade in front of the garage door. Wisting assumed they had picked up their daughter.

Allan Broch-Hansen opened the door, swinging it wide to usher Wisting inside.

'Is this a suitable time?' he asked.

'I saw your message,' Allan replied. 'We got home with Adine just an hour ago. She's up in her room now.'

They moved into the kitchen, where Irene was standing with her back to the worktop in front of the window.

'I just wanted to find out how you were doing,' Wisting said.

Allan cleared his throat. 'We're not very sure whether it was the right thing to do, picking her up,' he said. 'She should maybe have had a professional with her.'

'How did she react?' Wisting asked.

Irene crossed her arms. 'That's the problem with her,' she said. 'She doesn't show any emotion.'

Wisting shot an oblique glance at the floor above. 'Does she have any questions?' he asked.

Irene moved away from the worktop. 'I'll see if she wants to come down.'

Wisting laid aside the folder of photos from the discovery site and sat down at the kitchen table.

'Coffee?' Allan offered.

Wisting accepted gladly. A machine on the worktop ground the beans, filling the silence. Soon they heard two sets of footsteps descending the stairs.

Adine Broch-Hansen was wearing a soft, grey hoodie with matching trousers. It had been seven years since Wisting had seen her last. It seemed much longer ago. The years had set their mark on her face, like the map of a long, inconsolable existence. All the same, there was something appealing about her. She radiated a kind of melancholy that still made her appear attractive.

Wisting stood up. Adine reached out her hand, like a child who had been told how to greet people and was behaving exactly as instructed.

Even after more than thirty years as a detective, Wisting was unsure of what to say to people who had been affected by such major trauma. There was always a danger that whatever he said would make a bad situation worse.

'Nice to see you,' he said.

Adine nodded her head. Her gaze was lacklustre, and she had a faraway look in her eyes, as if she was thinking about another time, another place.

All four of them sat around the kitchen table. Wisting spoke up, sticking to factual information about the case. One hand rested the entire time on the folder containing documentation from the discovery site.

'I've brought some photographs,' he said, moving his hand away. 'If you'd like to look at them.'

These were printouts of a selection of overview images, made on ordinary photocopy paper. Looking at them would make the case seem more real to them, even though the details were more indistinct than if he had shown them on a screen.

Adine and her mother shook their heads, but Allan was

73

keen to see them. Wisting picked out four sheets of paper and slid them across to him.

'More coffee?' Irene asked, getting to her feet.

Wisting refused the offer. His cup was not yet empty.

Allan took his time examining the photographs. His daughter began to pick at a fingernail.

'Are we done?' she asked, looking at her mother.

'If you don't have any questions, then yes,' Wisting replied.

Adine simply shrugged before sliding off her chair and leaving the room.

'What about the two of you?' Wisting asked, turning to face Allan and Irene.

Adine's parents shook their heads. Allan pushed the pictures back across the table.

'I'll come with you to your car,' he said.

Outside, they heard children's laughter from the neighbouring garden. Allan Broch-Hansen's steps were slow and deliberate, as if there was something he wanted to say but needed time to put it into words.

'Just phone if anything comes to mind,' Wisting said when they reached the car.

Allan moved to avoid having the sun on his face. 'What is Reidar saying about all this?' he asked.

'He's not saying very much,' Wisting replied, opening the car door. 'I went with him and Gunn Hilde to the discovery site earlier today. I think it was good for them to have some certainty.'

'Reidar was always so calm and collected,' Allan commented.

They chatted for a while before Wisting sat in the driver's seat and drove off. In the rear-view mirror he saw Allan Broch-Hansen staring after him.

If neither family got in touch with him again, he could now

wrap up the case. But he knew he would continue to dwell on it. After nearly forty years in the police force, he had developed an instinct for knowing when something did not stack up. He had that feeling now, but just couldn't pin down exactly what was prodding at his intuition.

14

Evert Harting sat out on the terrace, leafing through one of Ella's magazines and listening to her and their daughter chat at the kitchen worktop. Isabell was telling her about a colleague who wasn't much liked by the students. Something about comments with unacceptable undertones.

'It's unlikely that Dad and I would have got together nowadays,' he heard Ella say.

'What do you mean?' Isabell asked.

'Well, you see, he had a higher position than me when we met at work,' Ella replied. 'I remember him flirting a lot, but today it's not so easy to know what's just flirting and what's considered wrong.'

'That's different, though,' Isabell protested. 'You weren't his student.'

She carried out the salad bowl and put it down on the table. It was mango and avocado with ready-cooked chicken from the local shop. Ella arrived with a basket of sliced bread. She made a few trips back and forth with salad dressings and cutlery before she finally sat down.

Isabell passed him the salad bowl so he could be first to help himself.

'Have you found anything?' she asked.

Ella answered for him. 'He found an old nail yesterday,' she said. 'From the 1600s.'

'From the Fresjeborgen fortress?' Isabell asked.

Evert smiled. She had heard him talking about the old stone building every summer she had been here.

'Well, it's from that time, at least,' he replied, passing the salad bowl.

'I fancy a swim later,' Ella said. 'It's twenty-five degrees in the water.'

Evert took a slice of bread and buttered it. 'I also found some gold,' he added.

'Gold?' Isabell echoed.

'A chain that someone must have lost while they were in swimming,' Ella quickly clarified. 'Everything's turning up on the lake-bed now that the water's gone. They found a dead man on the other side of the lake. Someone who'd been missing for eight years. He was lying there with his motorbike.'

Isabell had not picked up this news. Ella repeated the details she had gleaned from the online newspapers. Evert studied her as she talked. She continually touched her temple, pressing two fingers lightly on the nerves there, a gesture she made when she was nervous or worried.

He felt a sudden surge of concern for her. She kept guiding the conversation away from the gold initial necklace, as if it was painful for her to speak of it.

Kjell-Tore was her younger brother. There had also been another brother between the two of them, but he had died of a congenital heart defect seven years before Kjell-Tore was born. That might be what had made the relationship between Ella and her brother extra close and affectionate. From when he was small, she had helped him with everything and taught him all about the world as she saw it. She was the one he had gone to if he encountered any problems in life, and she always took his side. Like the time when there had been complaints from the pupils at Brynseng and then what had happened on his very first trip in the motorhome.

At Brynseng he had been working in a temporary caretaker post. Evert was not familiar with all the details, but it had something to do with him locking himself into a teachers' cloakroom adjacent to the girls' changing room. He was accused of peeping through a crack beneath the door when the pupils were getting undressed and going for a shower. It had all been a misunderstanding, apparently. Kjell-Tore had been in the teachers' cloakroom to repair a dripping showerhead. He was taken by surprise when pupils had suddenly burst into the room next door and had locked himself in until they left. In any case, that was how Ella had presented it. She had helped Kjell-Tore with a lawyer who had managed to get it all hushed up.

A few years later Kjell-Tore had bought his first motorhome. He had travelled north to Lofoten in it and was accused there of assaulting a teenage girl. In the newspapers it had been described as attempted rape, but in the end he had been fined for sexual harassment.

Suddenly, Ella got up from the table. 'We have to take a photo,' she said.

She fetched her phone, persuaded them to smile broadly and took several snaps.

'I want to have one of both of you together,' said Isabell, taking out her own mobile.

Ella sat down again and leaned towards him. He put his arm around her.

'Smile!' their daughter commanded.

They all laughed.

'One more!' Ella insisted, changing position in her seat.

Evert remained there with his arm around her until they

resumed their meal. A stray thought made him chew more slowly. He wondered if Ella had in fact handed in the gold necklace to the police or if she had got rid of it by some other means. Part of him hoped the latter was true. Everything would be different if he just hadn't found that necklace. Now he could not shake off the idea that it was going to lead to something that would tear this little family of theirs apart.

15

The public area in the police station's foyer was deserted. Bjørg Karin sat at the reception desk behind a glass partition, leafing through some documents. She was the social glue in the station, with her mild manner and concern for everyone. At the same time, she had a comprehensive overview of everything that went on, but never got mixed up in any of it.

'There you are,' she said, with a broad smile.

Wisting came in, checked his pigeonhole and picked up the papers it contained.

Bjørg Karin drew a small plastic bag with a zip closure towards her. 'There's something here I thought you should take a look at,' she said.

Wisting looked down at the plastic bag in her hand. 'What have you got there?' he asked.

Bjørg Karin opened the bag, poured the gold chain into her palm and held it up between two fingers. The initial pendant dangled to and fro.

'It's an initial necklace,' Bjørg Karin said. 'It was handed in as lost property a couple of hours ago.'

Wisting took the gold chain from her, held it in his own hand and felt his breathing become shallower.

'Who handed it in?' he asked.

Bjørg Karin had the lost property form in front of her. 'Ella Harting,' she read aloud. 'Her husband found it with his metal detector at the water's edge up at Lake Farris.'

Wisting gave her a searching look as he ran his thumb over the initial letter.

A for Annika.

'You're thinking about the Swedish girl, I take it?' he asked.

Bjørg Karin seemed disconcerted. 'Well, she did have a chain like that,' she said, though she immediately brushed it off. 'But, of course, probably loads of them are made.'

She handed him the bag that had contained the chain. He took it and dropped the necklace back in.

'How long ago is it now?' he asked. 'Three or four years?'

'Four,' Bjørg Karin replied. 'The eighteenth of July.'

They had received a tip-off that summer. Someone thought they had seen Annika Bengt waving from the rear window of a motorhome.

'I'll look into it,' Wisting told her.

He put the bag and chain on top of his bundle of post and carried it with him up to the department. The corridors were quiet, since most of the investigators had gone home for the day.

The computer hummed as the onscreen image appeared. He logged in and spent some time locating the Norwegian alert sent out by the Swedish police. Bjørg Karin was right. It had been the summer of four years ago. Annika Bengt had been reported missing on 18 July. The message from the national police headquarters in Stockholm had been issued two days later. The picture of the missing fourteen-year-old filled half the screen. The initial chain necklace hung in the hollow of her throat.

Wisting took the necklace out of the bag and held it up to the screen to compare them. They were identical. To be absolutely sure, he drew it up against the original one in the photo. They hung in the same way, with the initial slightly lopsided.

His mobile buzzed as a message came in. It was Line, sending him a picture of Amalie with her in a car, en route to fresh adventures in the USA. Both their faces were wreathed in smiles.

Wisting closed the message and rang Nils Hammer.

'Yes?' answered his colleague at the other end of the line.

'Where are you at the minute?' Wisting asked.

'Sitting in my car, on my way home,' Hammer told him. 'Has something come up?'

'Not really,' Wisting replied, lifting the gold necklace. 'It's just that I have something I'd like you to take a look at.'

'What is it?'

'Something I think will interest you.'

There was a moment's silence.

'You're at the office?' Hammer asked.

'Yes.'

'Then I'll be there in fifteen minutes.'

Only ten minutes passed before Hammer took a couple of steps into the room. Wisting pushed the gold necklace out to the edge of his desk.

Hammer stared at it.

'Bloody hell,' he said, picking it up. 'Annika Bengt . . .' He weighed it in the palm of his hand. 'Where did it come from?'

Wisting repeated what he had learned from Bjørg Karin. 'What are your thoughts?'

'I have to admit I didn't really have much faith in it at the time,' Hammer answered. 'If it hadn't been Peter O'Doyle's wife who reported it, it's far from certain it would have been followed up at all. In fact, I thought they put too much emphasis on it. When it came to the crunch, it was just a young girl in the back of a motorhome. But that was before the Solifer man, of course.'

Wisting cast a glance at the computer screen. He had already called up the case of the motorhome owner who had been nicknamed the Solifer man.

Hammer laid down the gold chain. 'The Swedes got nowhere with it,' he said.

'Do you still have the report?' Wisting asked.

'I probably have a copy in some folder or other,' Hammer replied. 'I'll go and find it.'

16

One after the other, Isabell and Ella balanced on the planks leading out to the lake. The afternoon sun was low in the sky and cast long shadows across the arid foreshore that surrounded them. They each had a towel draped over one shoulder, which they left on a boulder. Evert waited until they were both splashing in the water before he retreated indoors.

Ella usually left the diary in what they called the junk drawer in the kitchen, the top drawer nearest the door. Evert yanked it out and found a number of instruction leaflets, old receipts and a few crossword magazines, but no diary.

When he had first thought of it, he had envisaged being able to find out what she had written about the summer of four years ago, but of course she kept a book for each individual year. The old diaries were at home in Asker.

He kept searching all the same, looking in the cabinets above the worktop and some of the other drawers, but it was nowhere to be found.

The bedroom was another possibility. Sometimes she wrote in it before she went to sleep.

He moved to her side of the bed. The novel she was reading, a romance set in France, lay on the bedside table.

The diary was at the top of the drawer in the bedside table. It had a soft leather binding with an elastic cord around it. Taking it to the window, he glanced out at the swimmers as he leafed through to today's date. The notes section was blank.

Yesterday had a line or two about the temperature, both in the air and the lake.

Spoke to K-T, she had also added. *Was in Flensburg. Arriving on Thursday.*

Underneath, she stated that Isabell had sent a message and would be here in the morning. At the foot of the page, she had noted that they had eaten pork chops for a late dinner.

The previous day contained the same kind of information about the weather and what they had eaten. Two days earlier she had also spoken to Kjell-Tore. At that time, he had been on the coast outside The Hague in the Netherlands. Prior to that he had spent a week in a coastal resort in northern France.

He put back the diary and went to clear the table on the verandah. Ella's mobile phone lay by her seat.

He could hear raucous laughter from the lake below.

Evert picked up the phone. Ella used the same pin code for everything. Both bank card and mobile. It was a combination of her mother's birthday and the month her father had been born. 1408. They had used the same code on the alarm in the apartment at home in Asker.

He keyed it in, and the phone obligingly opened up. Evert moved in towards the doorway and stood half-hidden behind the corner pillar of the verandah roof. His fingers worked away on the screen. He opened the photo album and scrolled backwards in time. One year, two years, three years. The summer of four years ago. In the first picture of Kjell-Tore, he was sitting at one end of the table down on the new barbecue area. It must have been taken the day he and Ella had returned to the cabin after their trip in the motorhome. The next few images were of him with Ella on holiday in Trøndelag and of their journey through Gudbrandsdalen. It felt like rolling back time to those summer days.

Then Kjell-Tore popped up again. He was standing in front of the cabin, waving. The picture had been taken through the front windscreen of the motorhome, on the day he and Ella had set off. The kitten he had brought from Sweden was curled up on the step beside him. Kjell-Tore had named it Tuffy, as he recalled. It had gone missing while he and Ella were on holiday in the motorhome. Caught by a fox or just lost in the woods.

Other photos showed the days prior to that. Almost all of them had been taken at some meal or another. One evening they had received a visit from Ludvig Nordvik, who had come over from his cabin in Munkrodden. He sat in a narrow-brimmed sunhat, raising a bottle of beer to the camera. In a couple of the photos, Kjell-Tore sat with the kitten on his lap, while in others he stood holding the car wash bucket at the door of the motorhome. Several photos showed Kjell-Tore unloading the van on the day he arrived. He waved a few bottles of spirits he had smuggled with him and put some duty-free bars of chocolate on the table. The phone showed that the picture had been taken on 19 July at 18:46 precisely, around twenty-nine hours since Annika Bengt had last been seen.

Ella and Isabell were still in the water. Evert stood lost in thought as he scrolled further back through the camera roll. A picture appeared of Isabell holding up her catch. Two large trout. She had aged in the last four years. Had gone past thirty and acquired some wrinkles on her forehead and around her eyes.

He scrolled further back, and summer changed to spring. These were photos from his birthday, and then it was winter.

Kjell-Tore turned up again in the pictures from Christmas Eve. They had celebrated together. Isabell had been in Gran Canaria with a recently divorced girlfriend.

After Christmas came autumn, with photos of the holiday he and Ella had spent in Spain. There were a few more birthday photos before it turned to summer again. Five years ago. These were the same kind of pictures, posing in front of the cabin or sitting around a dining table. Isabell was not in any of them. It didn't look as if she had been here that summer.

The roll of images stopped after Easter. The older photos were probably stored on a computer somewhere. Ever since he and Ella had got together, she had been skilful at assembling photo albums, but when the commercial developing of photographs had come to an end, that had put a stop to the albums too.

He scrolled forward again and saw some photos from last summer when he and Ella had been in Molde. They had met Isabell there – she had been visiting a friend from her student days. She too had been offered a loan of the motorhome by Kjell-Tore, many times, but it wasn't something that appealed to her.

Down at the lake, Ella stood drying herself off. Isabell was now on her way up.

He exited the picture album, put down the phone and gathered up all the dirty plates and cutlery. They did not have a dishwasher at the cabin, and with the well being empty, he had to boil some water for washing-up. That took time. He moved outside again while he waited.

'Twenty-six degrees,' Ella said, setting down the thermometer on the table. 'I don't think it's ever been as warm as that in the water before.'

She disappeared inside to get changed. Isabell stayed

outside to dry her hair with the towel. Her wet bathing costume clung tightly to her skin, pasted to each and every curve. Evert looked down at Ella's phone, thinking of the photos of his daughter and realizing he was pleased that she and Kjell-Tore had not spent the summers here together.

17

Nils Hammer returned with an open ring binder. He sat down on the vacant chair and unclipped the rings that held the sheets together.

The tip-off had been phoned in on 23 July, the day the Norwegian media had first covered the Swedish missing person case from Bovikstrand. The call had been transferred to Nils Hammer. It was from Nina O'Doyle, who was married to the Irish blues musician Peter O'Doyle. They had a cabin at Nevlunghavn, and every year Peter gave a summer concert at the guesthouse there. The music was not to Wisting's taste, but Nils Hammer had attended several of the concerts.

Nina O'Doyle explained that she and Peter had been driving south on the E18 motorway on 19 July. Near Sandefjord, they had hung behind an old motorhome that was driving just below the speed limit. They themselves were towing a boat and so it had proved impossible to overtake. At one point a girl appeared in the rear window of the motorhome. She had waved to them. Nina O'Doyle had waved back, and her husband had commented that it looked as if the girl was lying on a bed at the back of the van. She should have been sitting in a seat with a safety belt on. After that, the motorhome had wobbled about a bit before taking the second turn-off towards Larvik. Nina O'Doyle and her husband had done likewise but when the road divided, they had driven in the direction of Helgeroa and Nevlunghavn.

They had not thought any more about it until they heard

about the girl who had disappeared from a campsite in Sweden. Then it struck them that the girl may have looked scared and that she had not only waved at them but also banged her hand on the Plexiglas window in some kind of desperate attempt to tell them she wanted out.

Hammer read aloud the report he had written after his conversation with Nina O'Doyle. They had never looked at the registration number and could not provide any description of the motorhome except to say that the window was on the right-hand side at the back and there was some sort of ladder or bicycle rack on the left-hand side.

They were certain of the date. It was the day they drove to their cabin. Nina O'Doyle had sent a text message to her daughter as soon as they arrived. The time had then been 17:13. That meant they had seen the girl about twenty minutes earlier. The motorhome had therefore turned off for Larvik twenty-seven hours after Annika had last been seen.

'I think I read somewhere that the Swedish police had received tip-offs from all round the world,' Hammer said. 'People had spotted her here, there and everywhere.'

Wisting nodded. He remembered there had been something about a lorry on a ferry to Morocco and a sighting on the Tube in London.

Hammer produced another sheet of paper from the ring binder. It emerged from this report that details of the sighting had been sent to an email address at police headquarters in Gothenburg.

'I heard nothing back at that time,' Hammer said. 'The following year, the investigative group was disbanded.'

Wisting's screen had dwindled into sleep mode. He woke it up again.

The Solifer man owned a motorhome that fitted the

description given by Nina O'Doyle. A Fiat Solifer with a rear window and a bicycle rack. That was how he had been given the nickname when, in the summer of three years ago, he had been a wanted man and arrested by the police.

The case had begun three days after Midsummer. A teenage girl had gone missing from a campsite at Stretere. Her parents had started searching for her in the early hours of the morning. Other teenagers claimed she had been drunk and had fallen asleep on the beach. An older man had tried to help her. No one knew who he was, but some of them thought he belonged to a motorhome on one of the twenty-four-hour parking sites. Her parents had investigated and discovered that a Fiat Solifer had left the parking bay in the course of the night. That was when the police were alerted.

The parking space was rented out to Werner Rudi whose address was given as Haugesund, but it turned out to be a false name. There was no requirement for ID on checking in, and payment was made in cash for three days. The registration number provided was also false but there was general agreement that it had been an old Solifer van. An alert was issued for the motorhome and roadblocks were set up. An Emergency Squad patrol stopped the vehicle near Lake Femund in the Innland region. At that point the girl had just woken up, more than ten hours after she had been abducted.

Due to the rapid clearing up of the case and out of consideration for the young girl, the story had not been reported in the media. It turned out that the man's name was Ove Rudi Werner, but he used only Rudi as his first name. He blamed a misunderstanding for listing his name as Werner Rudi and claimed that he had simply confused the numbers on his vehicle registration. The investigation showed that he had stayed at four campsites earlier that summer and given different versions of his name. At one of these locations, a flasher had been reported, but no formal complaint had been made. The girl he had taken from Larvik had not suffered any injury, but the Solifer man was sentenced to two years and nine months behind bars for false imprisonment.

Hammer continued to thumb through the ring binder. At the time the Solifer man was arrested, he had owned the motorhome for two years. He stated that he had holidayed in it only in Norway but could not provide any exact route he had travelled. He did not take photographs, was not present on social media and had spent several nights at the roadside. It was too late to track most electronic traces, but they had discovered that he had also been in the district in previous summers. The only date they could pin down with any accuracy was that on 22 July the previous year he had reversed into another vehicle outside the retail park in the town centre and an insurance claim had been lodged.

On board his motorhome, the sum of almost 3,000 kroner was found in Swedish banknotes. His bank account statements showed that he had made two large cash withdrawals the previous year from a cash machine in Svinesund, just on the other side of the Norway–Sweden border. These withdrawals were made more than two months before Annika Bengt disappeared. The Swedish investigators were informed of this, but it had not led to any progress in the case.

Hammer let the ring binder lie open on the desk. Wisting drew it towards him. At the top of one of the sheets of paper, the name of the investigator who had received the information was printed.

'What did you have in mind to do about it?' Hammer asked, indicating the gold necklace.

'I think we should raise it to a higher level,' Wisting replied.

He changed the screen image on his computer to a newspaper article that featured an interview with the senior investigating officer in the case, Ingrid Sandell, at the Swedish Police Authority in Gothenburg. She had a round face and appeared to be in her early fifties. Her dark hair was cut short, and her eyes were fixed on the camera, wearing a severe expression. The intention was probably to convey determination, but in fact it made her look rather sad.

The interview had taken place in connection with the second anniversary of the investigation. In summary, the article stated that the police were no closer to a solution now than they had been on the day Annika Bengt had disappeared.

Wisting came up with a stored number for international enquiries at the operations section of the national police in Stockholm. He made the call, introducing himself and explaining who he would like to get in touch with and, after a few taps on a keyboard at the other end, he was given a direct mobile number for Ingrid Sandell.

It rang for a long time with no response.

'Holiday?' Hammer suggested.

The call was transferred to voicemail with the standard spiel. Wisting terminated the call without leaving a message.

The time was now almost half past four in the afternoon.

'I'll try again tomorrow,' he said.

Deep in thought, he sat with his eyes trained on the initial necklace.

'Can you find out as much as possible about Ove Rudi Werner in the meantime?' he asked Hammer before turning his gaze back to the computer. 'All I know is that he was released from prison three months ago.'

18

The washing machine had completed its cycle. Kicki Dalberg had been walking around in her underwear since she'd stuffed in the trousers and T-shirt she'd worn when clearing the fore-shore at Lake Farris. There was probably gunge from the dead cat on both.

The machine, containing only those two items, had been set to sixty degrees. She felt no shame about it. No doubt Mia would have complained about the waste of energy. She went about in the same clothes for days on end before getting round to washing them. Until they stank of her sweat, and then even longer than that. One washing machine more or less meant very little in terms of the big picture. You could wash clothes for a whole year compared with a single flight to London. And she never travelled anywhere.

Spotify jumped on to a new playlist. Kicki swayed to the rhythm as she hung her clothes on the rack and set it out on the verandah.

It was neither concern for the environment nor thoughts about the climate that had made her into an activist. It had more to do with a defiant urge to protest and revolt. She had needed a place where she could feel heard and seen, where she could channel her anger and find an outlet for her own pain.

When she flopped down in the deckchair again, she received a message. Mia texted that the story was out on the internet and sent her a link.

Drought brings unexpected opportunity to clean up Lake Farris was printed above the photo of herself and Jonas. *See what they found!*

The article had been published only ten minutes ago but already two other items had superseded it. The opening of a new hairdressing salon and a warning notice about a road closure for the laying of new asphalt – these were obviously more important pieces of news.

Kicki clicked her way in and read. It did not take long. The journalist had not included very much of what Jonas had told him.

These teenagers believe the dry summer can be blamed on climate change, he had written. As if the cause of this dry spell could be called into question.

She felt irritated. Christ, this was more than something they had simply taken into their heads to believe. Researchers all over the world had scientifically proven that climate change is caused by human activities. For years, they had highlighted the results that were obvious everywhere now. But not even an educated journalist seemed to have understood these facts. So it was far from strange that the majority of people refused to take it seriously either.

It seemed as if what was most important to the newspaper editor was to show readers all the odd objects that had been found on what had now become barren land. They had published a whole series of photographs showing rusty shopping trolleys and warped golf clubs. Even her photo that included one of the rusty old bicycles. If the journalist hadn't left before they found the dead cat, it would almost certainly have been a focal point in the crazy cavalcade.

She skimmed the text, scrolling down to the foot of the page. Nothing about the global challenges or what was needed in order to tackle the climate crisis, but there was a separate paragraph explaining how much each of the discarded electric scooters had originally cost.

The entire enterprise had really been a waste of time. Picking up rubbish from the lake-bed trivialized the crisis facing the world. She had participated in order to give a warning cry, but it failed to reach anyone. Most people who read the story would probably do so because they thought it had something to do with the dead body found yesterday. There was also a report about that in *VG*, as if it were significant news. Mum had even phoned home from Scotland when she read about it and told her all about the girl this guy had tied up and raped on the living-room floor before taking his own life.

A lawnmower fired up somewhere in the neighbourhood. Kicki lay back in her chair, adjusting her bra a little, and looked around. The nearest neighbour was a man aged over eighty. If he wanted to gawp, he was welcome.

A plane etched a white trail of condensation in the sky high above her head. Slowly it broadened out before it became diffuse and dissolved completely.

Her mobile gave another buzz. Kicki reached out her hand and saw it was another message from Mia. *Coming to Larvik,* she wrote, along with a link to a golfing magazine. *Talking to Jonas about doing something to mark the event.*

It was a recent interview with the new Equinor head honcho, André Odalen. The eighth in a long line of male chief executives. Along the way they had scrapped the original name, Statoil – as if distancing themselves from a name that included the word *oil* would have any impact on their corrupt activities that were so hostile to the climate.

The article stated that he was trying to spend as much of the summer as possible at his cabin in Stavern and he was looking forward to the annual golf tournament at Larvik Golf Club. He would be attending with several others from the management board of the Norwegian firm and their operations abroad.

Kicki stared at the picture of the stout man in his fifties who led one of Europe's largest companies in the oil and gas industry. Meeting his contingent with banners and shouts of protest would not lead to any change whatsoever. The time for that was past.

Putting down her phone, she continued to perch on the edge of her chair. The noise from the lawnmower rose and fell. Filled with a restless tumult of emotion, she realized it would not subside unless she did something with it. Something serious.

19

The door lock was sticky again, as if it had grown stubborn and obstinate with age. Wisting had to jiggle the key to get in.

The house had soaked up the summer heat. During the day, the air had become dry and close.

He walked from room to room, opening windows to let in some fresh air. Then he changed into a T-shirt and shorts.

In the fridge, there was a plate of leftovers from yesterday's dinner, but it didn't look tempting. Instead, he chose a can of beer and went out on to the terrace behind the house.

The air was just as oppressive there as indoors, but he could not blame the weather for his feelings of disgruntlement. Thoughts of the Swedish girl swirled through his brain like an undersea current.

He drew his finger along the cold metal edge of the beer can before opening it.

Probably thousands of those gold initial necklaces had been sold, both in Norway and in Sweden. He had not seen one anywhere other than in the photos of Annika Bengt, but it was most likely a teenage fad that had come into fashion after Line had grown up.

He took a drink from the can. Drops of condensation had formed beads on the smooth metal as if the can itself was sweating in the summer heat.

They had once faced a case involving a dismembered foot in a training shoe. He still remembered the name of the manufacturer. Scarpa Marco. The trainer had been produced in

China. Each year around 15,000 pairs were imported into Norway. In total just over 50,000 of them had been sold throughout the country. But they were made in eleven different sizes.

The customer base was not the same for jewellery as for shoes, but he followed the idea all the same.

If 50,000 initial necklaces had been produced, they would have to be divided by potentially twenty-nine different letters, corresponding to the Norwegian alphabet. That would be just over 1,500 of each initial letter. But it would be similar to the shoes, in that three times as many pairs of size 43 were sold than size 46. The letter A was probably one of the most common and most widely sold. If he multiplied by three, that would be 4,500 necklaces. This meant that, rounding the numbers off, approximately 2 per cent of Norwegian women would own an A-necklace.

A large passenger ship sailed west in the outer shipping lane. The smoke rising from the funnel dissolved into thin threads that drifted apart. Wisting sat down in his usual garden chair, drawing one of the other chairs towards him and removing the faded cushion so that he could rest his legs on the seat.

He was just playing with numbers, but the likelihood that someone might have lost the same type of necklace as the one belonging to Annika Bengt began to diminish.

He took another gulp of beer.

Besides, it dawned on him that both men and women wore trainers. The truncated foot they had found had belonged to a man who'd been reported missing from the local retirement home a year earlier.

His phone buzzed. A message from Line. It struck him that he had forgotten to respond to the previous message, when she and Amalie had been in a hire car on their way to the coast. Now they were in an amusement park. Amalie sat in the front carriage of something that looked like a convoy of safari jeeps driving through the jungle. He wondered whether he should send a picture in return but contented himself with writing that it looked like great fun.

While he had the phone in his hands, he checked his email and read the news headlines. The local paper, *Østlands-Posten*, had published a new story about the discovery of the dead body in Lake Farris. The content was much the same as in the original report, but they had now sent a photographer to the spot and spoken to a local historian who said that the water level had never been so low since the dam was built at Lake Farris in the mid-1700s.

Beneath this article, he saw a related snippet of news – *Drought brings unexpected opportunity to clean up Lake Farris* read the headline above a photograph of two solemn-looking teenagers. *See what they found!*

The linking of these two stories seemed tasteless, making it appear as if Morten Wendel had popped up from the lake-bed like any other piece of rubbish. It did not seem as if the staff in the newspaper's editorial team talked to one another, or else it was an embarrassingly desperate attempt to attract readers.

All the same, Wisting clicked into the series of photos to see what the youngsters had found. Much of it was old, possibly objects that might have been lost in the water at the time when timber floating was still carried out, while others were more recent evidence of vandalism – shopping trolleys and electric scooters that had obviously been tossed in from the shore.

As he looked up from his phone, his thoughts turned again to the initial necklace. It was now almost eight o'clock in the evening, but it was not too late to try the Swedish investigator again.

The number was already listed in his call log. He let it ring until the voicemail chimed in. Instead of reading out a message, he wrote a text explaining who he was and where he was calling from. To make the information even easier to understand, he attached an image of the initial necklace and added that he was keen to discuss this find with her.

The screen darkened while he sat clutching the phone. He laid it down and took another drink of beer.

Suddenly the phone rang. A Swedish number calling. The same one that he had tried a moment ago.

He answered in his usual fashion: 'Wisting here.'

'Ingrid Sandell, Gothenburg police.' Although soft-spoken, her tone was firm.

'Thanks for phoning back,' Wisting said. 'Have you seen the photo?'

Sandell came straight to the point. 'Where was it found?' she demanded.

Wisting explained about the lake that had dried up and the man with the metal detector. 'It doesn't necessarily mean anything or have any connection—' he added.

'It does mean something,' Sandell interrupted. 'You wouldn't have sent it to me if you didn't think it meant something.'

She was right, of course. He had that indefinable feeling, that tight knot in his diaphragm, which years of experience told him to rely upon.

'A tip-off was phoned in to us when Annika Bengt disappeared,' Wisting went on. 'Someone thought they'd seen her in a motorhome here in Larvik, not far from the spot where the gold chain was found. A report was sent to you at the time.'

There was a moment's silence, as if Ingrid Sandell was taking time to cast her mind back.

'We can't have given it priority,' she said, without making any attempt at explanation.

'The following year we had a case of abduction, when a man abducted an intoxicated girl in a motorhome, but no direct connection was found between him and Sweden,' Wisting told her. 'I'd like to confer with you about whether or not there was any evidence in your case pointing to Norway. And if you think this necklace may have belonged to Annika Bengt.'

'There were nineteen Norwegian families at the campsite when she went missing,' Sandell replied, as if she still had all the case details at her fingertips. 'In addition, there were a few boys on a motorbike holiday and a Norwegian guy who worked at the marina. But nothing pointed directly to Norway. Until now.'

'You think so?' Wisting asked. 'That the necklace could be hers, right enough?'

'Well, it's certainly worth checking out,' Sandell said. 'A Dutch jewellery firm has the design patent. There aren't so many of them. In Sweden, 468 A-necklaces were sold up till the time when Annika disappeared.'

'You've checked that out, then?'

Ingrid Sandell elaborated: 'Loads of tip-offs came in about A-necklaces, including from a female junkie in Kungsbacka who'd started wearing one a few weeks after Annika went missing. We tracked her down. Her name was Agneta, and she told us a friend had given it to her. We got hold of the friend. His story was that he'd bought it online. Eventually we managed to confirm that. It turned out that the Dutch company had online outlets in a number of European countries, marketing in Swedish and other relevant languages. When someone ordered a necklace with the initial letter A, one was stamped out and posted from a factory in Estonia. We received a list of all the Swedish customers. Agneta's friend was one of them. Annika's mother too. She had bought the necklace for her.'

'Do you happen to know how many of them were sold in Norway?' Wisting asked.

'No, but I'd think there would be even fewer,' Sandell answered. 'The Dutch firm had been selling them for nearly ten years when Annika disappeared. The initial necklaces were only a small fraction of their range. I have a contact person there, so I can check it out. You should receive a comprehensive list so that you can get in touch with the various individuals and ask if they've lost their gold chain. Naturally, that should be done, but we should also tackle this on a broader front.'

'We?' Wisting repeated. 'Do you think this is enough to justify reopening the case?'

Ingrid Sandell gave no answer.

'Larvik . . .' she said, hesitating. 'I passed it once in my sailing boat. It's not far from the place where the ferry lands at Strømstad, is it?'

'Twenty minutes away,' Wisting confirmed.

'I can be with you tomorrow, around midday,' Sandell said. 'Does that suit?'

Wisting told her it did, adding: 'Let's take it from there, then.'

When the conversation had ended, Wisting leaned his head back in the chair and fixed his gaze on the sky above. Summer always brought a kind of peace, a kind of hiatus in time. That had now come to a juddering halt.

20

Evert Harting sat outside the cabin, a cup of coffee in his hands and his eyes trained on the lake. A faint heat haze was slowly dispersing.

Now, in summertime, he drank nothing but coffee in the mornings. It had cooled down while he sat there but he took a sip all the same before getting to his feet and tipping the dregs over the railings.

The verandah timbers creaked as he walked inside. Ella had turned on the radio on her bedside table. That meant she was awake.

He set his cup aside on the worktop to refill when Ella got up. His mobile was charging. It was half past eight and he had one unanswered message, only ten minutes old.

Hardly anyone rang him nowadays, at least not numbers he did not have stored alongside names in his contact list. Days could go by without him speaking to anyone on the phone. If somebody wanted to get hold of him, they sent a text message or wrote an email.

Grabbing the phone from the charger, he took it out on to the verandah again, where he looked up the number and found it was unregistered.

For a second or two he considered returning the call, but then decided it could wait. If important, they would probably phone again.

'Good morning.'

Isabell was standing behind him. He had not heard her approach.

'Good morning,' he said, with an affectionate smile. 'Did you sleep well?'

His daughter stretched her arms as she stifled a yawn.

'I slept with the window open and woke to the dawn chorus,' she said. 'Then I fell asleep again.'

'There's coffee,' he told her.

'Later.'

She padded down the steps, out on to the grass, heading to the outside loo, in a long-sleeved sweatshirt that reached to mid-thigh.

Evert sat down and read the online news. *Aftenposten* first. No major news stories.

His phone rang silently in his hand while he sat there. The same number that had tried to reach him earlier. He let it ring twice before answering, without volunteering his name.

'I'm William Wisting,' said the man at the other end. 'I'm calling from the police in Larvik. Am I speaking to Evert Harting?'

His voice was calm, controlled and friendly, but nevertheless provoked a sense of disquiet.

'That's me,' Evert confirmed.

'I'm phoning in connection with a gold chain, handed in as lost property yesterday,' the caller continued. 'Do you have any knowledge of that?'

Evert swallowed uneasily.

'That's me,' he said again. All of a sudden, his words felt jumbled. 'I was the one who found it. My wife handed it in to you.' He hesitated slightly. 'Is anything wrong?'

The policeman avoided answering the question. 'I suppose you're familiar with the area where it was found?' he asked instead.

'We have a cabin here,' Evert replied and began to explain how they had inherited it from Ella's parents. Probably of no interest whatsoever to the policeman, he thought even as he was speaking. 'We took it over fifteen years ago and have been here more or less every summer for the last thirty years,' he managed to round it off.

'Could you possibly come into the police station?' the policeman asked.

Evert Harting had stood up without realizing it. 'Because of the gold chain?' he asked.

'Yes,' the policeman said. 'When can you be here?'

Isabell was on her way back from the toilet. He thought about the eggs he had planned to boil and the breakfast the three of them had intended to eat together.

'In half an hour,' he replied.

The policeman thanked him, adding: 'Ask for Wisting when you come in.'

Evert Harting slipped the phone into his pocket.

'Who was that?' Isabell asked.

'A detective,' he told her. 'They want to know more about that gold chain I found.'

'Was it valuable?'

'Maybe. I don't know. I have to go to the police station.'

Ella was standing in the doorway. She had heard what they had been talking about.

'Aren't you going to have any breakfast?' she asked.

'I had a slice of bread when I got up,' he lied.

The conversation around the breakfast table might be strained.

He patted his trouser pocket to check he had his car key.

'But you don't know anything else about that necklace,' Ella protested.

'It probably won't take long,' he assured her.

'Have you done something wrong?' Isabell asked.

'What do you mean?'

'Did you have permission to search where you did? There are probably rules about that sort of thing.'

He smiled. 'Everything's fine, from that point of view,' he reassured her. 'I'll take the detector with me, so I can do another search before it gets too late in the day. I'll try to be back before lunch. We can eat together then.'

He packed his equipment and got into the car before he could be bombarded with any more questions.

The steering wheel vibrated in his hands and shards of gravel sprayed up around the tyres. His thoughts were churning in every direction. By the time he parked outside the police station, he had made up his mind to follow the same procedure as in various preliminary meetings at work: share the least possible information.

The investigator who met him was older than he'd envisaged. A man who had reached the age at which what he said was listened to with respect. There was something familiar about him, possibly from the media. A man who led major, serious investigations. Not the sort of person who got involved in lost and found.

They went to his office on one of the upper floors. The sun shone in through the window, highlighting the shelves stacked with ring binders. The wide desk was covered in tall piles of papers. Some of the letters on the keyboard at the computer screen had worn away completely.

Evert Harting sat down in the chair opposite the police officer.

'Thanks for coming so quickly,' Wisting said.

His face was wide, rough and angular, his eyes dark and narrow.

'I was a bit taken aback,' Evert replied. 'What's all this really about?'

Wisting opened a folder.

'We're making some enquiries for the Swedish police,' he answered. 'They're wondering if this necklace you found could be connected to a missing person case.'

He laid down the photograph of Annika Bengt that had appeared in the press. Leaning forward, Evert Harting tried to pretend he had not seen it before.

'Looks like the same necklace,' he said.

Wisting gave him a résumé of the case, outlining it succinctly with simple, straightforward facts. Evert Harting listened and nodded his head.

'I remember the story,' he said. It would be wrong to distance himself completely. 'But do you have any reason to believe it belongs to her?'

'The Swedes have worked on this for four years,' Wisting replied. 'They don't want to leave any stone unturned.'

'But how do they think it could have ended up here?' Evert asked. 'Do they believe she was abducted? And brought here?'

'That's one avenue of conjecture, as good as any other,' the detective responded. 'Can you tell me how you found the necklace?'

He nodded, giving a full explanation and directions to the location. 'You can see where I've been digging, if you go out there,' he told him. 'But there's nothing else around that spot, at least not anything made of metal.'

Wisting jotted down some notes. 'How do *you* think it got there?' he asked.

'I thought maybe someone had lost it while they were swimming,' Evert replied. 'Apart from that, I've no idea.'

'Do people usually go swimming there?' the detective asked.

'People go swimming all over the place, as you know,' he answered. 'But if it's as you suggest, then someone could have thrown it from the shore.'

That was not saying too much. Mere speculation. Just as good as anything else.

'How far is the discovery location from your cabin?' the detective went on.

'About a kilometre, I'd say.'

'Is there much traffic along that road?'

He shook his head. 'There's just one more cabin on our side, then the track goes on to a croft that's been taken over by the scouts. People drive along there to go into the woods, and for fishing or swimming. The kayak club is also situated at the beginning of the track, there's a bit of coming and going along there. And then the dog owners' club has a place where they run training classes.'

'What about camping?' the investigator asked.

'There are tents there fairly regularly,' Evert replied.

'What about motorhomes?'

His throat suddenly felt dry and constricted. What did this policeman know, in actual fact?

'There's probably been the occasional one,' he answered.

That was true, at least. They usually drove all the way up to Fossane before turning. There were several places where it was possible to overnight in a motorhome.

The policeman fell silent, as if he wanted Evert to tell him more. But there was nothing more to tell, at least not now. He had no grounds to say anything further. Anyway, Kjell-Tore did not camp in the way the investigator was suggesting.

The silence began to feel oppressive. He was close to asking a counter-question, about whether the police had any reason to suspect someone in a motorhome, but decided against it.

'Were you at your cabin in July four years ago?' the investigator asked.

'We've been there every summer for the last thirty years,' he replied.

'Yes, you said that on the phone,' the policeman told him, nodding. 'Do you have any thoughts about the summer Annika Bengt disappeared?'

Evert Harting shook his head slowly, closing his eyes momentarily and breathing out noisily, as if he could blow away the question and all the thoughts that were churning inside his head.

'It's a long time ago now,' he said by way of excuse. 'Maybe when I manage to collect myself, but right now I don't have any ideas at all.'

'Who lives in the other cabin?' Wisting asked.

'Hmm?'

'You said there was another cabin on your side of the track,' the detective reminded him.

'Yes, that's Ludvig Nordvik. An old bachelor, but probably fifteen years or so younger than me. He bought the cabin ten or twelve years ago.'

The policeman made a few more notes before his questioning took a different tack. He asked about the metal detector and what other objects Evert had found. Evert told him about the silver coins and the hand-forged nail. As he spoke, his pulse rate began to slow down.

The meeting had lasted half an hour when the detective rose from his seat.

'I'll show you out, then,' he said.

Outside, in front of the police station, he produced a card

with his contact details. 'Call me if you think of anything,' he said.

Evert Harting took the card, glancing from it up at the detective. He thought he could make out an expectant glimmer in the man's eyes.

21

Wisting lingered behind the sliding doors, watching as Evert Harting drove off. The man had tried to be open with him and give answers to his simple questions. However, he had detected a slight hesitation that jarred somehow. The pauses after each question had been unusually long before he came out with incomplete responses. Normally this indicated that some details had been held back. Or else it was simply a bad habit, carried over from a lifetime of working closely with politicians.

On the stairs up to the department, he bumped into the summer temp, Daniyal Rana, who had been involved in the removal of the corpse at Lake Farris. He hovered on the landing above, as if to let Wisting pass.

Wisting put his hand on the banister and stopped for a moment, giving him a friendly smile.

'Have you made any progress with the safe?' he asked.

Daniyal Rana's face lit up. 'I think so,' he replied. 'It's of Danish manufacture, produced in 1988.'

Wisting nodded. He had seen for himself the metal plate with that information stamped on the steel, but he let the young policeman tell him about his findings.

'I drove around in that area yesterday, in the evening,' he continued. 'Went from house to house, you might say. Or from farm to farm. They had all read or heard about the biker and were full of curiosity. They were keen to talk.'

'What did they have to tell you?' Wisting asked.

'As you know, the safe lay underneath some coils of barbed wire,' Daniyal Rana went on.

Wisting remembered that. The young officer produced a notepad from his breast pocket as he ploughed on.

'The ones I talked to, thought that was something . . .' He found the name in his notes. '. . . Johnny Skautvedt must have dumped when he tidied up an old sheep pasture before selling his entire smallholding and moving to Porsgrunn. According to the population register, that happened in 2009.'

Wisting was about to say something, but held back to let Daniyal Rana draw his own conclusion.

'So the safe must have been stolen and dumped sometime after 1988 but before 2009,' he summarized.

'Well done,' Wisting commented. 'Well investigated.'

'That's still a lengthy period of time,' Rana continued. 'More than twenty years, but there were also a few sheets of corrugated iron in the mud under the safe. If I find out when they ended up there, then I can narrow it down a bit further. Perhaps enough to make it possible to search for potential cases.'

'Do you have anything to go on?'

'Maybe,' Rana answered. 'I have the name of someone who replaced their barn roof fifteen to twenty years ago, but it's fairly doubtful that he'll be willing to admit he dumped the sheets of roofing in the lake.'

Wisting took a tentative step up the staircase.

'Be patient,' he advised him. 'Don't make any accusations or attempt to force a confession. Give him time to find a way to tell you what he did without placing himself in an awkward position.'

Daniyal Rana seemed unsure what that might entail but thanked him all the same. Wisting moved on up to the department.

For the moment he and Nils Hammer were the only ones who knew about the new investigation in the offing. Wisting headed into his colleague's office and shut the door behind him.

'What do you know about the Solifer man?' he asked.

'There's good reason to go on calling him by that name,' Hammer replied. 'He doesn't have a new address since his release from prison, but he did buy himself a new Solifer. It's possible he's living in it.'

Wisting stood with his back to the door. 'No job?'

'He receives some disability allowance.'

'What address has he given?'

'Just as a matter of form, his mother's old apartment in Haugesund.'

'So we don't know where he is at present?'

Hammer shook his head. 'We have everything we need to trace him, though. Reg number, phone number and bank account number. But for that he has to be formally declared a wanted man.'

'We're not at that stage at the moment,' Wisting commented. 'We've nothing on him as yet.'

'We have one possibility—' Hammer began.

'What's that?'

'The motorhome he used for the abduction was impounded,' Hammer explained. 'It was sold back to the caravan centre in Heggdal, since that was where he'd bought it. It's been used as a hire van ever since then.'

Wisting moved to the window and looked out in the direction of the company Hammer was referring to, even though it was located beyond his field of vision.

'The crime scene technicians didn't do much other than take photos of it,' Hammer went on. 'But if Annika Bengt was held captive in it four years ago, then in theory there could still be some biological traces of her there.'

His body language betrayed Wisting's scepticism. 'In a hire van? After several years?'

Hammer showed him the webpage of the caravan centre on which the motorhomes for hire were displayed.

'It's probably not the most popular one,' he pointed out. 'It's available for hire until the fourth of August. I think it's worth a try. We could hire it out and get the forensics team to examine it.'

Wisting gazed at the screen. The booking could be made online.

'Do it,' he said.

It felt like taking a step in the direction of something meaningful.

'We can pick it up before lunchtime.'

22

The tyres vibrated monotonously on the bumpy asphalt. The engine made a constant thrum in the background. Usually driving the car had a calming effect, holding his hands on the wheel brought a feeling of control, while at the same time he could enter into some sort of meditative state. No matter what, the road would take him where he wanted to go. Today he could not shake off the thoughts rattling around in his head, a cacophony of doubt and worries.

A police investigation was under way, and he was part of it. Less than twenty-four hours after Ella had handed in the initial necklace, he had been asked to attend for interview. They must have some basis for this, something that had prompted the detective to ask about motorhome traffic along the track leading to the cabin.

His life had always been like a placid river, slowly meandering through the landscape of everyday activity. No significant events had taken place. Now he was caught in a chaotic whirlwind of his own making.

As the turn-off approached, Evert Harting slowed down and swung off the road. The needle on the petrol gauge had crept downwards. He would have to fill up on his way back.

The grass on the lawn at the housing cooperative was brown and dead. The pennant on the pole at the entrance hung limply, the colours almost entirely faded.

The apartment lay in semi-darkness, with venetian blinds

pulled down and curtains closed. To him, the silence seemed almost hallowed.

Ella had a special drawer in the wall unit in the living room where she kept her passport and other important documents. Evert pulled it out. The diaries were there, stowed away at the very back. He found the right one and took it to the chair in front of the TV, switched on the reading lamp and sat down.

The contents had the same abbreviated format as in the book he had read at the cabin. He riffled through to 19 July. *K-T arrived from Sweden around six o'clock*, it said. The weather had been fine, but not so very warm, he read. Only twenty-two degrees Celsius. The days before and after confirmed what he had seen in the photos on Ella's mobile phone. They had spent three days in Kjell-Tore's company before driving north in his motorhome. It mentioned the kitten he had brought with him, and that it had gone missing. It detailed what they had eaten, when he had left, and when the cabin was closed up at the end of the season.

His fingers had begun to quiver as he leafed through the pages — he was filled with a sense of doing something forbidden.

He went back to the days prior to Kjell-Tore's arrival. On Saturday 16 July, he had spoken to Ella on the phone. *K-T in Sweden, at Bovikstrand. Coming here on Tuesday*, was what she had noted. The three days prior to his arrival contained only brief jottings about the weather. A few days before his stay at Bovikstrand, he had travelled across from Poland by ferry to Ystad in Sweden. Throughout his journey he had reported home to Ella. It looked as if he had undertaken a circular trip that crossed Denmark and Germany but had spent most of his time in Poland before travelling back to Norway via Sweden.

Evert raised his head and stared at the wall above the TV set. Kjell-Tore had been at Bovikstrand on Saturday 16 July. Annika Bengt had gone missing in the early hours of Monday the 18th. On the evening of Tuesday the 19th, Kjell-Tore had arrived at the cabin. His name must be on some kind of guest list somewhere. Maybe the police had already made the connection and that had been why they had been so quick to call him in for interview.

Abruptly, he got to his feet and gave himself a shake, almost in an effort to throw off his paranoid thoughts.

It had become difficult to breathe, as if he had over-exerted himself or was wearing a tie that was too tight. He walked to the terrace door and peered out between two slats before opening it. The air outside was no different. Heat shimmered above the surrounding rooftops. His thoughts continued to wheel around in circles as if they had lost all sense of direction.

It would be easier if Kjell-Tore died in a road accident or was subject to some other kind of sudden death, rather than that his actions were exposed. Death was something they could get through. Even Ella could manage that. The other accusations would be more difficult to accept.

Shaking his head, he moved away from the terrace door and headed into the kitchen. He shouldn't think as if Kjell-Tore was guilty. Not yet at least.

He turned on the kitchen tap. The water had to run for a long time before it became cold. He filled a glass, took a long drink and filled it again before taking the glass with him back to the chair and the diary. It lay open at a week in May. *K-T in Kristiansand*, it stated. *Laying slabs.* He flipped back and forth through the pages. Several weeks later he had been at a similar job in Halden before leaving on the ferry for Denmark, as he had done every summer for the past few years.

What had he actually been up to on those trips? A single man in a motorhome. He hardly ever said much about it. It wasn't as if they heard many stories about things he had experienced or places he had been. It seemed as if he kept mainly to the coast, visiting beaches and campsites.

He took out his mobile phone and took a photo of the pages that told him where Kjell-Tore had gone before he arrived at Bovikstrand. Then he skipped back and took pictures of the notes referring to Kristiansand and Halden. He continued to flick through the pages and took more photos of all the instances where Ella had mentioned *K-T*. Afterwards, he went back to the drawer and took out the other diaries.

Last year Kjell-Tore had driven all the way down to Croatia. Evert recalled that he had told them the drive had not taken any longer than three days. According to Ella's notes, he had spent the night in Leipzig and some place on the Austrian border on his way south. He snapped some images of this and went on browsing through the book.

An hour later, he had documented all Kjell-Tore's travels, even the ones he had taken round and about in Norway. He returned the diaries to the drawer and carefully pushed it shut, as if terrified anyone would hear him.

23

'I've booked a motorhome,' Hammer said by way of introduction.

The girl behind the counter, in her mid-teens, was wearing a tight sweater with a slogan about saving the environment. *Planet before Profit.*

'Name?' she asked, turning to the computer screen as she continued to chew gum.

'Nils Hammer.'

The keyboard clattered. Wisting looked around the premises while the hire agreement details were registered. A fairly elderly couple stood in a section containing camping chairs and tables, but apart from that the place was empty. Outside, there were rows of new and used motorhomes and caravans with sales signs displayed in their windows. On the other side of the yard, he saw a workshop and a showroom with large plate-glass windows.

'I'll get Mr Pape to show you the van,' the girl said once the hire agreement had been completed. 'He's over in the new building.'

The name was writ large on the wall behind her as part of the company logo. Patrick Pape.

'Just go out and wait and he'll meet you there,' she said, picking up the phone.

Hammer brought the signed papers with him. Wisting walked a bit further along the concourse and located the old motorhome between two used caravans. It felt strange to see it. He remembered the tense hours when the hunt had been at its height until the van and the girl from Stretere had been found at Lake Femund.

He moved behind it and studied the window, picturing in his mind's eye the description of the girl who had been hammering her hand on the plastic pane. It must have been washed over four years. The van would be cleaned after each hire, of course, the cost of which was included in the charge.

The curtains were closed. All the same he moved closer, standing slightly on tiptoe, and peered inside. A dead blue-bottle hung with one of its legs, thin as thread, caught in the flimsy fabric of the curtain. The Plexiglas itself had some discoloured patches, both inside and outside.

He tried to think of when he had last washed the windows at home. Around Easter he had tackled the outsides, but the insides had been longer ago. He had never cleaned the insides of his car windows. He had owned the vehicle for nearly five years now and had probably wiped the inside of the front windscreen a few times, but never the rear.

This thought made him feel more optimistic than he had been when they arrived.

He walked back to Hammer just as a well-tanned man with sun-bleached hair emerged from the glass building opposite. A shaggy dog trotted along at his side.

'Well now, are you planning a trip?' he asked, shaking their hands in turn while the dog came forward and sniffed them eagerly.

The man was smiling in a way Wisting found distasteful. It seemed like a mask glued on, worn to conceal something.

He smiled back and gave Hammer a nod, as if to convey that he was the hirer of the van. 'I've just come along for company,' he explained, avoiding giving his name.

However, it appeared that Patrick Pape had recognized him. Although he retained his salesman's smile, behind it he discerned a sliver of apprehension.

'I can give you a better deal than this,' he said, holding up the agreement papers. 'A newer and larger van. I may be able to do something about the price too.'

'We've decided on this one, thanks,' Hammer said.

Pape lowered his arms, as if with a sense of resignation. His smile vanished.

'You know about this van?' he asked. 'It was previously placed at the state's disposal. I bought it from you lot.'

Hammer crouched down and scratched the dog's neck. 'That's right,' he admitted.

'So, what's all this about?' Pape wanted to know. 'Has the case been reopened, or what?'

'We may conduct a kind of reconstruction,' Wisting replied. It was a half-truth.

Hammer stood up again.

'A training programme based on the case,' he added. 'For the new police students who're starting this autumn.'

'I see,' Pape answered. 'I'll have to show you how everything works all the same.'

He ran through the instructions for use of the propane gas, the toilet facility and the water system before handing over the keys to Hammer.

'Has it been hired out much?' Wisting asked.

'More or less the whole season,' Pape replied. 'Mainly to people on a low holiday budget. This year, though, it's been mostly in the yard. People have become used to nothing but the best. They want the newest and most modern ones. I'm really trying to sell it off now.'

Wisting wanted to ask if he had a list of all the previous

hirers, but was unable to come up with a good reason why he might request that.

Hammer climbed in and sat behind the wheel. The motor-home started up with no problem. Patrick Pape's face broke into his well-practised smile.

'Call me if you need anything,' he said encouragingly as he headed back to the glass building.

Wisting stood on his own watching Hammer drive away. The curtains in the rear window swayed from side to side with the rock and rhythm of the van's movement. The sun glinted on bright metal somewhere along the side of the vehicle. When it had gone, the heat settled, quivering on the asphalt road surface.

24

Wisting had given directions while Hammer reversed the motorhome into the inspection garage. It only just cleared the roof.

It was in fact something Wisting fancied. Taking a road trip with a cabin on wheels. Simply following wherever the road took you, leaving the daily routine behind and waking up to a new location every day. Ingrid would have liked it too, he thought. He pictured himself in the driver's seat. They could have taken Amalie on a holiday, driving through mountains and glens, buying ice cream along the way and picking wildflowers in a meadow.

He slammed the door shut. The bang echoed around the brick walls.

The key was still in the ignition. Instead of locking up, he sealed the doors with tape and marked them with his name.

The senior investigating officer of the Swedish investigation had sent him a text message while he had been doing this.

A total of 403 A-necklaces sold in Norway, she wrote. *See you in a few hours.*

He confirmed receipt of the message and said that a room had been arranged for her at the hotel on the slope below the police station. Just then, Maren Dokken phoned.

'You wanted me to let you know about the ID work on Morten Wendel,' she said without any preliminaries.

'The family's waiting for confirmation,' Wisting said.

'The DNA tests may still take a while longer,' Maren

explained, 'but they've found fracture injuries on a leg bone that match his medical history. He broke his leg in a skiing accident when he was fourteen.'

Wisting thanked her for the information. 'Then I can tell them that if they ask. Otherwise, I'll wait until we know for certain.'

'There's actually something else I wanted to discuss with you,' Maren added.

'Yes?'

'Just something I was wondering about,' Maren said. 'It doesn't mean anything today, but the Broch-Hansen family were the nearest neighbours when Morten Wendel disappeared. All the same, it doesn't look as if they were asked about anything. I know of course that the situation was a bit delicate. He had raped their daughter, and their house burned down, but it would still have been natural to ask what they saw or didn't see the night he went missing.'

Wisting shifted his phone to the other ear. 'If you wait a moment, I'll come up to your office,' he said.

'Only if you have time.'

'Give me two minutes.'

He called into his own office and picked up the sealed folder marked with a minus sign and headed to Maren's office.

'They *were* asked, all three of them,' he said, taking a seat. 'It was only Allan and Irene who were at home the night Morten Wendel went missing. Adine was staying the night with an aunt who had a daughter of the same age.'

He broke the seal on the folder and located the two statements.

'They didn't have anything to contribute,' he went on. 'They had scarcely seen him after he'd been released from custody. Irene Broch-Hansen told the investigators she hoped he'd ridden out into the forest and hanged himself.'

Maren drew the papers towards her. Wisting waited as she skimmed through them. It did not take long. Irene Broch-Hansen had been out in the front garden watering the flowers, but apart from that they had spent the evening watching television together.

'Morten Wendel disappeared sometime between 19:15 and 21:30,' Maren remarked.

Wisting nodded. The time had been fixed because his parents had gone out around seven and when they returned, both he and his motorbike were gone.

'Their car was picked up on CCTV in both directions,' Maren added, mentioning the surveillance camera outside the sports centre further down in the residential area. 'Morten must have taken a different route.'

'That's right,' said Wisting. 'We collected CCTV footage from the whole town and looked through hours of recordings without spotting him. To be honest, it was all we had to work on.'

Maren glanced at the folder on his lap. 'You have more documents there,' she said.

'These are a few photos from the same surveillance camera that picked up when Morten's parents left and came back,' he replied. 'There's video footage too.'

He placed three sheets of paper in front of her, mostly showing the same thing, a white delivery van with a tail lift.

'That's Allan Broch-Hansen's vehicle,' Wisting explained.

'The time given is 05:48,' Maren pointed out.

The time stamp was clearly marked in one corner of the printout.

'It was just by chance I spotted that,' Wisting said. 'Maybe mainly because there were no other cars out driving at that time.'

He sat up straight. 'We kept extending the time window

of the material we were looking through,' he continued. 'The idea was that Morten Wendel could have driven around aimlessly all night. I sat one evening and played the recording at double speed, searching for motorbikes, but I thought there was something familiar about this van.'

Wisting put down another picture. 'He comes back one hour later.'

Maren sat with a photo in each hand. 'Where was he?' she asked.

'He wasn't asked about it until a fortnight afterwards,' Wisting answered. 'A lot had happened in the meantime. Their house had burned down.'

'But he must have had some explanation for it?'

Wisting shrugged. 'Just that he was out driving. He was suffering from insomnia after that business with his daughter. He used to lie awake all night long. When he became too restless, he went for a drive to get some air. Sometimes he parked beside the canal quay and walked along the quayside, other times he drove around in the Bøkeskog forest. He couldn't say where he had been that night.'

Wisting was aware of Maren's penetrating gaze. 'What do you think he was doing?' she asked.

He held back for a moment or two before responding: 'There's one detail you may have picked up on,' he said, pointing at the bundle of case documents. 'The neighbours usually heard Morten start up his motorbike. He'd probably tinkered with the exhaust system to improve the performance.'

Maren nodded. 'No one heard him drive off,' she said.

'One way that could have come about is that both the motorbike and Morten were driven away in Allan Broch-Hansen's delivery van,' Wisting said calmly.

He saw her thoughts begin to circle. She grabbed a pen,

as if getting ready to start writing in order to keep track of them.

'The time frame doesn't fit, though,' she said.

'Something may have happened that evening,' Wisting replied. 'Morten and his bike may have been placed inside the van then and lain there until the quietest part of the night.'

'But then it must have happened in the full light of day,' Maren objected. 'There are a number of neighbours there and traffic in the street.'

This was a counter-argument that had already been tested. A tall boundary hedge meant that the two properties were secluded, though there was free passage between the two gardens. Morten Wendel's motorbike was usually parked at the side of the house. Allan Broch-Hansen generally reversed his van into the courtyard. Using the tail lift, he could easily have managed to hoist both a dead body and a motorbike aboard and keep them hidden.

'So you mean he killed his daughter's rapist?' Maren asked.

'It's an unproven hypothesis,' Wisting asserted. 'But such things have happened before. This was six days after Morten Wendel had been released from custody. He was walking about freely, just a few metres from the walls of their house. Adine couldn't bear it. She was unable to go on living there. You can imagine how a father would feel, and what his mental state would be.'

'But didn't you do anything?' Maren protested. 'Wasn't it investigated?'

'We followed it up as far as we could,' Wisting answered. 'There's a reason for the existence of a minus folder.'

He put down the whole folder. 'The papers there are classified,' he explained. 'They belong to the clandestine investigation.'

'What did you do?'

'We brought in his van. Had it examined without him knowing or noticing anything.'

'How did you manage that?'

'We deliberately damaged it so that it had to be taken in for repair. While it was there, we used cadaver dogs to search the cargo space and got the forensics technicians to examine it.'

'I assume the case would have a different status if you'd found anything?'

'No reaction,' Wisting said. 'Not so much as a drop of engine oil.'

'But you're still unconvinced?'

Wisting swatted a fly.

'There is an explanation,' he said. 'The body doesn't have to have had contact with the floor of the van. It could have been placed in a cargo crate. That would have made it easier to handle.'

He was now perched on the edge of his seat. 'You said the forensics team had found old fracture injuries on his leg,' he said. 'Was there any mention of other injuries?'

Maren shook her head. 'The autopsy is not finished yet, but everything is being photographed and documented. I'll have the results sent over.'

She fiddled with her pen. 'What are your thoughts now that he's been found?' she asked.

'I'm not sure yet,' Wisting told her. 'It's plausible that he drove off to commit suicide, but I've given it a lot of thought. It's also entirely possible that his body was placed on the motorbike and the person who drove it sat behind him, accelerated and stayed with him beyond the water's edge, then swam back to shore.'

He saw that Maren was finding it difficult to digest this theory.

'Then there's this business of the fire,' he went on. 'The Broch-Hansen house burned down the day after Morten Wendel disappeared. If anything had happened in there that evening, all evidence of it went up in flames. There was no longer a crime scene. No crime scene and no body – until now.'

He sat gazing at the young detective. 'Well, what do you think?' he asked when she didn't say anything.

She shook her head, as if she had nothing important to contribute, but all the same she drew her notebook towards her and opened it at one of the last pages. It was punctuated with half sentences and keywords. One of them was circled.

Tape.

'I thought it striking that Morten Wendel was taped to the handlebars, almost in the same way that Adine was taped to the furniture when he raped her, but decided it wasn't so strange. He'd used that method once on her and was able to use it again on himself, but there could be an element of revenge in it. An eye for an eye, a tooth for a tooth.'

She paused for a beat before she rounded off: 'Maybe the dogs didn't react in the van because he wasn't dead yet,' she said.

This was an idea that Wisting had not considered. He sat in silence for a few minutes, taking this in. Then he got to his feet.

'We don't know what really happened,' he said. 'Or indeed whether anything happened at all. And maybe we never will.'

He tapped his fingers on the folder containing the classified reports as a sign that she should hold on to them.

'Things have a tendency to come to the surface, though, sooner or later,' he said. 'Make sure you're ready if that should happen.'

25

The Swedish investigator was suddenly standing in his office doorway. Bjørg Karin had shown her up.

'You have a visitor,' she said. 'From Sweden.'

Wisting rose from his seat and greeted her warmly. Ingrid Sandell looked different from her photograph. The slightly stern expression was replaced by a more vivacious demeanour.

'I'll get something for you to drink,' Bjørg Karin said. 'Do you want to remain in here or move to the conference room?'

'We'll stay here,' Wisting said.

Ingrid Sandell put down her travel case immediately inside the door.

'Do you have it here?' she asked once they were left on their own.

Wisting sat down and opened the bottom desk drawer. The initial necklace was still in the plastic bag Bjørg Karin had used. He opened it and poured the chain out on to a blank sheet of paper.

Ingrid Sandell produced a pair of glasses and leaned forward.

'Feel free to pick it up,' Wisting told her. 'It's been under water for a long time, buried in mud.'

She lifted it up. Her breathing was audible. The gold chain slid slowly between her fingers. The A lay for a moment on the back of her hand before she studied the catch.

'The link next to it is damaged,' she said, glancing up at him. 'It looks broken.'

Wisting had drawn the same conclusion. The gold chain had not simply been lost – it had been torn from the neck of whoever had worn it.

'You wrote that four hundred and three A-necklaces had been sold in Norway,' he said.

Ingrid Sandell still sat with the necklace in her hand.

'I spoke to the Dutch manufacturer,' she said. 'They need a court order before they'll hand over a customer list.' She made a face, looking discouraged. 'You know, privacy protection.'

Wisting made some notes. 'I can get the papers to the court by tomorrow morning,' he said.

The Swedish investigator moved the chain to her other hand.

'I've read the witness statement about the girl at the window and the report on Ove Rudi Werner,' she said. 'The Solifer man.'

'We know he was here the summer Annika disappeared,' Wisting summarized. 'We don't know if he was in Sweden, but three days after the witness observation, he was involved in a road accident here in Larvik.'

'And the following summer he abducted a girl from here in the town,' Ingrid Sandell rounded off for him.

Bjørg Karin returned with water and coffee as well as a plate of biscuits. Wisting thanked her and explained that Bjørg Karin had been the one who had taken charge of the A-necklace when it was handed in.

'Could the person who found it tell you anything more?' Sandell asked.

Wisting replied: 'Nothing except provide details of the exact spot where he found it.'

They were left alone again.

'Do you have a photo of the Solifer man?' Sandell asked.

Wisting turned to face the computer screen.

'We gathered in more than eleven thousand photos from the campsite and the surrounding area from the last twenty-four hours before Annika went missing,' Sandell added.

'Eleven thousand?' Wisting repeated in surprise.

'There were almost two thousand overnight guests at the site,' Sandell replied. 'They all took holiday snaps. If our man isn't to be found on the lists, he could well be in one of the photos.'

Wisting put Werner's mug shot on the screen, taken from the front and in profile. He was a skinny guy whose dark hair was combed back from his forehead.

'The NOA has adopted a facial recognition program,' Sandell continued, talking about the Swedish police's national operations department in Stockholm. 'It's used to find out if people on CCTV footage are registered in the photographic records, but it must be possible to use it in the opposite way too.' She pointed at the screen. 'They must be able to see if he's in the photos from Bovikstrand.'

'I can send you the image,' Wisting said.

Ingrid Sandell nodded. 'Apart from that, what are your thoughts, going forward?'

'We've taken possession of the motorhome,' Wisting told her, explaining how it had come about. 'The crime scene technicians will make a start on it tomorrow.'

Sandell seemed impressed by his efficiency. Wisting felt obliged to clarify the situation a little.

'You have to remember that this is one of Norway's largest camping areas,' he said. 'In addition, the main road between eastern Norway and the south coast runs through this district. There are other explanations.'

'But this is what we have to work with,' Sandell objected, describing it as the Norwegian lead.

Wisting helped himself to a biscuit.

'Do you have a list of all the Norwegians who were present at Bovikstrand?'

Sandell nodded and moved to her travel case to take out a folder she had prepared in advance.

'I went through it yesterday,' she said. 'The lists are based on the booking system at the campsite. I said there were nineteen Norwegian families in residence, but that only means there were nine Norwegian motorhomes. All the same, we've been in contact with them all. There are no single Norwegian men among them.'

'Does the perpetrator have to have been a registered guest at the campsite, though?' Wisting asked.

'I don't think he was,' Sandell replied. 'The campsite was chock-full. We know they turned away drop-in customers. Some of them camped in the surrounding area for a night or two. In the car parks and along the roadsides. Wild camping, as they call it.'

She took a sip of coffee. 'How well do you know the case?' she asked.

'Just through the media, really,' Wisting answered.

'Well, Annika Bengt was to spend the night in a caravan with two of her friends but headed off to call in at her parents' van,' Sandell explained. 'The quickest route there goes outside the campsite. Along a footpath, out on to the public road and back in through the main entrance. We're talking about a matter of eight hundred metres. We believe she disappeared somewhere along that stretch.'

'It would be easy just to push her in if there was a motorhome with its door open somewhere along that route,' Wisting pointed out.

He began to look at the documents in the folder. None of the names were familiar.

'There's an electronic version too, that you can search through,' Sandell said, laying down a memory stick. 'Can we go down now and look at the van?'

Wisting glanced at her cup. It was only half-empty.

'Of course,' he replied, rising from his seat.

They took the lift. The air down in the basement corridors was cool compared to the rest of the building. The ceiling light in the inspection garage came on automatically when they stepped into the room. The fluorescent tubes flashed a few times before the motorhome was flooded with light.

Ingrid Sandell made a circuit of the vehicle.

'Let's say it was her,' she began. 'I took four and a half hours to get here, but then I caught the ferry from Moss to Horten.'

Wisting had already calculated the travel route from Bovikstrand.

'Five hours if he drove via the Oslofjord tunnel,' he said.

'The sighting here was made more than twenty-four hours after she was last seen in Bovikstrand,' Sandell continued, but avoided mentioning what she thought had been done during those hours. 'We worked according to a forty-eight-hour time window when we were searching for her. There's an FBI statistic that says most abducted children are murdered within that time frame.'

'The girl abducted from here was found after ten hours,' Wisting said. 'She had traces of diazepam in her blood. It could have been something she used to get high herself, but an empty packet of Stesolid was found in the van's glove compartment.'

He pointed at the cab of the motorhome.

'Suppositories,' he added. 'Ove Rudi Werner used them to alleviate muscle stiffness and cramps. The girl was blind drunk and already in a helpless condition when he took her.'

'Was she examined?'

'She was taken to a rape reception centre,' Wisting answered. 'They found no sign of sexual assault. The suppositories were not under discussion at that point. It's possible they could have discovered something if they'd known what to look for.'

They walked behind the motorhome. Neither of them spoke. Wisting could picture in his mind how Annika Bengt had woken from a deep, drugged sleep and tried to attract attention from other cars on the road.

Ingrid Sandell withdrew a few paces to stand with her back to the wall, her head tilted slightly. Something about her gaze bore witness to hard-earned experience and acumen.

'What are you thinking?' Wisting asked.

'I think she's here somewhere,' Ingrid Sandell answered, turning to face him. 'If it was Annika Bengt who was seen in that window, he hasn't merely got rid of her necklace. This has to be where he's also disposed of her body.'

They exchanged a fleeting look, conveying a silent understanding that they shared the same thought.

Wisting thrust his hand into his pocket and took out his car keys.

'I can show you the discovery site,' he said.

26

A pair of scrawny roe deer trotted along a single tyre track. They hopped quickly off to the roadside and slipped in between the trees when Evert Harting came motoring along. It was as if the drought had forced them to search out new grazing grounds.

He dropped his speed even further before rounding the last bend and driving down to the cabin. Ella and Isabell were sitting in the shade on the verandah. Isabell waved to him.

The heat rushed into the car as soon as he parked. He first left all the windows slightly open to air the interior and then took his time retrieving the metal detector from the boot.

Isabell had a book on her lap. Ella was polishing her glasses.

'You've been ages,' she said, inspecting the lenses. 'We had to have something to eat.' She replaced her glasses on the bridge of her nose. 'The rest of yesterday's salad.'

The empty plates were still on the table in front of them.

'What did the police say?' Isabell asked.

'Not much,' Evert replied. 'They wanted to know how long we'd been here and whether I'd found any other jewellery.'

'Maybe it's from a major robbery or something,' Isabell suggested.

'Possibly,' he said. 'They asked about the traffic along the track. What kind of vehicles drove on it.'

'This summer?' Ella asked.

'Previous years as well,' Evert answered.

He saw an apprehensive expression cross Ella's face.

'There were two roe deer up near Ospebrekket,' he said, changing the subject. 'I've never seen them there before. They looked hungry and thirsty.'

Isabell glanced at the detector. 'Did you find anything more?' she asked.

'Just scrap metal,' he fibbed. 'Beer cans and loose screws.'

'Can I come with you next time?'

Evert smiled. His daughter had never shown any interest before.

'If there's a treasure trove lying there somewhere, I'd like to be with you when you find it,' she said.

'We can have a jaunt before dinner,' Evert promised.

He went indoors, putting the detector on to charge, and took a couple of slices of bread out to the verandah again. Ella was engrossed in one of her crosswords.

'Norwegian mountaintop with twelve letters?' she asked. 'Starts with GA- and ends in -EN.'

'*Galdhøpiggen*,' Isabell suggested.

Ella counted the number of letters. 'That fits,' she said with satisfaction and filled it in.

'Have you heard anything more from Kjell-Tore?' he asked, his mouth stuffed with food.

'He's in Denmark,' Ella replied without taking her eyes off the crossword. 'He's arriving on the ferry tomorrow afternoon.'

Isabell closed her book but used a finger to keep her place.

'You never mentioned that Kjell-Tore was coming,' she said. She always called him by his name, rather than 'Uncle'.

'You know he's here every summer,' Ella answered. 'Actually, he'd expected to arrive this evening, but apparently the ferry was full. Anyway, he'll stay outside in the motorhome for as long as you're here.'

She filled in another solution in the crossword.

'He's bringing some of those German sausages that Dad likes so much,' she added.

Evert took another bite of bread. He really had no idea what kind of sausages she was talking about. It was probably something he'd once said just to be polite.

He looked across at Isabell. 'How long are you planning to stay?'

'I don't know,' she replied. 'We'll see.'

'*Galdhøpiggen* is wrong,' Ella said. 'The ø doesn't fit.'

Isabell turned her attention to her book and Evert finished chewing another mouthful of bread.

'*Gaustatoppen*,' he said.

Ella turned her pen upside down to erase what she had written. Evert stole a glance as the letters disappeared and new ones were written in.

'That's it, then,' she said. 'So the vegetable must be *parsnip*.'

Isabell swatted a fly as Evert got to his feet.

'I'll go and sit at the computer for a while,' he said, taking the plates to the kitchen sink.

'Can't you bring it out here with you?' Ella called in to him.

'I can see better in here rather than in daylight,' he told her.

He sat down at the kitchen table and conducted an online search for the incident in Lofoten that had ended with Kjell-Tore being arrested for what the newspapers had described as an attempted rape, but that had ended up with him being fined for sexual harassment. It was difficult to come to any clear understanding of what had really taken place. The police statement was too evasive, and the news reports were too vague for that.

Ella's diaries did not go so far back. The oldest book he had found was six years old. He cast a glance out at the verandah and checked the picture on his phone. At the end of April Kjell-Tore had been working in Stavanger. It didn't say what he had been doing, but it was most likely laying some kind of paving stones. That would fit with the time of year.

Using his subscription to *Aftenposten*, he could also read the *Stavanger Aftenblad*, including the historical newspaper archive.

On Monday 16 April, there was a report about an incident at the weekend. A teenage girl on her way home from town had been offered money by a man who had exposed himself to her. The same thing had happened again an hour later. The man was described as slim, around five foot nine in height and spoke with an east-Norway accent. The police had scoured the area without finding him.

The location was west of the city centre. Evert Harting looked it up on the map. Stavanger was a city of 150,000 inhabitants and this was the sort of thing that happened now and then.

A noise outside from the verandah made him look up. Ella was sitting in the same place. She looked hot in the sun that glittered on the green foliage behind her.

He sat for a while longer before shutting down the browser and closing the laptop.

27

Ingrid Sandell flipped down the sun visor as they drove out of the Larvik tunnel. The summer traffic whizzed by in the left lane. Wisting flicked on his indicators. He had taken them out on the E18 north of the town to follow the same route as the O'Doyle couple and the motorhome they had been following.

'The lake's down there,' he said, pointing to the right.

Ingrid Sandell craned her neck to look over the top of the concrete barrier. Wisting followed the road to the round-about where Nina and Peter O'Doyle had turned off towards Helgeroa and Nevlunghavn, while the motorhome had turned in the direction of Lake Farris.

The rutted gravel track narrowed the further they drove and was full of potholes.

After a kilometre or so, Wisting turned out on to the yellowed grass at the edge of Lake Farris. The car rocked and squealed. Ingrid Sandell rolled down the window on her side and they could hear the tyres crunch on the parched earth.

He drove into the shadow below the branches of a solitary beech tree and let the Swedish detective step out of the car first. She walked down to the line of rowing boats situated where the water's edge usually lay. From there, the ground sloped slightly, out towards the water that was left.

'The lock gates that regulate the water were damaged by frost last winter,' Wisting explained, pointing in the direction of the dam beneath the motorway bridge to the south. 'In order to repair them, the water had to be drained out and since then there's been hardly any rain. The lake hasn't filled up again, just dried up more and more.'

The sun played on the depleted water surface.

'It's the drinking water source for two hundred thousand people in the region,' Wisting went on. 'Twenty million litres every twenty-four hours. You can see it diminish with each day that passes.'

Sandell took a step out on to the cracked earth crust. Wisting touched his hand to his forehead.

'We'll be able to see the spot where he dug up the gold necklace,' he said. 'It's supposed to be around twenty metres out.'

'Over there,' Sandell said, pointing.

They could follow the footprints of the man who had found it. They led to a refilled depression in the ground.

Ingrid Sandell hunkered down, picked up a handful of sandy soil and let it run through her fingers.

'He virtually guaranteed there were no other objects made of metal here,' Wisting said.

'How deep was the necklace buried?' Sandell asked, scooping up another handful of earth.

'About thirty centimetres,' Wisting replied.

Sandell straightened up and walked further out, towards the water's edge where the ground became more sodden, and her feet sank into the mud.

'I can bring dogs here tomorrow,' Wisting said.

The Swedish investigator drew back, moving closer to dry land.

'He must have used a boat to dump her body,' she said.

Wisting half-turned towards the row of boats behind them.

'They're probably locked up,' he said. 'Even though the locks would be easy to break open, it would have been several

146

hours from the time Annika Bengt was seen at the van window until it grew dark.'

They set off back to shore. Wisting crouched down and picked up a stone on the way. When they had returned to where the perimeter of the lake used to be, he wheeled around and threw it with all his might. Dusty earth sprayed up when it hit the ground a couple of metres from where the gold chain was found.

Ingrid Sandell pointed to the gravel track they had driven along.

'Where does that track lead?' she asked.

'A few kilometres further inland,' Wisting told her. 'It goes to some cabins, a couple of smallholdings and a scout camp. The local dog owners' club also has premises along there.'

He realized they were both thinking along the same lines. The most likely scenario was that Annika Bengt had been dumped and hidden somewhere further along the track, and then the killer had got rid of what had been left of her in his van on his way back. Thrown shoes, clothes and other belongings out into Lake Farris.

'We can drive out there and see,' he said, making for the car.

The interior was baking hot and Wisting rolled down the window as the car trundled back on to the track.

They drove slowly on. A scatter of birds flew up from the bushes at the roadside. Soon they had lost sight of the lake and there was forest on both sides of the track. After a few hundred metres, a narrower track turned off to the left.

'The man with the metal detector stays in a cabin along there,' Wisting explained.

He let his left hand dangle out of the window. The occasional branch brushed against it as they swept past.

The track was narrow, but every few hundred metres or

so there were passing places, small spaces at the side of the track where a motorhome could park without causing an obstruction.

Eventually a smallholding appeared, with a gate that prevented ingress. A rusty wire net fence accompanied them for a few metres before the track veered off to the left. The long grass between the wheel tracks rubbed against the chassis underneath them.

The woods changed character and became gloomier, turning from light-filled, leafy trees to dense spruce forest. They could just make out the water between the tree trunks.

The scout camp, situated on a promontory, was deserted. The track continued for a few hundred metres further before it ended at a turning space. A footpath led even further into the forest.

'They extracted timber here at one time,' Wisting told Sandell. 'This was where it was piled up before being transported.'

A small workman's hut with a chimney lay abandoned beside a heap of gravel. The windows were smashed, and the door hung askew from the top hinge. Straggly weeds grew tall around it. The entire place had become overgrown. Along the outer edges, litter was strewn: empty cigarette packets, plastic cups, takeaway containers and other rubbish.

Wisting turned the car around.

'Where is Ove Rudi Werner now?' Sandell asked.

'We're working on finding that out,' Wisting said. 'He was released three months ago but has no fixed address. What we do know is that he bought a new motorhome. He's probably living in it.'

He continued to drive slowly. Chunks of gravel rattled in the wheel arches.

'Have you checked in?' he asked, referring to the hotel room he had booked for her.

'Not yet,' Ingrid replied.

She leaned towards the front windscreen and looked up at the sky.

'Do you have any plans for this evening?' she asked.

He shook his head. 'Why do you ask?'

Ingrid Sandell leaned back in her seat with a heavy sigh.

'I've had this case for four years now,' she said. 'The past two, I've been on my own. Now something's happening and I don't want to sit all alone in a hotel room, just waiting. I need someone to share my thoughts with.'

Wisting did not say anything.

'What if we have dinner together?' Sandell suggested. 'Spend the time talking over the case. Discussing theories and possibilities.'

Wisting was about to answer that this was a good idea, but didn't get as far as saying anything before Sandell caught herself.

'Sorry,' she said. 'You probably want to go home for dinner.'

'I live alone,' Wisting told her. 'And I do have to eat.'

They drove on for a while.

'Do you have any wine?' Sandell asked.

He looked across at her. 'I'm sure I have some in the cupboard,' he replied.

'Then I'll bring something we can eat with it,' she said. She glanced at the time.

'Let me check in at the hotel first, and then I'll be with you at five o'clock,' she said. 'We'll have the whole evening ahead of us.'

Wisting smiled. He liked her decisiveness. He was not used to other people taking charge. He was normally the one who

149

directed others and made all the decisions. But he had to admit he liked it.

'Herman Wildenveys gate number seven,' he said. 'Five o'clock. See you then.'

28

Two crows were hopping around on the barbecue area. Evert Harting leaned back in his chair, watching them. It looked as if they were trying to poke some food scraps out of a crack in the concrete. They were pecking furiously and flapping their wings, taking turns to chase each other.

Isabell put down her book. 'Shall we go for a drive?' she asked.

'With the detector?'

'Yes. We won't have dinner for another couple of hours or so, will we?'

Evert Harting stood up. 'Let's see if we can find anything, then,' he said with a smile.

Ella remained seated. 'Don't forget the sun cream,' she said.

Evert collected the metal detector from the charger. Isabell put on a pair of shorts and a T-shirt. Both of them rubbed on some high-factor cream before leaving.

Dust from another vehicle still hovered above the track. They saw it ahead of them on the long stretch before the dog owners' club.

'We can continue from where I found the gold chain,' he said, pointing out the spot. 'The water has pulled back even further.'

He parked the car in the shade of the only tree in the area. They changed into boots and walked down to where the water's edge had formerly been.

'You take it,' he said, passing the detector to Isabell.

She took it from him and found a comfortable way to carry it.

'You can see my tracks,' he said, pointing to his footsteps on the dried-out mud. 'We'll start just below that.'

They walked down to the undisturbed area. The sunken rowing boat that had lain stern-down in the water for a few days was now stranded on totally dry land.

Isabell began to swing the detector to and fro.

Evert had brought a coin from the centre console of the car. He tossed it a metre ahead of her. The detector beeped, the noise increasing as the detector approached.

'It's working!' his daughter said, beaming. She picked up the coin.

'Finders keepers,' he said.

She moved on. Evert Harting followed behind her and slightly to one side. The bone-dry earth crunched beneath their feet.

They walked parallel to the old search area, up to the rocky hillside in the south, before turning and walking back again without producing any result.

'It's a matter of working systematically,' Evert told her.

They moved off in a different direction. When they were level with the old rowing boat, the detector gave a loud beep.

'There's something here!' Isabell called out eagerly.

She swept the detector back and forth to determine the exact spot.

Evert produced the trowel from his tool belt and crouched down. He scooped up a few spadesful and explained how the pinpointer tool worked.

'Try it now,' he said.

Isabell put down the detector and searched with the sensitive probe in one hand while scraping soil aside with the other.

Very soon she found the cause of the reaction. A carabiner clip attached to a short length of rope.

'Your first find,' Evert said. 'I'll bet it comes from the wrecked boat.'

Moving on, they circled a few times, side by side, without any results. His thoughts ranged back in time, to Isabell and her uncle down through the years. He had looked after her when she was a little girl, spending the night with them when required. Kjell-Tore had always been at their disposal, always there for them, as part of their close family. Birthdays, Christmas and other special occasions. He had often turned up with magnificent, expensive presents. But Isabell had moved away from home at an early age and contact with her uncle had diminished.

'You hadn't realized Kjell-Tore was coming?' he asked.

'Mum didn't mention it. That's how it was last year too. All of a sudden, he was here.'

'Don't you like him?'

Isabell didn't answer immediately.

'Well, I've only got one uncle,' she said. 'But I wouldn't say he's my favourite.'

They reached a patch where the earth was damp, and their feet sank into the mud. Evert skirted around it while Isabell walked straight across.

'Is there any particular reason why you don't like him?' Evert asked when they met on the other side.

At that moment the detector gave a signal that was difficult to interpret. The sound seemed to burble out of the little microphone.

'There must be loads here!' Isabell cried.

'Let's see,' Evert told her.

The screen indicated that it was made of brass.

'What does that mean?' Isabell queried.

'It could be something very old,' Evert said. 'A coin or an item of jewellery, but it sounded like something bigger. It should be easy to find . . .'

He gave her the trowel again. She knelt with her back to the sun. The compacted earth split when she began to dig. Evert crouched beside her. The first few scoops contained nothing interesting. She tossed aside another couple of spadesful and looked across at him, as if expecting something or someone to emerge from the nothingness.

'It's probably a bit deeper,' he said. 'Around twenty centimetres below the surface.'

Isabell kept on digging. An odd smell rose from the dried-out sludgy bottom. The trowel struck something soft. It did not pass through, just nudged it further down into the earth.

She laid the trowel aside and used her fingers instead. It was a scrap of cloth.

'Wait a minute,' Evert said, suddenly afraid of what they had found.

He produced a small brush to sweep it clean. Fresh crumbs of earth drizzled down from the edges. Isabell gathered them up and threw them away.

'It's a shoe,' she said.

She was right. They had uncovered parts of the upper and sole of a black fabric shoe with eyelets of metal, coated in verdigris. The laces looked as if they had once been white. The sole was narrow, obviously not an adult size.

Evert used the back of the little brush to pick off some soil around the heel. Isabell, eager, did not understand his caution. She took hold of the tip and pulled it free.

It came out easily. Nothing else accompanied it.

'The eyelets must be made of brass,' she said.

'Most likely,' he replied.

He took the trowel and dug further down where the shoe had been. Isabell took the metal detector and swept it around.

'I think there's only the one,' she said.

'You're right,' he said, straightening up.

'What should we do with it?' she asked.

He looked at it. 'Throw it back in again,' he suggested.

She did as he said and swept the earth back into the hole with her foot.

'That's how it goes,' he said, smiling. 'Most of what's lying about round here is just junk.'

She smiled back and looked around. A mild current of air wafted a cloud of grey dust that swirled along the ground.

'But you never know,' she said, refusing to give up hope.

29

The wine he owned was a gift he had received after delivering a talk at the Norwegian Bar Association. That had been over a year ago, but he expected they had bought something fairly expensive that could safely be kept in reserve. He had a couple of other bottles, but they were even older, and he was unsure where they had come from.

They decided to sit outside but had to walk through the house to access the terrace. Wisting tidied up a little, shaking the cushions on the garden furniture and wiping down the table.

His guest was punctual.

'It's going to be pizza,' she said, handing him the box at the door. 'Is that OK?'

'Pizza's fine.'

She was about to remove her shoes, but Wisting told her to keep them on. 'We're going out on the other side,' he said, leading the way.

Birds took off from the lawn and flew in various directions when they came out. Ingrid Sandell walked up to the railings and took hold of the banister.

'What a view!' she exclaimed.

Wisting put aside the food.

'It's Stavern,' he said, pointing out the landmarks – the old military barracks, the red garrison church, Hotel Wassilioff, Citadel Island, the lighthouse at Stavernsodden, the Hall of Remembrance, and the Tordenskiold statue at Mølleberget.

Beyond the small coastal town, the dark blue sea stretched out, turning almost white as it reached the horizon.

She remained standing while he brought out the wine. When they sat down, he let her sit facing the view, allowing her to gaze out across the vista.

'Are you sure you want to open this just for pizza?' she asked, indicating the bottle.

'I have some beer too,' Wisting said.

Ingrid Sandell nodded her head. 'Then let's save the wine.'

He left the wine out but went inside and came back with two cans of beer.

'It'll take some time to run the facial recognition,' Sandell told him. 'NOA have started on it, but they must first build a database of all the photos from the campsite.'

Wisting placed the beer cans on either side of the table.

'Two crime scene dogs are arriving tomorrow,' he said. 'I think it's worth a try around that turning area at the end of the track. They'll do it as a training exercise, quite informally.'

Sandell began to tuck in.

'How many cases have you had where the body's been buried?' she asked.

'Not many,' he replied.

'It's something that happens mostly in books and films,' she said. 'It's possible it has to do with burial rites, but in reality, it's both impractical and exhausting. Most corpses are concealed in other ways. Hidden under something or dumped in water.'

'But you don't think Annika is in the water?'

'The turning area is a good spot. Beyond the tracks, she could lie in open terrain without being found, maybe just covered over with twigs and branches.'

She told him about the searches for Annika Bengt and places they had been tipped off that she might be hidden.

Everywhere had been thoroughly combed without producing any results.

'Did you conduct any searches up at the border crossings?'

Ingrid Sandell shook her head. 'We should have done,' she said. 'We should have had lists of registration numbers of all the cars that drove out of Sweden at that time, but we don't. What we do have is hours of footage from cameras on all the roads round about. We just didn't really know what we were looking for. Not until now.' She lifted another slice of pizza. 'I'll get one of my officers to start on the job, but it was certainly possible to leave the area unobserved.'

The pizza was one Wisting liked. Cheese, ham and mushroom, with a thick crust.

'The Annika case has been like a big boulder,' Sandell said, swallowing. 'Impossible to shift.'

She began to list all the leads that had been pursued in vain.

'Nothing came of any of it,' she rounded off. 'Nothing. It's as if she was simply devoured by the void, as if she had never existed at all.'

Wisting could hear how the case had taken hold of her.

'A podcast producer is working on a documentary series about Annika,' she said, putting down a half-eaten slice of pizza. 'Have you ever experienced that? One of your cases being researched in that way? Where you've done everything you possibly could, your very utmost, what you believed to be right, but where you nevertheless end up getting the blame?'

'Not like that, no,' Wisting replied.

'The top brass have asked me to come for interview,' Sandell continued.

'When is that?'

'In four weeks.'

'A lot could have happened by then,' Wisting commented.

He cleared away the pizza box and brought out a couple of wine glasses and his notebook.

'We have a name,' he said.

Ingrid Sandell spoke it aloud: 'Ove Rudi Werner.'

Wisting ran through what they knew about him. He also produced his iPad to call up a photo from the police system. It was taken in connection with his arrest three years earlier and showed the forty-six-year-old man from the front and the side.

He looked older than his age suggested. His hair was receding on either side of his forehead, his eyes deep-set, with a shadow of desperation about them. It made him look both threatening and vulnerable at the same time.

He did not have to be the one who had abducted Annika Bengt. The investigation would have to focus just as much on producing certainty that it could *not* have been him. Often that was a simpler task than proving the opposite.

They drew up a shared plan without paying any attention to land borders or formal restrictions. Making an indentation for each step in the investigation, Wisting jotted down keywords for significant elements and references to specific documents. Eventually he had built a structured approximation of the case and a clear direction for their work to take in the immediate future.

They emptied the wine bottle as they worked. Wisting went inside and brought out another one.

'My wife was also called Ingrid,' he said, without really knowing where that had come from. 'She died fourteen years ago.'

Ingrid Sandell kept her eyes on her glass while he refilled it.

'I'm sorry to hear that,' she said.

Wisting smiled. 'My granddaughter's named after her. Ingrid Amalie. She's in the USA just now with her mother.'

Sandell picked up her glass and sat cradling it on her lap. 'How did she die? Your wife?'

'It happened in Africa,' Wisting replied. 'I've never heard all the details of what happened, but it was a road accident. She was working as a teacher at the high school here in town but had a leave of absence to take part in a teaching project targeting young women in Zambia. The accident occurred on a trip to Angola, to examine the possibility of extending the project to other African countries. The car went over a cliff. Two local workers also died.'

He had seen pictures of the wreck and the accident site. It had been a sheer drop of about twenty metres. It must have taken around three seconds from the time the vehicle drove over the precipice until it hit the ground. These were thoughts he always tried to push from his mind, but he knew that three seconds was more than enough time to appreciate the situation and be overcome by fear of death.

The sea and sky were reflected in the living-room window behind Ingrid Sandell. In the hazy image it was difficult to see a dividing line.

He took a gulp of the new wine to break the atmosphere he had created. It tasted more full-bodied than the previous bottle.

'Have you been on your own since then?' Ingrid Sandell asked.

'For the most part,' Wisting said. 'I had a relationship that lasted a couple of years, but that's also quite a long time ago now.'

He took another mouthful. 'What about you?' he asked. 'Are you married?'

'I have been,' she answered. 'To a police officer. He became my boss eventually. That didn't go so well. We divorced eight years ago. Now he works for the NOA, in Stockholm. The equivalent of your Kripos.'

'Do you have children?'

'We have a son – he's thirty-five now and in the police too. And also divorced.'

She hid a smile behind her glass. 'What does your daughter do?' she asked.

'She's a journalist – she worked for a number of years as a crime reporter.'

He laughed himself at the incompatibility of this and had to explain how their professional roles had sometimes overlapped.

'Once she had Amalie, though, she worked on various documentary projects as well as some true-crime podcasts, in fact. I also have a son, Thomas. They're twins, actually. He's in the armed forces, stationed abroad.'

The sun went down as they continued talking about families and their colleagues.

'Have you ever regretted becoming a police officer?' she asked him.

Wisting shook his head. He had always felt his job as a detective suited him down to the ground, even though he also felt it was beyond his capabilities to change anything in a global sense.

'The dead are still dead,' he mused, looking down into his glass.

He knew he had made a difference in the lives of some individuals. He had helped victims and their family members, given them certain answers and maybe some kind of closure. He had obtained justice for some, but it was as if it was never enough. He could not save everyone, and he could not change the world all by himself. However, he was pleased to have been there when it mattered.

'What about you?' he asked.

'I don't know what else I could have been,' she replied. 'Probably there is no other profession in which the weight of another person's death is pushed upon you to the same extent.' She took a drink from her glass. 'But I usually like to say that my job has taught me little about death, but a lot about life. How fragile it can be.'

'A slender thread,' Wisting said, nodding in agreement.

A thread that, without warning, could be cut. In a single second everything could change. You never knew when you might find yourself in the wrong place at the wrong time.

His neighbour's water sprinkler turned itself on. The monotonous sound trickled out into the evening darkness.

Ingrid Sandell put down her glass. 'I should call a taxi,' she said. 'We've a long day ahead of us tomorrow.'

30

The darkness that had settled outside the cabin windows matched his own state of mind, he thought.

His reflection stared back at him. He looked pale in the blue glow from the computer screen. His eyes were shining and the stubble on his face was dark and dense, covering the whole of his stiff neck.

He had found nothing specific about Annika Bengt's shoes in the missing person report, other than that they were made of black cloth. At some point the police had dressed a headless mannequin in the clothes she had been wearing. A simple white T-shirt with a sports logo on the chest and a pair of pink knee-length cotton shorts with a cord tied at the waist.

He glanced at the blank window again. It felt as if he had roused something dormant and inevitable when he found the gold chain necklace. Something that refused to give him any peace of mind.

'Aren't you coming to bed?' Ella called out from the bedroom.

'Staying up a bit longer,' he replied.

She would fall asleep soon. He had seen her take one of the tablets from the blister pack in the kitchen drawer, a prescription she renewed a couple of times a year. Sleeping medication. She took them only when anxiety got the better of her. In addition, she had drunk three vodkas to his one.

Evert turned back to the computer screen and the diagram he had drawn up, a combined timeline and incident record.

He double-checked the information he had compiled. After Stavanger, Kjell-Tore had worked on a job in Kongsberg. That same week, there was a report about a man ogling a group of teenagers at a beach in Vingersjøen. Blue shorts and a white T-shirt was all the description given. Admittedly, it was a common style of clothing, but Kjell-Tore did have blue swimming shorts in some sort of synthetic material. Ella had a few photos on her mobile of him wearing them, sitting down beside a lake in the mountains.

There were no similar reports in either of the next two locations, but in other places he found sporadic coincidences between various accounts of sexual harassment, as the police called it in the newspapers, and towns where Kjell-Tore had been staying.

Two years ago, he had been in Halden. Ella had added: *The fortress*. Evert remembered Kjell-Tore talking about a major job in the old military base. It had been carried out in several stages, and he had been across the Swedish border fairly often for shopping while based there. One of these stays corresponded with staff at a care centre for underage asylum seekers reporting a man in a motorhome to the police. He had offered one of the girls there money to go with him in his van.

He closed the laptop lid and got to his feet without making a sound. The door to the bedroom was open a crack. Padding across, he strained to hear Ella's regular breathing. The door to Isabell's bedroom was shut. She was probably reading in bed.

The floorboards creaked faintly when he turned around. Leaning against the door, he slipped his feet into his sandals and moved outside. The door slid silently shut behind him.

The night air was fresher than inside at the computer. He

166

drew in a couple of deep breaths, but it failed to relieve the pressure in his chest.

He walked down the steps from the verandah and took a few paces out across the soft grass. The sky was spattered with stars. The waxing moon was already big enough to bathe the landscape in a blue-tinged light.

He walked along the path down to the lake, past the barbecue area and onwards, to where the water's edge was usually situated. His thoughts were spinning. Distant memories of previous summers popped up. The sound of laughter and refreshing cool dips in the lake. A time and circumstance he was unable to resurrect.

A feeling of regret washed over him. Many years had passed since he had twigged what the situation was with Kjell-Tore – he had felt the rough outlines of it, but let it pass. Had never said anything or taken any action. Now, in retrospect, he thought the signs were even clearer, but he had no idea how to handle it.

Above his head he heard the flapping wings of a bat. Several of them, in fact. He saw their shadows silhouetted against the night sky. The wings were elongated in elegant curves and sent a faint susurration out into the night. They flew with precision and flexibility, guided by signals he could neither see nor hear.

He turned and looked up at the cabin and the soft light from the living-room windows.

The restlessness that had driven him outside had been provoked by an article in the *Smaalenenes Avis*, a local newspaper in Askim, last autumn. A thirteen-year-old Afghan girl was reported missing from the same care centre where a man driving a motorhome had tried to bribe one of the young girls to take a lift with him the previous year.

It was more or less by chance that he had come across the report. He had tried searching for more details of the man in the motorhome and found an article about the missing underage asylum seekers. In total, there were several hundred children and teenagers who had arrived in Norway without their parents, and who in the course of the last few years had disappeared from refugee reception centres and care facilities. The thirteen-year-old girl who had gone missing from the centre in Halden had been highlighted as a concise example. Her name was not given. The article simply stated that most of her belongings had been left behind in her room.

No one had written about her actual disappearance. That was part of the problem under discussion in the article. No one had searched for her. It had taken days for her to be missed, and weeks before she was recorded in the police computer systems. It had been assumed that she had travelled to join family in Sweden, but no one had followed that up. No one knew whether she had fallen victim to some crime or anything about her present whereabouts. Even whether she was still alive.

A shooting star sped across the sky in the west in a streak of brilliant light, leaving a trail as it faded and died. Evert Harting dipped his head and walked slowly back, well aware he would get little sleep that night.

31

Dust swirled up when she poured the dry cement into the bucket. She had portioned out six kilos in advance and now mixed this with water from two large bottles.

Kicki Dalberg adjusted the light on her head torch, turning the beam into an inconspicuous narrow strip.

The cement was harder to mix than she had anticipated. She used both hands to stir it with a long stick. In the end the mixture formed a viscous mass.

She stood up and scanned her surroundings. A nightlight was shining in the motorhome parked at one end of the car park. Its secluded position ensured it was screened from almost all view from the road. Anyway, there was no traffic.

The hood on her sweatshirt muffled all sound. She pushed it back from her head and stood, straining her ears. All she could hear was the rhythmic pulsing of the sprinkler system, 240,000 litres every night, according to the report in the local newspaper. The subsequent discussion in the comments had been ferocious when it became clear that the golf course had been granted exemption from the water restrictions. Anger had raged but no one had seen past their own small patch of brown lawn. No one had argued for the bigger picture, and no one had done anything about it.

She switched off her head torch. Even though the night was now at its darkest, the sun was not far below the horizon. That made it easy to find her way about, but also easy to be seen.

A gust of wind rustled the leaves on the nearby ornamental shrubs. With its well-trimmed lawns and sumptuous floral borders, the golf course was a blatant symbol of human excess and recklessness, she thought. A legitimate target.

The first hole lay between a sandy bunker and a small artificial dam. The ground was still damp after receiving its allotted ration of water. The little flagpole was inserted in the middle of the hole. Kicki scouted around in the gloom before pouring out the contents of the bucket. The cement spewed into the hole, making a gurgling noise as it filled it.

Her adrenaline level soared. It felt as if the rebellious hormones seething within her became satisfied and infused her with a sense of justice being served.

The hole gobbled more of the mixture than she had calculated. The bucket would not plug much more than four holes before she would have to mix more.

She set it down and produced a spray can from her rucksack. The ball bearing rattled inside when she shook it. The orange spray paint formed an even layer on the green, well-trimmed fairway as she drew the letter *T*.

To make sure she got it right she had to switch on her head torch again.

TURN OFF THE TAPS, she wrote in large letters. *CAP THE WELLS*, she added to be sure everyone would understand that this referred not only to water. That filling up the golf holes was also a symbolic act.

Her fingertips were stained with spray paint. She wiped them on her T-shirt before shaking the can again.

STOP OIL, she scrawled, taking a step back to examine the result. It would be a superb welcome flourish for the new Equinor boss.

The concrete would not be properly set for another twenty-four hours, but play would be ruined for many days to come, perhaps even until the end of the season.

A car drove past out on the main road. The headlights swept across the fairway. Covering the head torch with her hand, Kicki crouched down. Once the vehicle was out of sight, she produced her mobile and took some photos.

Hole number two lay beside a small stand of trees that obscured the moonlight. *THE EARTH IS BURNING* she wrote on the grass before embarking on filling the hole. She used only one hand to decant the contents while she used the other to film what she was doing. Some of the cement landed on the grass. She scraped it up with her foot and pushed it down around the flag. Like planting a seed of protest, she thought.

Hole number three was further away. She skirted the periphery of the trees and shifted the heavy bucket of cement from one hand to the other while she carried it. A noise made her pause in the shadows. It sounded like a car door slamming somewhere, but it was difficult to localize. As she listened, the sprinkler system on the area to her left stopped abruptly before it started up somewhere further off.

She stood still for a while longer before sneaking forward and filling the hole without turning on her head torch. *STOP EQUINOR* she wrote this time and then withdrew into the shadows again.

The bucket was becoming lighter to carry, but she did not know how far the cement would last. Her plan had been to fill all eighteen holes, but she now realized this would take too long.

On her way from the fourth hole to the fifth, she walked past the wooden fence that screened the operations plant. She stood staring at it. There was no lighting in there, and no cameras.

She sauntered around the timber slats and into the open area. Two motorized ride-on lawnmowers were parked beneath a canopy, alongside two heavy-duty lawn rollers and other machinery used for maintenance of the turf. Somewhere behind them an engine was chugging, the water sprinkler system, perhaps.

Kicki approached the nearest lawnmower, unscrewed the petrol cap and lifted the bucket up to the rim. A hollow thump was heard when the cement dropped into the liquid inside.

She replaced and screwed on the cap and wiped some spillage from the rim before moving on to the second lawnmower. She inhaled a deep breath of the pungent odour before pouring in the rest of the cement and straightening up.

It would be OK to stop now, she thought. Before anyone spotted her.

32

Wisting stood at the kitchen window, rolling up the sleeves of his pale linen shirt. The weather outside was monotonous and familiar. Cloudless sunshine.

Despite having plenty of time, he was keen to make an early start on the day. He left his cup of coffee half-empty on the worktop and moved out to his car.

The traffic was sparse. During one of the heaviest snow-falls last winter, it had taken him three quarters of an hour to drive into town, but now he managed the same trip in only ten minutes.

At the vehicle entrance to the back yard of the police station he had to steer in a wide arc to avoid a magpie, pecking at something on the kerbstones. Undeterred, it merely flapped its wings a couple of times as he drove past.

He let himself into the basement and entered via the inspection garage where the motorhome was parked. The technicians had said they would come and look at it some-time after twelve.

The large safe had been pushed into a corner. Leaning against the wall, he saw a sheet of corrugated metal, caked in clay and mud. Beside that was a coil of barbed wire. Daniyal Rana must have gone back and collected these from the sludgy bed of Lake Farris.

On top of the safe was a collection of items – an old wrist-watch with a metal band, a sheet of plastic pockets filled with coins, an album cover, a sheath knife and a leather strap with a buckle. They all bore signs of having been submerged in water for a long time.

The safe had been empty when it was lifted out, but it made sense to believe that some of the contents could have been scattered around beside it.

Wisting lifted the watch to take a closer look. The glass was covered in a cloudy bloom. *Longines* was marked on the face and the hands had stopped at seven minutes to two.

The band was intricately made, the links coupled together with tiny joints. Dry earth crumbled and drizzled on to the floor when he ran his thumb along them. On the back, the case was etched with a picture of a ship with three masts and billowing sails. It looked valuable, something the owner would probably need to store in a safe. The same applied to the plastic pockets of collectors' coins.

The album cover was inside a plastic protector. The cardboard had disintegrated completely, but the vinyl record itself looked undamaged. If it had been stored inside the safe, it must have been a rare edition.

The knife was obviously hand-crafted, but there were no inscriptions on either the shaft or the blade.

The leather strap had a metal buckle at one end and punched holes at the other, but it was too short to be a belt. It looked more like a dog's collar. In the middle of the strap, he saw a metal disc on which a name had probably been engraved. The first letter looked like a V, but the others were almost totally worn away.

These finds told him something about the owner of the safe, suggesting they had most likely had an interest in music and once owned a pet called something beginning with V. If they did not find a crime reported in their own records, it might be useful to use the newspapers to ask the public for help.

The silence between the concrete walls was broken by a series of muffled thuds from the shooting range further back in the basement. Sometimes the officers in the patrol section rounded off their night shift duties in there if they had no reports to write.

Wisting went upstairs to the duty room. Daniyal Rana sat at one of the desks and at first only glanced up fleetingly from his computer screen. When he realized it was Wisting, he rose from his seat.

'Good morning.'

Wisting returned the greeting and told him what he had seen down in the inspection garage. Daniyal Rana explained that he had done some rummaging at the discovery site.

'Good thinking,' Wisting said. 'Have you made any progress in finding out the owner of the safe?'

'I think I've discovered when the sheets of roofing ended up in the water,' Rana replied. 'The farmer I was tipped off about told me he had laid a new roof in the autumn of 2001. The total number of sheets seems to match the size of the barn. He'd hired someone to do the job for him, he said. The arrangement was that they should take the old sheets of metal to the waste disposal site, but he thinks they must have dumped them in the lake.'

'So the safe most likely ended up there between 2001 and 2009, then?' Wisting calculated.

'I'm going through the records,' Rana said, indicating the computer screen with a wave of his hand. 'There's no separate category for theft of safes. I have to open up each individual case to see what's been stolen. It's taking time, and many of the reports are incomplete. What's more, it's far from certain that the safe was stolen in our police district, or that the robbery was reported at all. People who keep money squirrelled away at home instead of depositing it in the bank have usually earned it illegally.'

Silent images from a news channel were rolling across a TV screen behind him.

'That's what criminal inquiries mostly entail,' Wisting told him. 'Time-consuming investigation in which the majority of results lead nowhere.'

'It would probably be easier to make a public appeal for the owner in the media,' Rana suggested. 'Publish photos of the safe and its contents.'

'Let's try our own channels first,' Wisting said. 'Call me when you get to the bottom of it, or if you don't succeed in doing that.'

As he turned to leave, he realized the young summer temp had something else on his mind.

'Why has the motorhome been brought in?' he asked. 'There's no mention of it in the operations log.'

Wisting grew evasive. 'We're going to undertake some investigations into an old case,' he answered.

'Concerning the Solifer man?' Rana asked.

Wisting smiled. 'You've heard of him?'

'Not before last night,' Rana told him. 'I checked the reg number and saw that he and the motorhome had been the subjects of a police alert three years ago.'

'That's right,' Wisting said, nodding.

'Is he suspected of something else?' Rana asked.

Wisting checked his mobile phone to provide some distraction.

'We'll see what comes of the examination,' he replied, heading for the door.

'He's out of jail again,' Rana went on. 'Do you know what he's up to now, or where he is, even?'

'No,' Wisting managed to answer before Rana was summoned over the police radio.

A car had driven off the road at Hallevannet and an ambulance was already on its way.

Grabbing his utility belt from the desk, Rana slung it on. Wisting stood watching as he dashed out.

The mute TV screen on the wall showed a weather warning – rain was forecast for the weekend.

33

The others were still asleep. Evert Harting sat on the top step beside the verandah, a cup of coffee in his hands. Two roe deer, their chestnut coats gleaming in the sunshine, stood at the water's edge, drinking. They slaked their thirst at a leisurely pace before raising their heads in unison and gazing around. Then they trotted back towards the forest.

Evert got up slowly. Balancing the half-full cup on the ledge, he moved down to the barbecue area. It was four metres wide by five metres in length. In one corner, a barbecue pit had been built. Around the table, there was room for eight, even though they'd never seated as many as that here.

Shrubs studded with red berries were growing along one side. Evert broke off a branch. He stripped it of leaves and stood peeling off the bark while his eyes studied the largest crack in the concrete. His belief was now greater than his doubt. He thought the worst of Kjell-Tore and was no longer able to camouflage the idea. Instead, he took it to its logical conclusion – if K-T had taken the Swedish girl, in that case, what had he done with her? And the girl from the asylum centre in Halden, what about her?

He prodded the stick into the nearest crack. It slid down as far as ten centimetres. He tried again in one of the larger cracks that ran all the way across. The stick penetrated far down, stopping at a soft base. He pulled it up and studied the residue of grey cement left on the tip.

The crack was largest in the middle, under the table.

He pushed it slightly aside and crouched down beneath it. He pushed the stick down and stirred it around before hauling it up and running the tip between his thumb and forefinger. The debris transferred reminded him of the dried mud down at the lake. He held his fingers under his nose and sniffed – a faintly sour odour, probably from the bark on the wood.

A black beetle came scuttling up from the crack he had investigated. Evert Harting took a step back. He knew of detectors that could penetrate concrete and create images of what lay underneath. The contractor who had laid fibre cables in the housing cooperative had used one to locate pipes and cables before they began to dig up the asphalt in front of the apartment block. He had been treated to a demonstration. It must be possible to hire such equipment, he mused.

Turning around to look back at the cabin, he was startled to discover that Ella had come almost all the way down to where he stood.

'Have they grown larger?' she asked.

Evert followed her gaze under the table.

'Not since spring,' he answered.

Bending down, Ella took off one of her Crocs and shook out a stone.

'Kjell-Tore will sort it,' she said. 'He's just been waiting until there are enough slabs left over at one of his jobs so that he can get them cheap. If not, we'll just have to buy some.'

She turned around, heading for the outside loo.

'We'll discuss it with him when he arrives,' she called over her shoulder. 'First he needs to fix the incinerator on the new toilet.'

Evert watched her as she walked between the trees and up to the red-painted hut.

Before they had acquired the incinerating toilet, they'd had to empty the outside loo every fourth year. It was always Kjell-Tore who had undertaken this task. Evert had accompanied him on only one occasion. They had dug a hole further into the forest, and filled it with a couple of barrowloads of muck before covering the hole again.

Climbing the steps to the verandah, he tipped out his cold coffee and filled the cup halfway again.

Ella returned and washed her hands in the basin on the stool beside the steps. The sun glinted in her silver hair.

'It's going to be hot again today,' she said.

Her face creased as she smiled, squinting up at the sun. During the works function held when she had retired, the Permanent Secretary had made special mention of her smile and said that she had always shone a light in the darkness. Approving of the description, he had always felt that her wrinkles had been formed by laughter and her constant good humour. Now he understood they were down to the worries she had never shared with him.

'I was thinking of warming some bread rolls for breakfast,' she went on, drying her hands on a towel. 'Isabell will probably be up soon too.'

He was standing two steps above her now and leaned forward to kiss her on the forehead.

'Excellent,' he replied. 'I have to take my turn as well,' he added, motioning in the direction of the outside loo.

Ella went inside. Evert considered changing into rubber boots but left his sandals on instead.

The weeds grew tall behind the cubicle. The opening left for shovelling out the muck was overgrown with stinging nettles. Birds flitted about in the trees above him. The sun flickered between the leaves overhead, creating a pattern of shadow and light along the forest floor.

They had not gone far that time he had assisted with the emptying. Scarcely more than twenty metres into the woods. He was unable to find the spot again, but it was easy to read the terrain. The vegetation was marginally different and there were small ridges where the earth had been opened up. These varied in size, depending on how much had been filled into the hole. One of the hillocks was slightly higher than the other and not quite so overgrown.

He broke off a somewhat stronger branch than he had used down at the barbecue area and pushed it down into the heaped-up earth. It moved easily through the upper layer of turf. Evert added some extra pressure and the stick sank deeper, almost a metre down before it met resistance and eventually refused to penetrate any further.

Black earth clung to the stick when he drew it up again. He held the tip in front of him but could not discern any odour. The earth seemed damp, but not especially dense. The signals from the detector would reach a good distance down and be strong enough to indicate metal in a zip or trouser button. However, it would be difficult to do that while Ella was at the cabin. And Kjell-Tore was expected this afternoon. Maybe he could suggest that the two of them take a trip into town.

He tossed the stick aside and retraced his steps. Isabell was up now and sat outside in her pyjamas while Ella set the table.

'Isabell's going home today,' she said.

'Today? So soon?'

Evert dipped his hands in the basin of water. 'You only arrived on Tuesday, didn't you?'

'I can understand her,' Ella said. 'Three days without a proper shower and toilet and only us old folks for company.'

Evert grabbed the towel, glancing at his daughter as he

turned down his mouth. An attempt at a subtle gesture of fellow feeling, no matter what her reason might be.

'I texted a bit with Mona yesterday,' she explained, talking about a friend Evert had never met. 'We're invited to a party on the quayside at Nesodden this evening.'

'That sounds nice,' Ella said, putting down a cheese slice. 'Anyway, rain is forecast from tomorrow night. They just announced it on the radio. A downpour of heavy rain.'

Isabell pushed out her chair and excused herself, saying she was going to get dressed.

'Dad and I are intending to head north in Kjell-Tore's motorhome in a few days, regardless,' Ella went on. 'I think we'll leave on Sunday.' She glanced across at her husband. 'Don't you think?'

Evert Harting nodded.

On Sunday. Three days more. A great deal could come to pass before that.

34

The computer screen was damaged in the top left-hand corner. Various colours and shapes flickered on the display. The affected area looked as if it had spread since the previous day, but not so much that it prevented him from using it.

Wisting had written his earliest reports on a typewriter. He had still been a young police officer when the first computers were adopted. New machines with greater capacity continually came into use, but some of the most important data systems were still the same as twenty years ago. Wisting was familiar with all the functions. Filtering a search to home in on the exact information was a skill in itself. Strictly speaking, he had plenty of other calls on his time, but he spent a few minutes searching for the case of the stolen safe. Among the crimes that fulfilled the search criteria, one in particular stood out and explained why he had no memory of the incident. In September 2006, there had been a break-in at the premises of an excavating contractor in Kjosebygda, about ten kilometres from the centre of town. That was the autumn Ingrid had died, and Nils Hammer had been put in charge of the department while he was granted a few weeks' compassionate leave.

He opened the files. No suspects. The burglary had taken place while the owner was on a construction project in Østfold, and his wife had reported it. A police patrol had examined the crime scene and described how the theft had been committed. This must have included the use of a pallet truck to make off with the safe. It was clear that photographs had been taken at the crime scene, but these had not been stored electronically. In order to view them, he would have to collect the paper files held down in the archives section. The most interesting aspect was that the complainant reported that, in addition to around 100,000 kroner in cash, the safe had contained a collection of knives and some signed LPs.

Wisting made a note of the case number but left it at that. He had established that the case did exist in the system but would let Daniyal Rana have the satisfaction of finding it for himself.

He flicked through to a fresh page in his notebook and made a start on the routine daily tasks. Each morning, he ran through the incoming cases and the status of ongoing investigations. This helped him to maintain oversight of progress and to manage the resources within his department. However, nothing demanded action from him now.

When it was almost 9 a.m., he rang the dog handler responsible for the search for Annika Bengt. They would be on the job within the next half-hour.

Wisting got to his feet and switched off the computer. He had arranged with the Swedish investigator to pick her up from the hotel so they could both be present during the search.

He was looking forward to meeting her. He seldom entertained such feelings, but he was certainly filled with pleasant anticipation at the thought of seeing Ingrid Sandell again. Thinking of her had distracted him completely from the first moment he awoke. Yesterday had made him curious about her and he was keen to spend more time in her company. He had tried to rein in his thoughts but there was something about her that kept surfacing.

She was waiting outside the main hotel entrance, dressed in practical clothes – trainers, beige trousers and a grey T-shirt.

'Thanks for yesterday,' he said when she got into the car.

'Likewise,' she replied. 'We must do it again.'

He could not bring himself to say anything, and simply threw a glance over his left shoulder as he turned the car around.

The drive took only ten minutes, and their conversation was focused on the case. It flowed smoothly, as if they shared an understanding that really needed no words.

The dog patrol vehicle was parked in the shade beside the turning space at the end of the track. The dog had already been released and was crouched on the ground behind the van. A black German shepherd with prominent, stiff ears. It made no move as Wisting and Ingrid Sandell stepped from the car and spoke to the two handlers. Wisting already knew the older of the two, Torgny Holmann, and was aware that his dog's name was Sheriff.

'Thanks for doing this at such short notice,' Wisting said.

Holmann brushed an insect away with his hand.

'It suited our programme for the week,' he answered. 'It's a good idea to make an early start, before it gets too hot.'

'What's the reason you want to search here?' his colleague asked.

'It's based on an old witness statement,' Wisting told him. 'Annika Bengt may have been spotted in a motorhome that turned off towards Larvik. It was just one of many tip-offs at the time and wasn't really followed up in any detail, but three days ago a necklace identical to hers was found on the dried-up foreshore of Lake Farris. The track beside that location leads here. We don't have anything more to go on than that.'

'So you don't believe she's somewhere out there in the mud?' Holmann asked.

'That is a possibility, of course, but it would have been much riskier.'

'I get it,' Holmann agreed. 'We can look there afterwards. That's easier terrain, completely open and undisturbed.'

He took out the GPS device used to track the dog's search.

'Is any part of this area more likely than anywhere else?'

Wisting shook his head.

'I'd think about ten metres out from this spot, around the whole turning area,' he replied, fanning his arm in an arc to demonstrate.

Holmann studied the area in question. 'Five hundred square metres,' he estimated. 'That should be doable.'

He called the dog to him with a single sharp command. Sheriff sprang up, sat at his owner's feet and looked up at him, eyes filled with energy and expectation. Holmann activated the tracking device and attached it to the dog's harness. With a light pat on its back, he sent the dog out to search. It trotted forward off the leash and first roamed around the perimeter of the turning spot. Its nose trailed along the ground, came across some litter and then moved on. Wisting picked up the empty plastic package left on the ground. It appeared to have lain there for a winter or two, but the writing on it was still legible. The contents had been German rye bread. A couple of beer cans and an empty jar of frankfurters also bore witness to tourists from Germany.

'Do you fancy holidaying in a motorhome?' Wisting asked.

Ingrid Sandell hesitated for a moment.

'I prefer sailing,' she said. 'Feeling the wind in my hair and the waves beneath my feet. That's a feeling of freedom you can never get on land.'

'I've never tried it,' Wisting admitted.

Sailing seemed complicated to him. You needed knowledge of wind and weather, navigation and the mechanics of a boat.

'A motorhome sounds so simple and practical to me,' he said. 'Free and flexible.'

'Where would you go?' she asked him.

He used the tip of his shoe to prod a faded drink carton on the ground and flipped it over.

'I don't think I'd make too many plans,' he replied. 'Just sit behind the wheel and drive to out-of-the-way places, searching for hidden gems not accessible by other forms of transport.'

'That sounds lovely,' she said. 'But I wouldn't like to travel on my own. It doesn't bring the same pleasure when you can't share your experiences with someone.'

Wisting agreed. He hadn't travelled anywhere since Ingrid died, apart from occasional work-related journeys.

Sheriff had reached the old tumbledown workers' hut. He seemed to show some interest in something stuffed down between two lidless metal barrels. His tail was quivering.

Holmann marked the position on the tracking device before pulling out a multicoloured hand towel.

'You have to remember he's trained to mark blood, semen and the smell of a corpse,' he explained. 'This is probably a location where there may be lots of different kinds of body fluids.'

He threw the towel to them. 'You can see if that's something you want to log.'

Wisting shook his head. The stiff hand towel was still brightly coloured and did not appear to have been there long.

Holmann directed the dog into the woods. Wisting and Sandell stayed behind on the turning area.

'I have a house in Spain with a small sailing boat,' Sandell said. 'A little place on the east coast called La Sella. I inherited both from my father. I stay there for a few weeks every autumn. You can come and pay me a visit. I can teach you how to sail.'

The phone rang in Wisting's pocket and, taking it out, he saw it was a number he had saved. *Siri Klopp, VG*.

'A journalist,' he said, letting it ring. 'Surely they can't have found out about this yet.'

He answered, wearing a frown.

'It's about the climate protest at the golf course,' the journalist said. 'What's your take on that?'

Wisting glanced across at Ingrid Sandell.

'I don't know anything about any climate protest,' was his response.

'We've received a video and a number of photographs from last night,' the journalist clarified. 'The protestors have filled some of the holes at the golf course with cement. They're now demonstrating against the top brass of Equinor who were supposed to play at a tournament there today.'

'As I said, I know nothing about it,' Wisting replied. 'If there's something going on there now, you really need to take that up with the duty officers at HQ.'

'I've spoken to them,' the journalist told him. 'They've two patrols out there. I wanted to know how you intend to investigate the crime.'

'As of now, we've still to receive a report,' Wisting said.

As he rounded off the conversation, it crossed his mind that the protestors had achieved exactly what they'd hoped for. They had been noticed in a totally different, more spectacular fashion, rather than simply picking up litter from the lake-bed.

'It didn't have anything to do with us,' he said, flashing a smile at Ingrid Sandell.

Returning his phone to his pocket, he strode over to the car and took out a bottle of water for each of them. Sandell read out the name on the label.

'*Farris?*'

'Yes, the same name as the lake,' Wisting confirmed. 'But the mineral water doesn't come from there. It's drawn from a natural source, a spring under Bøkeskog forest.'

They stood chatting as they heard the dog handlers moving around among the trees. Wisting had been on two work trips to Spain. Once fifteen years ago to follow up a lead about a sailing boat drifting, abandoned, in the sea just beyond Stavern, and again only two years ago to search for a Norwegian woman who had disappeared from a small town in Catalonia, called Palamos. He liked the country, the climate, the people and the relaxed atmosphere.

Ingrid Sandell now brought the conversation back to the case in hand.

'The anniversary is in two days' time,' she said. 'I usually call Annika's mother to tell her about progress in the case. Not on the actual anniversary, but a couple of days in advance. She'll expect me to do that this year too.'

Wisting checked the time, more or less as an automatic reaction.

'The day has just begun,' he said. 'Everything might look totally different by this evening.'

Sandell nodded but said nothing.

From where they stood, they could hear the dog team working in among the trees. From time to time, at regular intervals, Holmann and his dog returned to the original spot before disappearing into the woods once more.

The search continued for almost an hour before they finished. Holmann gave Sheriff plenty of water to drink while his colleague held out an iPad with a map and the GPS data.

'We've been over it all,' he said. 'With no reaction whatsoever.'

The map image showed the zigzag trail the dog had followed. More than the agreed area was shaded to indicate that it had been searched. No locations were marked.

'What do you think about a search on the lake-bed?' Wisting asked.

He looked down at the dog, lapping up the water it had been given. Wisting took a few sips from his own bottle.

'His capacity is probably slightly reduced, but I think we should give it a try,' Holmann said.

They packed up and drove in convoy back to Lake Farris. Wisting pointed out the spot where the initial necklace had been found.

'That's good,' Holmann said, kicking at the barren earth. 'He can get his nose right down without being hampered by vegetation.'

He returned to his van and let the dog out. It was not quite as frisky this time, but instead moved precisely at Holmann's command and worked in specific sectors radiating out from the discovery site.

'The detector man's been back,' Sandell said.

She pointed at the water's edge. Wisting gazed at the new footprints. There were two pairs of them now, one slightly larger than the other.

'They've been digging here,' Sandell added.

She walked towards what had been a sunken rowing boat, now covered in algae and other deposits from its time submerged beneath the water. A gaping hole showed where something made of metal must have been uncovered.

'I can phone him and find out what he found there,' Wisting said.

He looked around to see if they had been digging anywhere else. Obliquely across from them, one spot looked as if the earth had been disturbed. The sun was glittering brightly on the water's surface behind it, making it difficult to see.

Wisting cast a glance at the dog before they moved forward. It looked as if this had been a bigger hole than the other one, but it had been refilled. A corner of black fabric was protruding from the little mound of earth. Ingrid Sandell tugged at it and pulled out a shoe.

'Converse,' she said, rubbing her thumb over the faded logo inside.

Her voice dropped, as if this was a decisive moment. Wisting had no wish to disturb that and simply looked from her face down at the shoe.

As Sandell turned it over, loose soil drizzled down.

She used her fingernails to scrape off the mud to reveal a number on the rubber sole – 5 ½.

'Same size as Annika,' she said. 'Corresponds to thirty-nine in Sweden.'

'Is that the kind of shoe she wore?' Wisting asked. Sandell nodded.

'Yet another indicator,' she said, unruffled, as her eyes scanned the area. 'I'm really starting to believe she's here somewhere.'

35

Evert Harting waited beside the steps while Isabell gave her mother a hug.

'Anyway, you can come again towards the end of summer but before teaching starts up again,' Ella suggested. 'It's to rain for the whole of next week, so the problem with the well will sort itself out. And Kjell-Tore will fix the toilet while he's here.'

Isabell smiled at her. 'We'll see,' she replied. 'Thanks for having me.'

Taking her bag, Evert walked to the car and set it down on the back seat.

They drove with the windows open. Isabell sat with her elbow jutting out into the breeze. The gravel rattled around the tyres.

'Are you leaving because Kjell-Tore's coming?' Evert asked.

No answer was forthcoming. He glanced across at her. Isabell leaned towards the open window and rested her head on her hand. Her hair fluttered in the breeze.

'Mum's fond of him,' she said. 'He's her brother, after all.'

Evert changed his grip on the wheel.

'That doesn't matter,' he said. 'If he's done anything to you, I want to know about it.'

Isabell brushed her hair back from her face.

'He hasn't really,' she replied. 'It's just awkward being in his company.'

They drove for a while in silence.

'What happened?' Evert asked.

'It was a long time ago,' Isabell answered. 'Nothing worth talking about.'

They had reached the long stretch beside the dog owners' club. Two vehicles were parked on the flat area beside the bay where he had found the initial necklace, one with its rear doors open. As they came closer, they saw it was a police van.

Isabell pulled her arm back through the window.

'They're searching for something,' she said.

Evert dropped his speed. A police dog was scurrying about on the barren lake-bed, under the supervision of two uniformed police officers. One of them had taken off the top half of a pair of overalls and tied it around his waist. Two other figures were watching from a distance. One male, one female. The man turned around as they approached. It was the detective he had met the day before. William Wisting. His eyes followed them until they had passed by.

'It must have something to do with the gold chain,' Isabell said.

Glancing in the mirror, Evert began to say something but found himself unable to articulate the words. He had to clear his throat to get them out: 'They think it may belong to a girl who went missing.'

His daughter looked at him.

'Eh?'

'Annika Bengt, from Sweden,' he said. His throat was dry. His voice vanished like sand between his fingers, and he had to repeat her name. 'She disappeared four years ago.'

Isabell sat up straight and swivelled round in her seat. Once the police officers were out of sight, she flopped back down again.

'What makes them think that?' she asked.

'It was a special necklace,' he replied, and went on to tell her about the initial chain and the girl's disappearance.

'I remember when it happened,' Isabell said. 'They thought she'd been abducted.'

Evert swung out to avoid a pothole on the road. Isabell turned around again, but there was nothing more to be seen.

'There hasn't been anything on the news about it,' she commented.

'It's not the sort of thing they announce unless they know something for certain,' Evert told her.

They turned out on to the asphalt surface of the main road. Evert rolled up the window and looked across at his daughter. He saw she was preoccupied.

'Did the police say anything else when you were with them? Whether they had a suspect, for instance?'

'No, they asked me about traffic on the track and who stayed in the area.'

'You should have told them about the shoe,' Isabell said. 'After all, it could be hers. It was a small size.'

She rolled up the window on her side too and ran her fingers through her hair.

'Good Lord,' she groaned. 'We could have trampled over her. She might be lying down there in the mud.'

Evert did not reply. He was wondering what her thoughts were about her uncle but could not bring himself to ask. And there were other possibilities. Among the online searches he had made, he had turned up a case of a man who had abducted a girl from one of the campsites out near Stavern. That had been the year after Annika had gone missing. He had been stopped in his motorhome near Lake Femund, and the girl had been found lying in the back of the van, drugged and fast asleep. That man had been from Haugesund, but he had a connection to the area, and the modus operandi had seemed similar.

Traffic was crawling towards the town centre, but when he turned off in front of the railway station, there were still ten minutes left before Isabell's train was due to depart. He could not let her leave without speaking out about Kjell-Tore.

He cleared his throat again and had to take a couple of deep breaths before speaking.

'I'm afraid things may have happened that I didn't see or understand when you were little,' he said. 'And I appreciate that you'd prefer to put them behind you, but I do need to know.'

An oppressive silence hung between them.

'I won't tell Mum or take it up with Kjell-Tore if you don't want me to,' he went on. 'But we can't be sure that this is something that only affected you.'

Isabell reached out for the door handle but remained seated.

'No good would come of it,' she said. 'He'll still be Mum's brother, but nothing will be the same. Everything will be spoiled.'

Evert stared straight ahead. Passengers were beginning to throng on the station platform.

'You're not the one who's spoiled anything,' he said. 'Nothing is your fault.'

She sighed audibly.

'It's not as bad as you think,' she said. 'He didn't rape me. It's not anything like that.'

He felt relieved when she said that, but at the same time it was confirmation of his suspicions. Something had happened. He sat in silence, waiting for her to tell him more.

'I was little and don't remember very much about it,' she began. 'But he exposed himself to me, that sort of thing. He wanted me to be naked too.'

Evert felt a wave of emotions, a mixture of anger and

sorrow. He clenched his jaw tightly to hold back the tears. Isabell noticed.

'It's fine,' she said, putting a hand on his shoulder. 'It's a long time ago. I've put it behind me now, but it's embarrassing to be in the same room as him. Nothing worse than that.'

She opened the car door. Outside, the train departure was announced over the tannoy.

Evert felt his breath tremble as he exhaled. He felt far from certain that she had told the story exactly as it had occurred, but he could not work himself up to ask any more questions.

'You can't say anything to Mum,' she said as she stepped out. 'Or to K-T.'

He followed her out and lifted her bag from the back seat. The train arrived at the platform and waiting passengers prepared to board.

Isabell put her arms around him. 'It's OK,' she reassured him again.

'I really wish . . .' he began but was simply unable to put his feelings into words. 'Know that I'm here for you if there's anything I can do. I'll support you.'

With a smile, she took her bag and walked towards the train.

Taking a few steps back, Evert leaned on the car bonnet. In the course of a few minutes, his world had changed. He had always wanted the best for Isabell, wanted to protect her from everything, but he had failed. He had let her down.

A combination of rage and despair clashed within him, fighting for his attention. His eyes misted over. He could not see if Isabell was at any of the windows as the train left the station, but he raised his hand in a gesture of farewell all the same, hoping that her burden would be slightly easier to bear now that she had shared it with him.

36

Holmann and his dog turned back to the starting point. Sheriff's expectant behaviour had been replaced by some sort of subdued resignation. The dog handler shrugged and flung out his arms to sum up the fruitless search.

'It doesn't necessarily mean she's not here,' he said.

Wisting thanked him for his efforts.

'Let us know if there are other possible areas worth searching,' Holmann said.

As he and Sandell walked back to the vehicles, Wisting looked at his watch.

'Let's go for lunch somewhere,' he suggested. 'The technicians are coming to examine the motorhome in an hour's time. They can assess the shoe as well.'

They put the paper bag in the boot of the car.

'Water has a special propensity for erasing the past,' Sandell commented. 'To wash away all traces.'

Wisting also did not believe it would be possible to secure DNA to prove that this was really Annika Bengt's shoe. Nevertheless, the discovery did support the theory they were working on.

The air conditioning quickly lowered the temperature in the car. He parked in the back yard at the police station and took Sandell to a restaurant near the square. Excusing herself, she went to the ladies while Wisting sat down at a table in the shade.

His phone rang before the waiter arrived at the table. A

number not stored on his mobile. He considered letting it ring out, but in the end decided to answer.

'It's Pape,' said the man at the other end. 'Vestfold Caravan Centre. You called in here yesterday.'

'That's right,' Wisting replied.

'One thing crossed my mind,' Pape went on. 'I'm not sure if it has any significance for you, but I thought I should mention it in any case.'

'Oh, yes?'

'Yes, it has to do with the original owner. Ove Rudi Werner. You probably know he's bought himself a new van, a more up-to-date Solifer?'

Wisting did not say anything. Pape hesitated, as if not quite sure how to go on with his explanation.

'Well, there was some chat after you left,' he continued. 'I actually thought he was still behind bars, but Roy in the workshop said he was here with it on Monday. There was a fault in the cooling system.'

'Three days ago?' Wisting queried.

'Yes, he first called in on Saturday, but there was no one here who could look at it, so he was given an appointment on Monday. Half past twelve.'

Wisting nodded at the waiter who put down two menus.

'So he's holidaying in this area?' he asked.

'It looks that way,' Pape replied. 'I see he has an address in Haugesund, but his new motorhome was bought at Kroken in Kristiansand. Of course, he could just have driven there, if he was heading along that road. They have a workshop.'

'Did he say anything about why he chose you?'

'I didn't speak to him myself. Roy didn't have much of a conversation with him either. But it was a job that took an hour. It turned out to be a steering relay that wasn't working as it should. Nothing more serious than a bad contact. He sat inside at the coffee machine and waited while Roy fixed it. Kicki probably chatted a bit with him. She was the one who arranged the appointment at the workshop. He may well have said more to her, about where he came from or where he was going.'

'Kicki?'

'You spoke to her as well,' Pape explained. 'She's my niece. She works at the customer reception desk. Kicki Dalberg.'

Wisting remembered her. She had adopted the Goth style and had hard black make-up around her eyes.

'Haven't you spoken to her?' he asked.

'She doesn't work every day. I tried to call her just now before I phoned you, but I didn't get an answer.'

'I see,' Wisting said, shifting in his seat.

Pape realized that Wisting was interested. 'Is this information that's useful to you?' he asked.

'I appreciate you getting in touch,' Wisting replied. 'Do you have Kicki's number handy?'

'I can send it to you,' Pape suggested. 'If you want to get hold of this Werner guy.'

'Send me her address too,' Wisting requested.

It would be easier to speak face to face with her rather than over the phone.

'OK,' Pape said. 'She lives with her parents, but they're away just now.'

He gave an address on the east side of town but promised to send it by text also.

'Let me know if there's anything more I can do for you.'

Wisting thanked him again and rang off just as Ingrid Sandell returned.

'We need to talk to a girl called Kicki Dalberg,' he said, giving her an account of what Patrick Pape had told him.

'If we find any trace of Annika Bengt in the Solifer man's old motorhome, I'd like to know where he's hanging out. Kicki Dalberg may know something.'

The waiter approached them, ready to take their order.

'Can't we just have something packed to eat in the car?' Sandell asked.

Nodding, Wisting looked up at the waiter, who suggested two wraps.

Ten minutes later, they were back in the car again. Wisting was familiar with the location of the street where Kicki lived. It was situated opposite the bay where Fridtjof Nansen had launched his polar ship, *Fram*.

Number 14 was a charming brick-built house with a modest driveway. Wisting took one last bite of his food and crumpled the paper before driving up in front of the garage doors.

They heard the cry of gulls from the sea-facing side as they stepped out. Wisting walked up to the door. A shabby bike was propped against the wall.

'She's seventeen,' Wisting said, with a nod of the head.

They could hear the doorbell out on the steps, but no one came to open the door.

Wisting tried again and followed up by knocking loudly, but there was still no response.

'We'll go round the back,' he suggested.

The garden was larger on the other side of the house, with a massive verandah built of stone in front of the living-room windows.

'Everything's locked up,' Sandell said. 'She doesn't seem to be at home.'

Wisting moved up to the sliding patio doors. The sun glinted on the glass. A clothes airer was visible on the inside, and beside that garden cushions were piled up on the floor.

'I think you're right,' he agreed.

He took out his phone and keyed in her number but was immediately directed to voicemail. Wisting wrote a message giving his details and asking her to call him back.

Before they returned to the car, Wisting moved to the door and tried the handle, but it was locked.

A boy with a skateboard barrelled past out on the street, but apart from that the neighbourhood was quiet. There was no one to ask.

They got into the car, shutting the doors in unison. Wisting reversed the car slowly out from the courtyard.

Ingrid Sandell glanced up at the house.

'My colleagues in Sweden usually tell me I'm far too distrustful,' she said. 'I generally believe the worst of people. That everyone tells lies or that something is wrong.'

'Occupational hazard,' Wisting commented.

'Presumably,' Sandell replied. 'Call it a gut feeling, but I don't like the idea that we haven't got hold of her.'

Wisting nodded. His own internal barometer was moving in the same direction.

37

The two forensics technicians donned white overalls while Wisting provided a summary of the case. Two frame-mounted work lamps flooded the motorhome with a harsh white light. Their own van was parked with the side door open, making all the necessary equipment accessible.

The pair were colleagues Wisting knew from other cases, David Eikrot and Gina Lyng. They were both thorough and worked with great precision and exactitude, but they were also both known for being self-willed.

'Four years,' Eikrot said, seeming sceptical.

Wisting looked across at Gina Lyng to see what her point of view would be.

'It's possible, though,' she said. 'It depends totally on how the van was used afterwards and what sort of biological material we're talking about. We found blood from a victim in the back of a vehicle used in a murder case seven years ago, even after the perpetrator had removed the mats from the boot and cleaned out the entire space.'

'Are we talking about blood in this case?' Eikrot asked.

'We don't know anything, really,' Wisting replied.

David Eikrot walked over and gazed down at the safe in the corner of the inspection garage. Flakes of caked mud had slid on to the floor.

'What's this?' he asked.

Wisting related the story while Eikrot studied the objects Daniyal Rana had retrieved from the surrounding sludge.

'It would be fun to try that on a turntable,' he said, glancing at the LP record.

Ingrid Sandell had remained in the background. Now she took a few steps forward and peered in through the door of the motorhome, as if to remind them why they were here.

'Will we have any answers today?' she asked.

Gina Lyng lifted the lid of an equipment case and checked the contents.

'It's not a job we can complete in just a couple of hours,' she said. 'It'll take a few days.'

'I'd like you to start at the rear window,' Wisting said.

Eikrot seemed to resent receiving instructions about his work procedures but made no comment.

'Anyway, it's not as if technical evidence comes with a date stamp on it,' he said. 'We'll most likely find some physical traces, but to build a full picture you need to have a list of all the people who've hired the motorhome and anyone else who's had access to the van.'

'For elimination purposes,' Gina Lyng added.

Wisting nodded. Pape would be able to get that for him.

His phone rang. It was the *VG* journalist who had called earlier in the day. He turned down the volume and let it ring.

The technicians spent more time preparing their equipment before donning face masks and setting to work.

The motorhome rocked when Eikrot stepped inside. After photographing the back window, he knelt on the bed and shone an ultraviolet light through the curtains. Wisting had not thought so far ahead, but if Annika Bengt had pushed her head in under the curtains, there could be hair still clinging to the fabric.

These investigations yielded no results. He unhooked the curtains and directed the light on the Plexiglas from various angles. The paper-like material of his overalls made a rasping noise every time he moved.

'Nothing visible to the naked eye,' he summarized, exchanging the light for a DNA sampling set.

He moistened one of the cotton swabs and ran it over the window before sealing the swab in a sterile plastic tube. He repeated the process three times. The analyses would not be available until long after summer if they turned up nothing more specific to give the case priority.

Wisting was most excited about the fingerprint testing. This could give them a direct link to Annika Bengt.

Gina Lyng used a fine brush to apply a dusting of black powder to the back window. From time to time, she stopped and examined her handiwork. From where they were standing, it was impossible for Wisting and Sandell to obtain any impression of the result.

'There's *something* here,' the technician finally said. 'But no lines, nothing that could be used for identification purposes. It's more like just a smudge.'

Wisting and Sandell moved behind the motorhome to view it from the outside. Approximately in the centre of the windowpane, the powder had attached itself to an oval blotch. In that spot, they could see traces from one of the cotton swabs used to secure DNA.

Ingrid Sandell cocked her head. 'As if someone has rested a forehead on the glass,' she remarked.

Wisting had harboured hopes rather than expectations of something more specific. The result was disheartening all the same.

Gina Lyng came out to join them and tugged down her face mask.

'We've only just begun,' she said. 'If anyone was in the back of the motorhome while it was in motion, they'd most likely have had to support themselves with their hands along the way. Fingerprints can always turn up in unexpected places.'

'You have to be patient,' Eikrot advised. 'The case is four years old. Nothing is urgent any longer.'

Wisting and Sandell exchanged glances.

'Let us do things thoroughly instead of rushing,' Gina Lyng added, flipping her face mask up again.

With a brief nod, Wisting took out his phone and turned to face Sandell. 'I'll try phoning Kicki Dalberg again,' he said.

Her number was saved but it did not sound as if it was connecting.

Coverage within the brick walls of the garage was poor. They moved out to the car park in the back yard. Intense heat rose from the asphalt. Wisting blinked in the sunlight as he tried the call again, but the connection failed once more.

Sandell leaned back and folded her arms, as if she felt cold.

'I'll try the uncle,' Wisting said.

Patrick Pape answered at once. Wisting was reluctant to alarm him.

'You asked me to let you know if there was anything further you could do for us,' he began.

'Of course.'

'It's to do with the motorhome,' Wisting said. 'We may need a list of all the people who've rented it or used it.'

Pape hesitated. 'That's not as easy as you might think,' he replied. 'I don't have the kind of system that allows me just to tap a few keys. It's a manual job. I need to go through all the rental forms and pick out the ones that apply to that particular van. It's going to take some time, at this point in the middle of the summer season especially. I'm more or less on my own at the reception desk here.'

The DNA analyses would also take time.

'I don't need it until next week,' Wisting told him. 'Have you managed to track down your niece?'

'No, and you haven't either, I assume,' Pape answered. 'Earlier it did at least ring out, but now it seems as if her phone is switched off.'

Wisting said that they had paid a visit to her home, but nobody had been there.

'Her parents are at her brother's in Scotland,' Pape explained. 'He's studying over there and has met a girl. I haven't wanted to bother them. They'll be home in a week or so.'

'When was the last time you spoke to Kicki?'

'That was yesterday, here at work. We close at four.'

'Did she have any plans?'

'Not that she mentioned to me, but after all, the weather's good. She's probably out with her friends. A boat trip or something like that. It's typical of her to go off without having much charge on her phone. She's very messed up and impulsive.'

Wisting gave this some thought. There were numerous logical explanations.

'Do you know her friends?' he asked.

'Not the ones she hangs out with now, but they're these save-the-environment folk,' Pape replied. 'I don't have children myself, so I used to tag along to handball games and that sort of thing when Kicki was smaller, but it's different times now.'

'Please tell her to phone me as soon as you see her,' Wisting requested.

'I'll do that,' Pape answered. 'Anyway, she'll be back at work on Saturday.'

The conversation ended. Ingrid Sandell had been watching

him as he spoke, and an expression of frustration had come over her face.

Wisting checked the time. It was almost two. He never felt so uncomfortable as when he was forced to wait. This was one of many difficulties associated with his job in the police force. It involved physical risk, confronting traumatic incidents, pressure of work, public exposure, bureaucratic burdens and lack of resources. As far as he was concerned, the silent waiting was worst of all. It represented time that vanished into nothingness.

Squinting at the roasting hot sun, he let out a groan from his innermost depths and turned to Sandell.

'Let's go inside,' he said.

38

Beads of condensation had formed on the outside of the glass. Evert Harting sat with his eye fixed on one of them.

'Weather phenomenon in seven letters,' Ella said. 'Begins with T.'

Evert blinked. 'Hmm?'

He was having difficulty switching his thoughts to her world.

'Weather phenomenon in seven letters,' Ella repeated.

The letters began to form into different combinations and possible solutions. Maybe that was why Ella had resorted to crossword puzzles. The playful mix of logic and language and ambiguous clues provided a distraction that meant her thoughts were not taken up with anything else.

'What about *thunder*?' he asked, without taking his eye off the drop of liquid. 'That would be seven letters.'

He heard her pen on the paper.

'That doesn't actually fit,' she said. 'Though it does start with T.'

The drop broke free, sliding slowly down the glass and adding to a little puddle on the tabletop.

'Tornado,' Evert said, raising his glass to his mouth.

'There you have it,' Ella said, delighted.

Evert went on sitting with his glass on his lap. Kjell-Tore could arrive any time now. All he felt was a constricting sense of powerlessness, a grudge against the past that had shaped Isabell into the person she was today. How her whole life would have been different if only Ella's brother had not been part of it. They could have had grandchildren by now, running barefoot on the grass in front of the cabin.

His eyes grew moist, a mixture of sorrow and anger.

'Energy in eight letters,' Ella continued.

If he was going to talk to her about it, he had to do it now, before her brother arrived. Or else he had to let it drop, just as he had promised Isabell.

He blinked repeatedly and got to his feet.

'I'm going for a walk,' he said.

Ella looked up. 'Now?' she asked, glancing at her watch. 'Kjell-Tore will be here any minute. The ferry gets in at two o'clock.'

'Just down to the cove,' Evert replied, pointing.

'Do you think there's something there?'

He fetched the detector from the charging unit, put on his boots and walked down to the jetty. The old oil barrels now lay on dry land. He set off towards them, swinging the search coil from side to side. Every step he took was laboured. Desperation sat like a stone inside his chest. The past could not be changed. The injustice could not be righted.

The detector emitted a loud signal. Around ten centimetres down.

The signal continued further out, unusually clear and distinctive.

He laid aside the detector, took out his trowel and began to dig. The cracked mud of the lake-bed crunched, and dust whirled up in the air. Isabell would have been overjoyed if she had been with him.

After a few turns of the trowel, the blade struck something hard. He changed to using his fingers and uncovered the end of a heavy chain. It was too firmly attached for him to pull out, and he had to go on digging. His hands became filthy, covered in a layer of dried earth that clung to every pore on his skin.

The links of the chain slanted slightly downwards. Link by link it came to light. He felt as if he was not just digging into the earth but into his own mind, looking for an understanding of something that had lain hidden and neglected.

'Evert!'

Ella was shouting from the cabin.

He put one hand on the small of his back and straightened up. Ella had risen from her seat and was standing at the foot of the verandah steps, waving. Kjell-Tore came driving along. The motorhome rocked from side to side on the pockmarked track. Billowing dust hung in the air behind it.

Evert took a deep breath and exhaled slowly in an effort to hold his emotions in check. Then he brushed off the dried mud and strode up to the cabin.

Kjell-Tore, in shorts and a crumpled blue T-shirt, gave Ella a hug and then put his hands down by his side.

'I must say, there's not much water,' he said, looking past Evert.

'More than five metres below the norm,' Evert replied.

'It's to rain at the weekend, though,' Ella broke in.

Evert tucked the detector in under the verandah. Kjell-Tore was watching him.

'Looks like you could do with a cold beer,' he said.

He disappeared into the motorhome and emerged with two bottles of beer with German labels.

'Here,' he said, handing one to Evert.

He produced a mini switchblade knife from his pocket. When the blade shot out, he flipped off the lid and exchanged bottles with Evert.

'Would you like some?' he asked, looking at his sister.

'I'll wait until we eat,' she answered.

'Yes, we must have a barbecue,' Kjell-Tore said, grinning. 'My fridge is chock-full of goodies.'

He clinked his bottle against Evert's and put it to his mouth.

Evert took a swig but could not avoid thinking it tasted bitter.

Kjell-Tore studied the thermometer that hung on the inside of the verandah pillar, beside the steps.

'Twenty-eight degrees,' he read out. 'It's even hotter down in Europe, but it didn't really feel like it.'

'The air's so still here, you see,' Ella explained. 'We'll sit in the shade.'

They sat down around the table on the covered verandah. Ella began to quiz him about the places he had visited during his trip. Kjell-Tore told them about beautiful beaches and charming villages in northern France, a music festival in the Netherlands and a road accident in which he had given some assistance, on the autobahn in Germany, all things he had already spoken about on the phone to Ella, and she had noted in her cabin diary.

Evert sipped the beer and listened without saying anything. Kjell-Tore stretched his legs out under the table and looked from him down to the metal detector below.

'Have you found anything this summer?' he asked, pointing with the bottle in his hand.

Ella answered before he had a chance to speak.

'An old nail,' she said, with a chuckle. 'You must show him.'

Evert remained seated. He took another swig of beer and felt a nerve vibrate in his temple.

'I found a gold chain in the bay beyond the dog club,' he said. 'An initial necklace.'

He thought he saw the muscles on Kjell-Tore's face crease before he hid behind the beer bottle.

'An initial necklace?' he asked, swallowing hard.

'The letter A,' Evert replied.

He struggled to read anything further in Kjell-Tore's expression. He blinked a couple of times, that was all.

'Ella handed it in to the police station,' he went on, noticing that Kjell-Tore compressed his lips. 'After that, I was called in for interview.'

Kjell-Tore screwed up his eyes, as if the sunlight was bothering him.

'Why was that?'

Evert Harting answered only the truth: 'They had a few questions about the location of the find. Wondered whether I knew how the necklace had ended up there and whether I'd seen anything.'

He half-turned towards Ella.

'The police were busy with something down there when I drove Isabell to the train,' he said. 'They were searching with a dog, so there must be something afoot.'

The atmosphere suddenly felt tense. Ella's head jerked in what looked like an involuntary twitch. Clearing her throat, she put both palms down on the table and pushed herself up.

'Is this a good time for you to start unpacking?' she asked.

'Yes, and I need to plug in the electric hook-up to the van too,' Kjell-Tore said.

'Evert will give you a hand,' Ella suggested.

She disappeared inside while Evert and Kjell-Tore went down to the motorhome. Kjell-Tore reversed it into place, with Evert guiding him. They set up the stabilizer legs and plugged in the electricity.

'Look here,' Kjell-Tore said, producing a duty-free carrier bag from the doorway. 'Chocolate.'

Evert thanked him and took the bag without looking inside. Kjell-Tore cast a glance behind him, into the van.

'I'll clean and tidy in here over the weekend, and then you can take it over.'

The plan was to drive to Namsos and further north along the Helgeland coast. Evert forced a lopsided smile but the thought of travelling and living in the same motorhome as Kjell-Tore did not sound inviting.

'No cat this time?' he asked.

Kjell-Tore hovered in the door opening, as if he did not understand the joke.

'Tuffy,' Evert explained. 'Wasn't that what you called him? The kitten you brought with you from Sweden that time. It wasn't exactly house-trained.'

Kjell-Tore's eyes narrowed and then he broke into gales of laughter.

'No, God forbid!'

He laughed as he stepped out and closed the door behind him.

'You should keep them chilled,' he said, indicating the duty-free bag.

With a nod, Evert carried the bag into the cabin while Kjell-Tore sat down outside. There were four bars of milk chocolate, a packet of Smørbukk caramels and two bags of Twist assorted chocolates. He stashed it all on the lowest shelf of the fridge.

The receipt was at the bottom of the bag. Just over 200 kroner. He took it out to give to Ella. She liked to pay him even though it was intended as a gift. The date and time were printed under the total sum. The chocolate had been bought on the ferry the day before, just after 9 p.m.

He looked up from the receipt and out of the window, to where Ella and Kjell-Tore were seated on opposite sides of the table.

Ella had told him that departure was full, and Kjell-Tore could not get booked on until today, but that was clearly not right.

There could have been a misunderstanding, but no matter what had been said, the receipt showed that Kjell-Tore must have come ashore yesterday evening. He had spent the previous night in Norway but let them think differently.

He checked the receipt one more time and felt his sense of disquiet increase. It was like a fever burning within him.

Outside, Kjell-Tore had risen from his chair. 'Another beer?' he shouted in to him.

Evert moved to the door. 'Not for me, thanks,' he replied.

Kjell-Tore headed into the motorhome and returned with another bottle. Evert took out his phone.

'I can transfer the money to you for the chocolate,' he said, placing the receipt on the table.

'No need for that,' Kjell-Tore protested.

Ignoring him, Evert keyed in the amount, but stopped abruptly, trying to avoid making it look contrived.

'I thought you came straight from the ferry just now?' he asked, looking straight at Kjell-Tore.

Kjell-Tore glanced down at the receipt and took another gulp of beer.

'No,' he answered, shaking his head. 'I arrived yesterday but went home first. Checked my post and did some washing in the machine. It builds up when you're out travelling, and you don't have any water here.'

Evert looked across at Ella. Her eyebrows were knitted together, and a tiny wrinkle had formed above her nose.

'I understood that sailing was full,' Evert continued.

'It was,' Kjell-Tore replied. 'I wouldn't have got on if I hadn't booked in advance.'

He took another swig.

'We should drive home too before we travel north,' Ella said. 'Have a proper shower and pick up some clean clothes.'

Evert agreed with that before turning his attention to his phone screen and completing the transaction. Putting down his bottle, Kjell-Tore wiped his mouth with the back of his hand.

'Well,' he said, getting to his feet. 'Shall we take a look at that dry toilet?'

'That would be great,' Ella said. 'The outside loo is starting to fill up.'

'It's probably just a simple electrical fault,' Kjell-Tore said. 'If not, it could be that the incinerator element needs to be changed. In that case, it would be covered by the guarantee.'

He disappeared into the cabin, with Evert following close on his heels. In the doorway, he stopped and looked at Ella. She had already picked up her pen and sat hunched once more over the crossword magazine.

39

The conference room was located on the shady side of the police station. It was equipped with a simple kitchen work-top. Wisting let the water from the tap run until it was cold, filled a glass and handed it to Ingrid Sandell before filling one for himself.

Nils Hammer entered and headed straight for the coffee pot, nodding to Wisting and then turning to face Sandell.

'Do you play golf?' he asked.

Ingrid Sandell laughed. 'No,' she replied.

'Me neither,' Hammer said. 'But the chief of police does.' The pot gurgled as he filled his cup.

'She wants to know who sabotaged the golf course.'

He shook his head and muttered something about prior-ities and use of resources.

'Do you have anything to go on?' Sandell asked.

'Well, we do know who it was,' Hammer said, drinking from the cup. 'The climate protestors.'

'What were you thinking of doing about it?' Wisting asked.

'Nothing,' was Hammer's terse response. 'Absolutely nothing.'

He left the room, coffee cup in hand. Wisting put his water glass in the sink.

'Let's go,' he said and accompanied Sandell to his office.

The damage on the computer had expanded. The pixels in the affected area were spreading like tangled roots and would soon encompass the whole screen.

'What are you looking for?' Sandell asked when he began to key in search words.

'Climate protestors,' Wisting told her, filtering his search. 'Kicki Dalberg was wearing a sweater with a picture of planet earth in flames when Hammer and I were at the caravan centre. Patrick Pape said she hangs out with save-the-environment folk.'

Two related cases from the last twenty-four hours appeared on the screen. One, reported as vandalism, concerned the plugged holes at the golf course. The other case referred to six people who had been reported for an illegal demonstration at the same place.

Wisting opened the file and scrolled through the list of names reported. Kicki Dalberg was not one of them.

He switched the screen image and opened the website of the local newspaper. Down the page there was a story about demonstrators on the golf course. They were photographed with placards and banners with inventive messages about leaving the oil in the ground and stopping fossil fuel crimes.

'There was another story too, I'm sure . . .' Wisting mumbled.

Sandell stood behind his back, waiting without a word while he navigated around on the computer. In the end he found what he was looking for, on a page containing a selection of stories about the drought. Three enthusiastic teenagers had collected rubbish from the dried-out foreshore of Lake Farris. They were pictured together in the main photo. Wisting put his finger on a dark-haired girl standing behind the handlebars of a corroded, rusty old bicycle.

'Kicki Dalberg,' he said. 'Two days ago.'

Ingrid Sandell found the names of the other two youngsters in the caption below.

'Jonas Lerum and Mia Ruud,' she read aloud. 'Were they at the demonstration today?'

Wisting returned to the list of local crime reports. Both names featured on the list of arrested demonstrators.

'So why wasn't Kicki Dalberg there?' Sandell mused.

Wisting noticed the name Jonas Lerum on the screen and wrote down the details of his address and other contact information.

'Let's ask,' he suggested.

They descended the stairs, down to the car. The address suggested that they were heading to one of the low-rise apartment blocks at Tagtvedt, directly east of the town centre. Entrance B, third floor on the left, according to the description.

The streets in the town centre were quiet. The heat vibrated above the warm asphalt. Sandell adjusted the vent on the air-conditioning system to direct the cool current of air at her face.

It was a short drive. 'That's the place,' Wisting said, pointing at a group of residential blocks.

He turned into an extensive car park and parked the car in the shade of one of the brick buildings. The noise reverberated as they slammed the car doors.

Wisting took directions from a noticeboard showing a simple map of the housing cooperative.

The doorbell buzzed in response to his prod and only a few seconds later, a voice replied from the grille on the panel.

'Yes?'

Wisting ensured he was visible on camera. 'We're from the police,' he explained.

This brought no reaction, and the lock did not click open.

'What's it about?' the man in the apartment asked.

'A case under investigation,' Wisting replied.

There was another pause. Two youngsters sitting on swings in a fenced-off play park were watching closely.

'We've already spoken to the police,' was the reply.

Wisting could understand his scepticism. After all, the police had broken up the demonstration at the golf course.

'This is about something else,' he clarified. 'An investigation that doesn't involve you directly.'

There was a further hesitation before they heard a click from the lock, followed by a door opening on the floor above. Jonas Lerum stood with his arms folded, waiting for them to come up.

'What's this about?' he asked again.

'Kicki Dalberg,' Wisting told him.

'She's not here,' Lerum said.

'Can we come in all the same?' Wisting asked.

The young climate protestor looked across at Sandell and back at Wisting before letting his crossed arms drop and nodding in the direction of the apartment door.

A younger girl had risen from the settee in the living room. She was wearing a T-shirt with colourful slogans. Wisting recognized her from the photo in the newspaper but could not recall her name.

'Mia Ruud,' she introduced herself. 'What's up with Kicki?'

A door leading out to a balcony lay open behind her. The curtains were fluttering.

'We need to speak to someone who might know where she's gone,' Wisting said.

Mia glanced at Jonas as he sat down.

'We don't know where she is,' Mia answered, returning to the settee.

Wisting drew out a chair so that he could sit too. Sandell followed suit.

'She's not answering our messages,' Mia added.

'When was the last time either of you spoke to her?' Wisting asked.

'On Tuesday,' Mia replied. 'We had a rubbish-clearing project at Lake Farris, because of the low water level.'

Wisting nodded, as if to confirm that he had read about it in the paper.

'Have you spoken to her uncle?' Jonas asked. 'She works for him, at least now and again she does.'

'She was there yesterday,' Wisting told him. 'He hasn't been able to get an answer from her on the phone either.'

'Has something happened?' Mia asked.

'That's what we're trying to find out,' Wisting replied.

'Was she meant to be at the demonstration today?' Sandell asked.

'I sent her a few messages about it, but she didn't answer,' Mia Ruud explained. 'I thought she was just in a bad mood.'

'Why would she be in a bad mood?'

Mia looked across at Jonas Lerum again. He was the one who answered.

'We had a bit of a discussion during the clear-up operation,' he said. 'She felt it wasn't sufficiently effective, so she left before we were done.'

'Then there was that business with the cat,' Mia reminded him.

He nodded. 'Yes, she found a dead cat. Someone had put it in a plastic bag along with some rocks and thrown it into the lake. The bag ripped open, and the contents splashed all over her.'

'That's when she freaked out, really,' Mia added.

'We buried it after she left,' Jonas went on.

Wisting sat gazing down at the tabletop as he pondered this.

'What kind of action did Kicki think you should be taking?' he asked.

No answer came.

'More extreme?' Ingrid Sandell suggested.

Jonas Lerum shrugged.

'Was she the one who blocked the holes on the golf course?' Wisting asked.

The young man in front of him looked away. 'I don't know,' he replied. 'Anyway, it's not our method of taking action. She wouldn't have told us about it in advance.'

Wisting nodded thoughtfully. He would prefer the explanation that Kicki Dalberg had gone into hiding after damaging a golf course rather than that she was in the new motorhome belonging to the Solifer man.

40

Meat was sizzling on the barbecue. Evert Harting waited until the first drops of blood trickled out, before basting it lavishly with a spicy sauce and flipping it over.

'You do that like a pro,' Kjell-Tore said as he drank from one of the green beer bottles.

Taking a step back from the barbecue, Evert picked up his own bottle and put it to his mouth.

'Five more minutes and they'll be ready,' he announced.

Ella had already laid the table and set out some potato salad.

'Evert was complaining about the concrete platform,' she said, rocking the chair she was sitting in to demonstrate how uneven the surface was.

Kjell-Tore ran the sole of his shoe over the rough concrete.

'Well, it's not really finished,' he said. 'There was so much rain last summer.'

'How long is it since you poured the cement?' Ella asked. 'Three years?'

'Four,' Evert answered.

'I'll get it done while you're away,' Kjell-Tore said. 'I'd really been thinking of crazy paving, but I think slate tiles will be just as good. Cheaper as well as easier and quicker to lay.'

'You know best,' Ella said.

Evert prodded the steaks and lifted one off for Kjell-Tore. He liked it slightly less well cooked than both he and Ella did.

'I was thinking about trading in the motorhome,' Kjell-Tore

said. 'I've had it for five years now, and it wasn't new when I bought it.'

'Is there anything wrong with it, then?' Ella asked.

Kjell-Tore sat down.

'Not really, but it's fun to have something new,' he replied. 'There have been a lot of developments on the motorhome front. I popped into the caravan centre in Larvik before I came here. They have loads of good ones.'

Placing Kjell-Tore's plate in front of him, Evert returned to the barbecue and served up the last two steaks.

Kjell-Tore took a mouthful and leaned back contentedly in his chair.

'You know that the amount of water on earth is a constant?' he asked them.

Ella looked out over the almost completely dried-up lake.

'The total volume of water on earth never changes,' Kjell-Tore continued. 'It turns into vapour and clouds, but comes back down again as precipitation – rain, snow or hail. Or it freezes and turns into ice that melts at some point. But the amount remains constant.'

He grabbed the bottle and waved it about.

'Some of it is made into beer, but that comes back out again.' He drank deeply. 'It's like an endless recycling system.'

Evert spent time moving the food around on his plate before finally cutting a portion of meat, pushing some salad on to his fork and putting it in his mouth.

'Most likely someone else has drunk that same water before you did,' Kjell-Tore went on, pointing at Ella's glass.

Ella laughed at this notion. Evert chewed and swallowed. This would normally be a hypothesis and discussion he would have taken pleasure in. He had no idea how many litres of water existed in the world, but purely theoretically, millions of years could go by before you needed to drink something that had already passed through another human being.

'You've maybe even drunk it yourself at some time,' Kjell-Tore added, pointing in the direction of the outside toilet.

'Don't you think that a drop or two of the contents in there will get filtered through the ground and end up in the well eventually?'

Ella smiled.

'Then I'd have to be unlucky for that drop to end up inside me again,' she said, blinking in the low afternoon sun. 'What's more, the well is dry. Evert fills containers with water at the new petrol station on the E18.'

'Water from Lake Farris, in other words,' Kjell-Tore said, waving his fork in the direction of what was left of the local source of drinking water. 'Then it's guaranteed that some of the contents of the outside toilet have leaked out and been brought back up again by the pumps. And think of all the folk who pee in the water when they swim in the lake,' he insisted.

Evert was playing with the piece of meat on his plate. Something he had read somewhere surfaced from the back of his mind. That there were a thousand times more molecules in a litre of water than there were stars in the Milky Way. From a geometrical probability distribution, it was almost certain that several molecules of what he drank would find their way back into his body.

Kjell-Tore took another swig of beer and looked across at him.

'Lost your appetite?' he asked, glancing at his plate.

Evert shook his head. 'They found a dead body in the lake here on Monday,' he said.

He deliberately avoided mentioning that the body had been male.

Kjell-Tore shifted in his seat. A flash of revulsion seemed to cross his face.

'Not exactly in the water, though,' Evert corrected, keeping his eyes fixed on his brother-in-law's face. 'They found it because of the drought.'

'A man,' Ella interjected. 'It was reported online. He'd been there for eight years.'

Kjell-Tore applied his fork to his steak again.

'I don't follow the news very much when I'm out travelling,' he said. 'There are probably lots of animals that have rotted away out there too. The purification plant takes care of all that sort of thing.'

'Let's talk about something else,' Ella said.

Kjell-Tore reached forward, putting his hand on her shoulder, and jovially rocked her back and forth. He had always been able to smooth her hair and exploit her empathy.

'You're right,' he said. 'Let's enjoy the evening. It could be the last one before the rain sets in.'

'They're expecting more than thirty millimetres,' Ella said.

'It won't take long, then, for both the well and Lake Farris to fill up again,' Kjell-Tore pointed out.

Evert peered out to where the strip of parched earth met the margin of the lake. *Panta rhei*, he thought. The wise saying of Heraclitus, the Greek natural philosopher. Everything flows.

He had always thought that was correct. Nothing lasted for ever. Everything was transitory. After sunshine came rain. Night turned into day. A young person eventually grew old. Everything living would die one day.

Slowly his gaze returned to Kjell-Tore.

Not everything blows over by itself, though, he reflected. Nothing changes without intervention.

41

'I know a guy who runs a motorhome park beside the marina in Stavern,' Wisting said. 'He can make some discreet enquiries among his colleagues in the trade.'

Ingrid Sandell flipped down the sun visor.

'Worth a try,' she replied.

'He also owns one of the best restaurants out there,' Wisting continued. 'I suggest we have a bite to eat while we're in the neighbourhood.'

The traffic was crawling from Larvik to Stavern. Wisting pointed out the golf course beside the road. The previous night's incident did not seem to have affected activities there. The manicured fairway was swarming with players. Ingrid Sandell sat quietly, immersed in her thoughts.

'A cat went missing from Bovikstrand at the same time as Annika,' she said after a while.

Wisting glanced across at her. 'A cat?'

Sandell tapped her head with her fingers. 'It was just a minor detail that occurred to me,' she said. 'It was never regarded as having any relevance to the case, even though Annika was fond of cats and wanted one for herself. But now I simply can't get it out of my mind.'

'You're thinking of the one the climate protestor found?' Wisting asked.

Sandell agreed. 'How far was that from where the gold chain was discovered?' she asked.

'Five hundred metres, as the crow flies,' Wisting told her.

'But Annika was surely a bit too old to let herself be lured into a van because of a cat?'

'Not if it was injured or needed help,' Sandell said, with a sigh. 'It's probably just a coincidence,' she said. 'Lots of people had brought their pets with them to the campsite. It wouldn't be so strange for one of them to go missing in the course of the summer, but we searched for Annika along all the roads and all the ditches. Nothing was reported about a dead cat.'

Wisting turned off the main road, driving out towards Risøya. Very soon the caravan park came into view.

'It's a storage yard for boats in winter,' Wisting explained as they drove slowly past. 'In summer, the motorhome tourists come in their droves.' The restaurant was located on the opposite side of the service building, right down on the edge of the quay. The salt sea tang made Wisting realize how hungry he was.

All the outdoor tables were occupied. The waiter suggested one inside and they sat down, almost alone in the restaurant.

'Is Arne Steen in?' Wisting asked when they were handed the menu.

'In the office, I think,' replied the waiter.

'Would you please tell him that William Wisting is here?' he requested.

With a nod of the head, the waiter left. Not long afterwards, the proprietor appeared.

'I can organize a table for you outside,' he offered.

'This is fine, thanks,' Wisting assured him and went on to introduce him to Ingrid Sandell. 'She's a colleague from Sweden.'

Arne Steen drew a chair over to the table and sat down. 'I recommend the halibut,' he said.

Wisting cast a glance at the menu. The halibut was served with mussel sauce and a side salad garnished with dill mayonnaise.

'The motorhome park looks pretty full,' he said.

'More than a thousand overnights so far this summer,' Arne Steen confirmed.

'We're looking for a particular van,' Wisting added. 'Could you look and see if it has been here with you?'

'Do you have the reg number?'

Wisting jotted it down.

'Could you possibly find out if it's been at any of the other campsites too?'

Arne Steen peered at him over the top of his glasses. 'You don't want to do that yourself?'

'We're trying to keep as low a profile as possible on this.'

'Then you most likely don't want to tell me why you need to get hold of him either?'

Wisting flashed a smile. 'I'm glad you're so understanding,' he said.

Arne Steen rose from his seat. 'If you also have dessert, I'll have an answer for you before you leave. Try the *affogato*.'

They had not been sitting long before the waiter arrived with their food. The restaurant windows were open, and they ate to the accompaniment of the lively background noise outside. They both had a view of the harbour, where the water glittered in the sun as boats sailed past.

'What's the name of your sailing boat?' Wisting asked.

'Hmm?'

'The one moored in Spain,' Wisting said. 'What's it called?'

She smiled. '*Justos Vientos*,' she replied.

'Something about justice?' Wisting made a tentative attempt.

'Almost,' Sandell answered. 'It's from a sailing expression. A wish for fair winds and following seas. Good wind is the near-est equivalent. I'm not sure if it's been correctly translated.'

'What kind of vessel is it?'

'It's getting on in years now, but it's a cabin cruiser, easy to sail, with five berths.'

She told him about ports along the Mediterranean coast she had visited. Some of the same glow from the previous evening came over her when the conversation turned to subjects other than the case. An indefinable ease made him feel elated.

'Dessert?' he asked.

Ingrid Sandell looked in the direction in which Arne Steen had disappeared.

'I don't think so,' she replied. 'Maybe just a coffee.'

As Wisting placed an order, his mobile phone vibrated on the table.

'Hammer,' he said, reading out the message. 'He's got hold of a geotechnical engineer who can bring some ground-penetrating radar tomorrow to scan the dried-up lake-bed.'

He looked up. 'It'd be good to get it done before the rain comes,' he commented as he tapped in a response.

'We should dig up the cat as well,' Sandell said. 'I can find out if the one that went missing from Bovikstrand came from a larger litter. A DNA test would tell us if it's actually the same cat.'

'I'll get that done,' Wisting said.

Arne Steen arrived at the table with their coffees.

'No result,' he said tersely. 'That motorhome hasn't been here or any of the other sites. There are a few places where I got no answer. I'll let you know when I hear anything, but I'd imagine the guy you're looking for is the kind of bloke who spends the night in lay-bys and suchlike where he doesn't need to pay anything.'

'You're probably right,' Wisting replied.

Ingrid Sandell glanced at her watch when they were left alone again. Wisting did the same. It was nearly 6 p.m.

'I should be getting back to the hotel,' Sandell said. 'I have to write a daily report for my bosses in Gothenburg. This lead is starting to look more promising, with the initial necklace, the shoe and the cat – and even a possible suspect. Then I'll have to phone Annika's family and tell them I'm in Norway. It's going to come out at some point, anyway.'

Wisting nodded. Outside on the sea, the white sails of a boat were billowing in the breeze as it slid into the harbour.

'What will you say to them?'

Smiling, Ingrid Sandell fixed her gaze on him.

'That the case is in the hands of one of the most conscientious investigators I've ever met,' she replied.

The words were totally unexpected and brought an immediate, involuntary flush to Wisting's cheeks. It was difficult for him to think of a response. Her compliment had affected him deeply. Instead, he got to his feet, laughing it off.

'Let's go,' he said.

42

Wisting left his hand on the steering wheel as he watched Ingrid Sandell walk towards the hotel. At the doorway, she turned and gave him a brief wave before stepping inside.

A bare-chested boy dropped a skateboard down on the street and used one foot to speed off. The hard wheels clicked on the uneven asphalt surface. Wisting waited until the lad had passed by before he drove out.

The gate at the vehicle entrance to the police station was open. Two officers stood inside checking through the equipment in the back of their patrol car. Wisting drove in and found a vacant parking spot. From the equipment depot he took out a spade and other items to use in order to bring in the dead cat. After placing these in the boot of his car, he headed into the inspection garage. The motorhome was still parked in the same place in a screened-off section, surrounded by police tape that indicated the forensic examination had not yet been completed. The safe from Lake Farris sat in the opposite corner.

He lifted the vinyl record that Daniyal Rana had found in the same location and made another attempt at reading the label, but all the printed text had worn off. However, the grooves looked undamaged. It might be worth trying to play it on his turntable at home.

He left a note with a message saying that he had taken the disc and carried it to his car.

A few clouds had gathered in the south as he drove off from the police station, but not enough to bring rain.

The road wound alongside the dried-up river-bed that usually carried the water out to sea. The river-bed was covered in smooth, round stones.

Up at the dam, the rubbish collected by the environmental activists was still lying on the ground. Wisting parked beside the pile of detritus before walking to the edge and peering down. Scars on the cracked earth showed where they had dragged items out from the lake-bed. It should be possible to find out where the cat was buried.

Over at the eastern dam gates, a ladder was bolted on to the stone blocks. Wisting took the equipment out of the car and clambered down.

The smell from the arid lake-bed was reminiscent of an old book, a combination of dust and age.

He ran his eye over the surrounding area and spotted a section a few metres away from the dam that looked as if it had been recently dug up. The earth crust crunched and split with every step he took.

On top of the scooped-out heap of mud, small pebbles were arranged in a cross formation. He took a photograph before plunging his spade into the soil.

The dead cat's grave was shallow, and the remains lay wrapped in what was left of the black plastic bag in which it had been thrown before being tossed into the water.

After taking another photo, Wisting put on a pair of latex gloves and lifted the whole bundle into the cardboard box he had brought with him. He unfolded the plastic to look at the cadaver. Most of the head had lost all its tissue. The mouth was just a crooked grimace showing discoloured teeth. On the animal's back, bones protruded through the patches of decomposed fur.

Breathing through his mouth, he moved the plastic further aside and took yet another photo.

The fur looked as if it had been grey with some white on the side. It seemed small, perhaps only a kitten, but it should be entirely possible to obtain a DNA profile from the carcass.

The bag contained nothing more to say where the cat came from. He wrapped it up again, closed the box and sealed it inside a biohazard polythene evidence bag.

The phone rang when he returned to his car. He tugged off his gloves and saw that it was a video call from Line.

A delivery van was parked at the side of the road, fifty metres away, but apart from that, he was on his own. He answered, calculating that it must be midday in Washington.

Line was smiling at him on the tiny screen. 'Hi,' she said, 'where are you?'

Wisting threw a glance over his shoulder. 'Beside Lake Farris,' he replied. 'The water level is five metres below normal, but rain is forecast for the weekend.'

'I read about the protest action at the golf course,' Line said. 'That they were protesting against the water sprinklers.'

'Against that and against the oil wells,' Wisting told her. 'The top brass in Equinor were supposed to hold a golf tournament there today.'

'Do you know who did it?'

'We have our suspicions,' Wisting replied. 'A sort of renegade from a local environmental action group.'

'They have at least attracted some attention,' Line said.

'Do you have Amalie there with you?' Wisting asked.

'Yes, wait a minute.'

Line shouted her daughter's name and moved forward with the phone in front of her. Amalie was on a settee with earphones on her head. She took them off when she saw her grandfather on the screen.

'Amalie's so good now at talking American,' Line said.

She addressed her daughter: 'Aren't you, Amalie? Say hello to Grandpa!'

Amalie, clearly embarrassed, made do with giving him a wave.

Wisting tried to persuade her to tell him what she had been doing, but she was not in the mood to chat.

'I can call you again in a few hours,' Line suggested.

'Good idea. Do that.'

'Then we'll have to hope nothing more happens,' Line said. 'So that you can enjoy a few leisurely summer days.'

'Let's hope so,' was Wisting's offhand response.

43

The bed creaked when he turned over. Evert adjusted his pillow and stared straight into Ella's face. The light was too faint for him to see her properly, but he knew how her eyes rested, how her hair spread out in soft waves over her pillow, and how the wrinkles on her face stretched out like small streams.

Her breathing was quiet and even. He tried to breathe at the same tempo, aware that the alcohol he had consumed had covered his thoughts in a thin veil, even though he had not drunk enough of it to produce any kind of sedative effect.

He felt cowardly for not having spoken to Ella and told her about her brother's true nature. He was not afraid of being disbelieved but was worried about hurting her feelings. Or rather – it was more than that. What held him back was a fear of changing something familiar and safe, of risking rocking the boat. It would entail undermining the confidence they had built up over the years, but the truth would destroy her world.

Three times in his life he had kept something secret from her. The first time was about a fairly brief relationship he had had with a married woman in the Department. It was while Ella was working there, but before they had caught each other's eye. The other woman had left and moved abroad prior to that. He and Ella had engaged in countless conversations in which it would have been natural to tell her about it, but it felt complicated and at some point in time it had become, in a sense, too late. All the same, it had always felt like a betrayal that he had kept silent about it.

The second thing he had never told her about was when he had sent confidential legal documents to the wrong recipient. They concerned a political initiative that involved the relocation and closure of government workplaces. The story had ended up in the media and led to the entire plan being overturned. He had been given a dressing-down by the Permanent Secretary and for a while had feared for his job. Internally, the incident had been hushed up and he had never mentioned his blunder to Ella, even though he knew she would have been supportive. She had been at home with Isabell at that time and it was totally unnecessary for his wife to share his worry about the consequences of his actions.

What had happened was still something that could bring him mental torment, but the third episode was the one that gnawed at him the most. It was while Ella's parents were still alive and living in their home at Jar. He was supposed to go there to drop off an electric hedge cutter he had borrowed. Usually he walked straight in, but the front door had been locked, so he had gone round to the back garden instead. He had heard his parents-in-law quarrelling on the terrace, but continued all the same. He rounded the corner of the house at the same moment that his father-in-law struck his wife. Not just once, but twice, with the flat of his hand.

Most of all he had felt bewildered. He had never before witnessed any kind of violence and simply stood there, filled with a shamefaced sense of distaste. Before they noticed they were not alone, he had turned tail and fled.

He did not know if this was something Ella had experienced while she lived at home. She had never told him about anything of that nature. What her parents had been arguing about he had no idea. The hedge cutter had remained in their house until the following summer.

Now he had that same cowardly feeling of having committed a sin of omission. Like a man who did not have the courage to look reality in the face.

He turned over on to his back again and stared up into the darkness. Some of what was weighing him down released its grip. Instead, he was filled with a kind of relief. Because he had already known for a few hours how he could protect Ella in the best way possible.

Kjell-Tore had to be removed from their lives.

44

By the time dawn came, Wisting had not slept for more than a couple of hours. The windows were open but brought no cooling effect. Outside, the birds had begun to sing.

He tossed and turned yet again and became even more tangled in the bedclothes. His thoughts ranged over all the events of the day, drifting between the cases without rhyme or reason, but always coming back to Kicki Dalberg.

The bed was warm beneath his body, and he lay for a while without any covers, but a little after 5 a.m. he got up. He swung his feet out of the bed and planted them on the floor.

One unanswered call on his mobile. Ingrid Sandell had tried to phone him just after he had gone to bed. His phone was set up in 'do not disturb' mode – only Line, the switch-board at police HQ and his closest colleagues could override that instruction.

It was too early to return the call. He padded out to the bathroom, wondering what she had wanted. His mind toyed briefly with the idea that his night could have gone differently if he had answered, but the call must have been about something related to the case. Most likely fresh information from Sweden.

In the kitchen, he checked the operations log on his computer while the coffee ran through the machine. The night seemed to have passed without any major incidents. He undertook a search on Kicki Dalberg but came up with no results. Then he keyed in the registration number of the Solifer man's new motorhome, but the only message that appeared was the internal alert with the instruction to report any sightings and keep him under observation.

Closing the laptop lid, he moved to the kitchen cupboard, took out a thermos mug and poured the coffee into it. Then he headed outside and got into his car.

He had forgotten to take in the LP from the safe to try out on his turntable in the living room. It was still lying on the back seat.

The radio played music with no chat between the tracks. On his way into Stavern, he encountered a road-sweeping vehicle with revolving brushes. It left a damp stripe behind it on the dry asphalt. Apart from that, the streets were deserted.

From the town centre, he made for the coast. He had lived here all his life and knew all the side roads and spots where a motorhome could park for a night or two.

At the entrance to a cluster of summer cabins at Lydhusstranda, he saw a German-registered van parked. He took a few sips from his thermos mug and drove slowly on.

Most of the side roads were closed off with barriers or rocks laid across to prevent vehicles from driving in. Before Hummerbakken there was a track leading into the hardwood forest on the northern side, where the grass that grew between the wheel ruts had been crushed and flattened. The track ended at a quarry that had never been profitable. One time in the past, a woman had been raped in a car along there.

Branches scraped the sides of his car as he drove. At the end of the track, an estate car with a roof tent was parked. Wisting had to drive all the way up to it in order to turn.

A grey-and-white seagull had settled on the white centre line when he turned on to the main road again. Flapping its wings, it took off as his car approached.

His thermos mug was empty now. The search continued without success. He had no idea whether or not the Solifer man was still in the area, and there were endless possibilities. What he was doing now was not much more than a distraction.

At Tveidalskrysset, a side road turned off to the right, where a barn had once stood. When Wisting had been driving around in a patrol car almost forty years earlier, a car used in a robbery had been set on fire inside it. The barn itself had collapsed on top of Wisting when he had searched through it.

The road meandered forward, just as he recalled. Further along, the sun was glinting off something. Wisting sat bolt upright in his seat. On the patch of ground in front of the remains of the barn, a motorhome was parked.

Wisting stopped twenty metres away. The van was an old Solifer with faded paintwork. The curtains were drawn, and an internal sun shade covered the front windscreen. The registration number had the same combination of letters, but in other respects did not correspond with the van they were seeking.

He began to back out, but something gave him pause. Sunlight dappled through the foliage around him. The radio was playing music from some James Bond film or other. Wisting switched it off and took out his phone. It was 06:43, he noted, as he took a photo through his car windscreen. Then he called the switchboard at HQ.

'I need the owner details for a motorhome,' he said, reading out the reg number.

He heard a keyboard clatter in the background.

'A Peugeot Solifer 1996 model,' the operator replied. 'Two hits for the agent – the registered owner is Vestfold Caravan Centre in Larvik.'

Wisting explained where it was parked and that he was alone in his car.

'I'll go out and check and will report back in the next ten minutes.'

'Roger that,' the operator acknowledged.

Wisting tucked his phone into his breast pocket and pushed open the car door. He sat for a few moments listening to the silence that enveloped him when he turned off the ignition. Not even birdsong could be heard.

He walked up to the motorhome and tried to peer inside, but even though there were gaps in the sun shade cover, he could not make out anything.

The paintwork was flaking off the door. Wisting knocked on it, but there was no response from inside. He knocked again, a bit harder this time.

'Who is it?' he heard someone ask.

A female voice.

'The police,' Wisting answered.

Silence. A face appeared at the side window. Wisting moved back to let her see him and felt relief wash over him when he saw Kicki Dalberg on the other side of the Plexiglas.

The curtain fell back again and after a few minutes, the door opened.

'What do you want?' she demanded.

She stood in a black T-shirt that reached to her thighs. Her arms were crossed. They were covered in white lines, self-harm scars. Her hands bore traces of orange spray paint, and the tips of her fingers were yellow, just like a habitual smoker.

'Are you on your own?' Wisting asked, indicating inside the motorhome.

Kicki Dalberg's reply was defiant. 'Why, what's it to you?'

Wisting ignored her question, saying instead: 'We've met before. I was at the caravan centre on Wednesday.'

She nodded mutely.

'We collected a motorhome that had belonged to a man who was previously convicted of abducting a young girl,' he continued. 'You'd met him a few days earlier. Ove Rudi Werner. He was back with a new motorhome that required service. A Solifer. It was in on Monday. The owner sat at the coffee machine while the vehicle was in the workshop.'

Kicki Dalberg looked at him. 'Is that why you're here?' she asked.

'Do you remember him?' Wisting insisted.

'He was horrible,' Kicki said.

'Why do you say that?'

'He smelled foul, probably hadn't showered for days. And he kept staring at me.'

She tensed her folded arms.

'Did he say anything?' Wisting pressed her.

'He was talking the whole time, about all sorts of things. About the weather and about his van.'

'Did he say anything about where he had been, or where he was going?' Wisting asked.

'I wasn't really listening to him,' Kicki said, leaning against the door frame. 'But I don't think he had any specific travel plans,' she added. 'Why do you ask?'

'We're looking for that man,' Wisting told her. 'Do you recall if he said anything that might help us locate him?'

It looked as if she was really giving this some thought.

'Has he abducted someone?' she asked.

'That was three years ago,' Wisting replied. 'But we need to talk to him.'

She ran her hand through her tousled hair.

'What happened to the girl who was abducted?'

'She came to no harm – he didn't injure her,' Wisting answered. 'But we don't know where he is or what he's doing now.'

Kicki Dalberg shook her head.

'Sorry, but I can't help you. I've no idea where he might be.'

Wisting felt his sense of anticipation turn to disappointment. He asked a few more questions about her meeting with the Solifer man, but nothing came of them. She had been uninterested in his prattle and had merely held a brief conversation out of sheer politeness.

Most of all Wisting felt relieved, nonetheless. During his sleepless night, he had imagined a different outcome to Kicki Dalberg's sudden disappearance.

'You must come with me,' he said.

'Why's that?' she countered.

'Since you're not old enough to drive this.' He nodded at the motorhome. 'And because we've a couple of other things to discuss before you're due at work.'

She stood obstinately in the doorway before heading inside and returning dressed in shorts and carrying a bag. Her shoes showed traces of what looked like grey dried cement.

She locked the door and tried the handle a couple of times before accompanying Wisting to his car.

'No one has seen me drive,' she said when she sat down inside.

Wisting held out the palm of his hand for the keys. She dropped them with a theatrical sigh.

'It's my uncle's van,' she said. 'He won't miss it. No one wants to hire it, and nobody wants to buy it either. It's just an old heap of junk he can't get rid of.'

'He was worried about you,' Wisting said as he started up the engine. 'I'll drive you to him now.'

She rolled her eyes.

'I'm not a child,' she protested. 'You can drop me off at home.'

Wisting avoided looking at her arms and simply shook his head. He could not leave her to her own devices.

'What will you do with the motorhome?' she asked after a lengthy pause.

'I'll get someone to check it out,' Wisting replied. 'Secure evidence of cement and spray paint.'

He pointed at her hands that lay in her lap. She did nothing to hide the paint stains on them.

'I stand by what I've done,' she said. 'It was a symbolic act. The folk that have all the money and power don't see how they're destroying the planet. I've ruined a little bit of their world just as they're ruining ours. It's a matter of making them understand.'

Wisting shot a glance in the mirror without saying anything. His phone rang in his breast pocket. It was the switchboard at HQ. He answered and put the phone to his ear instead of transferring it to the loudspeaker in the car.

'Have you a follow-up report?' the operator asked.

'The vehicle is linked to the damage at the golf course last night,' Wisting replied. 'I'm driving an underage girl home to a carer. Transfer the message to me and I'll log the details and further information when I come in.'

The operator confirmed this and ended the conversation.

The remainder of the drive was strained. Wisting tried to explain what lay ahead in terms of an investigation into her actions. She had countered with arguments based on values and comments of no relevance to the law or how the criminal process operated.

As they approached the town, he had to ask her what route to take to her uncle's house and she reluctantly provided directions.

A dog began growling inside the house as soon as they

stepped out of the car. It grew even more insistent when they rang the doorbell.

It did not take long for Patrick Pape to appear, in a brightly coloured dressing gown. He stood in the doorway in front of the dog without saying a word.

Wisting explained the situation.

'I told him he could just drive me home,' Kicki Dalberg said.

Patrick Pape seemed to be still half-asleep.

'I'd soon be getting up and leaving for work anyway,' he said. 'You should too,' he added, glancing at his niece.

Wisting took a step back.

'A detective will follow up with both Kicki and her parents,' he concluded.

Pape had no questions. Kicki squeezed past him and approached the dog. Heading back to his car, Wisting flipped down the sun visor and backed out. It was now past 7 a.m. The day was about to begin.

45

A weather forecaster was talking about the rain that was expected at last but warned that the torrential downpour could produce flooding and landslides.

When the music resumed, Wisting turned down the volume on the car radio and entered Ingrid Sandell's number on his phone. Her voice sounded echoey, as if she was in the bathroom.

'I saw you'd tried to call me last night,' Wisting said. 'Sorry I didn't answer.'

'That's OK.'

'What was it about?'

The background echo changed, and he could now hear a Swedish newsreader. He pictured the hotel TV set being switched on.

'I wanted to warn you,' she replied.

Wisting braked for a car that swung out from a street on his right.

'About what?' he asked.

Ingrid Sandell did not answer at once.

'You're in your car, I expect,' she said. 'Have you had breakfast yet?'

'Just a cup of coffee,' Wisting replied.

The TV was turned off.

'I'm on my way down to the breakfast room,' she said. 'If you're in the neighbourhood, I could explain it to you while we eat.'

'I can be there in five minutes,' Wisting told her.

Ingrid Sandell hesitated again.

'Don't take the call if anyone from police management phones you in the meantime,' she requested.

That sounded dramatic, but Wisting did not ask any more questions.

'Five minutes,' he merely repeated, and accelerated towards the traffic lights as they changed to amber.

Outside the hotel he parked in the area restricted to dropping off and picking up passengers.

Ingrid Sandell was seated at a table on the far right of the breakfast room. Her outfit was more formal than the previous day – long black trousers and a cream-coloured, loose-fitting shirt. She had helped herself to breakfast cereal but had not started eating.

'What's happened?' Wisting asked, pulling out a chair.

Sandell wrapped her hand around a glass of orange juice.

'I had a long telephone conversation with my boss yesterday evening,' she replied. 'Several conversations with several bosses, in fact. They're keen to publicize the latest information.'

Wisting said nothing but had expected something like this to happen.

'Tomorrow is the four-year anniversary of Annika's disappearance,' Sandell continued. 'The major media outlets have already prepared stories about the failed investigation. The Norwegian lead implies a possible breakthrough.'

'I have bosses like that myself,' Wisting remarked.

'My boss is telling your boss about it this morning,' Sandell said. 'Then you'll get a phone call about how they want you to respond to the Swedish press.'

It seemed as if she had hung back from telling him this.

'I see,' Wisting said. 'It won't damage our investigation, but it's bound to arouse false hopes for the family.'

'They've been informed,' Sandell told him.

Wisting turned around in his chair and scanned the room before spotting the coffee machine.

'They deserve some modicum of hope,' he said, getting to his feet. 'Coffee?'

She nodded. Wisting brought back a cup for each of them. Sandell leaned back in her chair when he sat down again.

'In Sweden we have more than one hundred murders every year and clear up only a little over eighty per cent of them,' she said. 'In the most recent statistics the number of unsolved cases passed eight hundred. But the Annika case is not one of many. She was a child. The other cases deal mostly with criminals who shoot one another. People don't bother much about that, but Annika has never been forgotten. It's a case that provokes outrage and demands for justice.'

Wisting took a drink from his cup. They did not have the same negative developments in the Norwegian homicide statistics, but the consequences of a case such as the one involving Annika Bengt remaining unsolved would be exactly the same. It created uncertainty and mistrust.

'Kicki Dalberg has been found safe and sound,' he said.

Ingrid Sandell's face brightened with relief.

Wisting gave her an account of how it had come about before going to fetch a bread roll with cheese for himself. Afterwards, the conversation took on a lighter note. He told her how he had found the buried cat and about Line calling him just as he was packing up its dead body.

The other tables filled around them while they chatted. Wisting kept an eye on his watch. When it was almost eight, he decided it was time to leave.

'I'll make some phone calls from my hotel room,' Sandell said. 'Then I'll come up to the police station.'

Wisting walked through the reception area and out. The air had become more oppressive in the half-hour he had been sitting at the breakfast table. The horizon was now grey and hazy. Rain would come before the day was over.

46

He had spent a restless night, but when he awoke, Evert Harting nevertheless felt relaxed and refreshed. Some kind of liberating peace suffused him, as if he could finally breathe freely again, having held his breath for a long time.

Ella laid the table outside for breakfast. She boiled eggs and heated frozen bread rolls in the oven. Kjell-Tore came padding out from the motorhome when the breadbasket was set down. He disappeared off to the outside toilet between the trees before arriving at the table with a 'good morning'.

'Sleep well?' Ella asked.

'Extremely,' Kjell-Tore replied.

It didn't really look as if he had. His red-rimmed eyes and pale complexion told a different story.

'Let's have a morning dip after we've eaten,' Evert suggested.

'Maybe,' was Kjell-Tore's lukewarm response.

He split a roll – it was so hot that the butter melted as soon as he spread it.

'There's a chain down there,' Evert said. 'I found it with the detector yesterday but couldn't reach the end of it. I might need some help to haul it up.'

Ella smiled as if pleased to hear that the two men had a shared project.

'Do you need to pull it up?' Kjell-Tore asked.

'It's more a case of me wondering what on earth can be at the end of it,' Evert answered with a smile.

Kjell-Tore nodded without confirming whether he agreed to help.

They had a leisurely breakfast. The sun had drifted above the crest of the forest in the east by the time Evert rose from his seat.

'I'll go and change,' he said, picking up the bathing shorts that were hanging to dry over the verandah railings.

Kjell-Tore was still sitting at the table when he emerged again.

'I'll come too,' he said, heading into the motorhome.

Evert collected his spade while Kjell-Tore was gone and then they walked together down the grassy slope and out on to the arid landscape, forsaken by the lake, that now looked like a desert. Each step sent small clouds of dust up into the air.

'It could just be a chain, you know,' Kjell-Tore said. 'There doesn't have to be anything at the end of it at all.'

'True enough,' Evert replied. 'But don't you feel curious?'

Kjell-Tore chuckled. 'Not really,' he said.

They had reached the spot where Evert had finished digging the day before. Kjell-Tore took hold of the rusty chain and tugged at it but couldn't free it.

'We two are different,' Evert said. 'I'm the sort who likes to mull things over.'

He put the spade into the ground and scooped up some of the hard-packed earth around the chain.

'Do you never wonder what happened to that kitten you brought with you from Sweden?' he asked.

Kjell-Tore yanked at the chain again, but it was still stuck fast.

'It crossed my mind here the other day,' Evert went on. 'A cat ran across the road at the dog owners' club. It was grey and white, exactly the same as Tuffy.'

This was not true, simply something he said to see how Kjell-Tore would react.

'There's not much to wonder about,' he said.

Tossing aside some more of the sandy sludge, Evert glanced at his brother-in-law and watched as a sly smile curled around his lips.

'Do you know what happened to it, then?' Evert asked, leaning on the spade.

'Perhaps,' Kjell-Tore answered.

'Did you kill it?'

'In a humane way,' Kjell-Tore said. 'After all, I couldn't keep it when I started work again.'

Evert stood with the spade tucked under his arm.

'I drowned it,' Kjell-Tore told him. 'It's said that's a pleasant way to die.'

'So they say,' Evert replied and began to dig again.

As for himself, he imagined it would involve a ghastly fight for life. Holding your breath until you had to give up and ingest water. In his youth he could hold his breath for more than one minute. That was a long time when you were battling against fate, and even once your lungs were filled with water, it would take time before death occurred.

'I put it in a bin bag along with some rocks and threw it out into the lake,' Kjell-Tore rounded off. 'But best not to say anything to Ella. You know what she's like.'

Evert agreed. 'I do know what she's like.'

His fingers clenched on the shaft of the spade as he disposed of another couple of spadesful before straightening up.

'It makes you think, though,' he said.

'What do you mean?'

'I've sometimes wondered what became of that kitten . . .'

'Now you know.'

Evert resumed digging with the spade.

'It just made me think about the lad they found on the other side.'

From where they now stood, they could not see where the dead motorcyclist had been discovered, but all the same Evert shifted his gaze, as if to tell Kjell-Tore where he meant.

'He wasn't old,' he continued. 'Only sixteen years of age. Think what it must have been like for his parents through all these years. Not knowing anything.'

Kjell-Tore wrenched the chain.

'It's not the same,' he said. 'Besides, the cat was wandering around on its own at the campsite when I took it with me. Nobody was bothered about it. The owners had left it behind.'

Evert looked at him. There was no sign of reflection to be seen on his face. Nothing to indicate that his thoughts had turned to Annika Bengt.

He wrapped the chain halfway around his waist and leaned back. Earth crumbled at the end of the sloping hole.

'It's loosened a bit now,' he said. 'Give me a hand here.'

Evert took hold of it with him. More of the compacted sludge loosened around the chain. Then the mud gave way, and they hauled out a small anchor.

'Obviously from a boat,' Kjell-Tore commented. 'We should have realized that.'

Evert held it up and shook the soil off it.

'It doesn't look as if it's lain here for many years,' he said.

Kjell-Tore agreed.

'Things quickly sink into the mud around here,' he said.

Evert glanced up at the cabin to see if Ella was watching, but she had gone inside.

'Shall we take a plunge?' he suggested.

'We need one now,' Kjell-Tore replied.

His face and body were dirty, a result of the shower of dirt from the dig.

They moved to the timber walkway Evert had constructed, and out into the lake. Kjell-Tore ducked down and swam a few metres under water before lying on his back and pulling out to deeper waters. Evert swam a few strokes after him before he took a breath, curled his back and dived under.

He kept his eyes open. The water was murky. It was difficult to see anything, but he could discern the movement of Kjell-Tore's legs above him.

The lack of oxygen began to press on his chest. He kicked off, broke the surface and took in a deep gulp of air.

'Hi there!' Kjell-Tore yelled.

Evert realized this was not directed at him. He turned while treading water. Ella had got changed and had come down to join them.

'I thought I should look after you both,' she said. 'It's not a good idea to swim just after eating.'

'I'm pleased to have you here, then,' Kjell-Tore said, swimming back towards the shore.

'Thanks, me too,' Ella replied as she entered the water.

The sun glittered on the waves around her. She smiled at the two men, as if she hadn't a care in the world.

47

The chief prosecutor had phoned before half past eight. By then Wisting had already gathered the most important pieces of information into a short summary. They ran through the case and chose details that could be passed on to the media.

Daniyal Rana appeared at the office door while they were speaking. Wisting signalled to him to wait.

'A ground-penetrating radar instrument is arriving today,' Wisting said into the phone. 'We should give some information about that. I'll make sure there's a patrol at the locus to set up a cordon around the area.'

'Fine,' the lawyer replied. 'Just don't forget that this case belongs to the Swedes. We can only answer for how we're providing assistance.'

They continued speaking back and forth about the content of the press release before Wisting was able to usher Daniyal Rana into the room. Where he stood, a shaft of sunlight from the window fell across his chest.

'I've found the case,' he said, producing a note with a case number. 'You wanted me to let you know.'

Wisting took the note but waited for the young officer to continue.

'The safe was stolen in 2006,' he said. 'But the theft was not investigated. The police attended the scene and opened a case file, but the complaint was withdrawn.'

Wisting had not looked so closely into the case when he had called it up on his computer screen.

'Why was that?' he asked.

'I don't know,' Rana answered. 'There's a reference to a letter from the victim, but it hasn't been filed.'

'It's probably somewhere in the archives,' Wisting said.

'The safe contained more than a hundred thousand kroner as well as signed LPs,' Rana went on. 'The owner handed in a detailed list of everything that was stolen, but that's not been scanned and included in the case files either.'

'It sounds like a crime worth investigating,' Wisting said. He got to his feet and grabbed the bunch of keys from his desk. 'Shall we go down to the archives and find it?'

'Do you have time?'

'I'll make some time,' Wisting replied.

They took the lift down to the basement and let themselves in through two doors and finally into the long-term storage section of the archives. The ceiling light flickered a few times before it came on. The old cases were deposited in a roller storage system that optimized the floor space. Wisting moved down the row and found the appropriate year number. In order to reach the shelves, he had to push the other units aside, using a manual crank handle.

'At what time of year did it happen?' he asked.

'September,' replied Rana.

Their voices echoed down here between the brick walls.

Wisting walked along the rows of shelves, checking the note with the case number, and eventually found the relevant archive box. Opening it, he leafed through the papers to locate the case he was looking for. A slim folder with a green cover. The name of the victim was written above the list of contents: *Jonny Bakker*.

'Let's see,' he said, starting at the back.

There was a handwritten sheet of paper with three lines on

it. The text was obviously an instruction to fulfil the formal demands required to withdraw a complaint. No reason was given, just an additional note to the effect that the person in question had been informed that he could not subsequently submit a report on the same crime.

He located the list of what the safe had contained, written in the same handwriting. In addition to company documents, there was a collection of knives, three valuable wristwatches and a small collection of coins, as well as some signed LPs by Frank Sinatra, Louis Armstrong, Bing Crosby and Dean Martin.

'They must have been worth a lot,' Rana said.

'Well, he did at least keep them in his safe,' Wisting replied. He closed the folder.

'Why do you think he withdrew the complaint?' Rana asked. 'We're talking about over a hundred thousand kroner.'

'It sometimes happens,' Wisting told him. 'As a rule, it's because they've found out for themselves who was behind it and come to some arrangement with them. Other times it can be that someone in the family was responsible, and they don't want the person punished.'

'So, you think he knows who stole the safe?' Rana continued with his questions.

The light above them flickered again. Wisting looked down at the papers in his hand and let his thumb run over the signature and stamp confirming that the case had been dropped.

'I wonder if I might have some idea too,' he said.

Daniyal Rana looked at him with incomprehension. 'Who, then?'

Wisting did not reply but instead looked at the time. Two hours to go until the search with the ground-penetrating radar.

'Come with me,' he said, tapping the young officer with the document folder in his hand. 'Let's go and ask the owner.'

48

'Shouldn't we have phoned first?' Rana asked. 'We can't be sure he'll be at home.'

'Sometimes it's best to arrive unannounced so they don't have time to think through what they're going to say or not say,' Wisting told him.

He turned into a side road. They passed a farmyard on the left, then some farm buildings appeared that they recognized from the photos in the old case folder.

The door to a massive garage space was wide open. A lorry, several plant machines and scrap vehicles had been dumped outside.

A tall tree cast a long shadow over the courtyard. Wisting parked beside it.

'Looks like we're in luck,' he said, pointing.

A bearded man in his early sixties emerged from a blue shipping container that appeared to be in use as a tool shed. His T-shirt was grubby and oil-stained.

Wisting stepped out. The rough gravel crunched beneath his shoes.

'Jonny Bakker?' he asked.

'That's right.'

Wisting introduced himself and Daniyal Rana.

'We've found your safe,' he said. 'The one that was stolen in 2006.'

Jonny Bakker looked at them. 'My safe? Now?'

'It was dumped in Lake Farris,' Wisting explained. 'It's turned up because of the drought.'

'My goodness.'

'It was broken into,' Wisting continued. 'Some of the contents lay scattered around in the same place. The money was gone, of course, but we retrieved a knife and a watch and some LPs.'

'They belonged to my father,' Bakker told them.

'Everything's ruined, but you'll get your things back if you want them, of course. But I was wondering if you could tell us a little about the theft first.'

Jonny Bakker scratched his neck. 'The complaint was withdrawn,' he said.

'All the same, we'd like to have a chat with you about it,' said Wisting.

A table and a few camping chairs were set out just beyond the garage. He indicated that they should sit down there.

'Well, it was a long time ago,' Jonny Bakker began. 'I'd been away for a week on a construction job in Østfold. When I came home on the Friday, the window had been removed. My wife had also been away that week. She arrived home just before me and had called the police.'

He pointed at the main building and repeated what had been in the police report.

'Why did you withdraw the complaint?' Rana asked.

The camping chair creaked as Jonny Bakker shifted position.

'There was so much going on at that time,' he replied. 'The company I ran then had gone bankrupt. I had a lot on my mind.'

'The case is time-barred now anyway,' Wisting pointed out.

A cat sloped across the gravel yard, found a spot in the sun and settled down to lick its fur.

'What kind of company did you run?' Rana asked.

'Mainly the same as nowadays,' Bakker answered. 'Excavator work, uplift of materials and other transport business. Snow clearing in winter. Except that these days I don't have any employees. I hire myself out on larger projects.'

'Did you owe much money after the bankruptcy?' Wisting asked.

'Not much once the machinery assets were sold off.'

'What about your employees?' Wisting ploughed on with his questions. 'Did they receive their money?'

'Eventually,' Bakker replied. 'There's a wage protection fund to take care of that.'

Leaning forward in his seat, Wisting folded his hands and rested his arms on his knees.

'Did the theft have anything to do with the bankruptcy?' he asked.

Jonny Bakker stared at him. 'You ask as if you already know the answer,' he said.

Wisting stared straight back, but did not receive any other response.

'Did Allan Broch-Hansen work for you?' he pressed him.

Daniyal Rana looked at Wisting in surprise when he mentioned the name of the father of the girl Morten Wendel had raped.

'Yes,' Bakker replied.

He looked uncomfortable, as if he wanted to get up and leave.

'Both Allan Broch-Hansen and Reidar Wendel worked for me then. I had a major contract for the construction of the new E18. They did a lot of driving, plus I had other jobs on the go as well.'

Now he could no longer manage to sit still. He pushed

himself up out of the chair and produced a pack of cigarettes from his trouser pocket.

'I owed them money,' he said, lighting up. 'They knew I had cash in the safe. In those days it sometimes happened that people were keen to settle up in cash on the spot if we dug a ditch or levelled a plot. Allan and Reidar made a bit of extra money on that as well.'

'Black money,' Rana commented.

Jonny Bakker nodded and took a drag.

'I wasn't here at that time,' he added. 'As I said, it was my wife who discovered it and reported it to the police.'

He took another drag and blew the smoke out again in what sounded like a sigh.

'Of course, I knew it must have been the two of them,' he said. 'There was no point in making a court case out of it. Then it might have looked as if I had tried to withhold money from the bankruptcy assets. Anyway, they paid me back what I didn't owe them, and I withdrew the complaint.'

'What about the other items in the safe?' Wisting asked.

'I wanted them back as well, of course, but it wasn't possible, they said. They had got rid of it all and now I understand what they'd done with it.'

In one of the neighbouring properties, a power saw started up. The noise rose and fell as Jonny Bakker sat down again.

'Do you have any contact with Allan and Reidar these days?' Wisting asked him.

Bakker shook his head.

'Of course, they lost their jobs because of the bankruptcy,' he said. 'I could have taken them on again when I started up my new company, but I don't think any of us was interested in doing that. They sorted themselves out again fairly quickly. Allan bought a delivery van and set up on his own. Reidar got into long-haul transport and drives regularly to Sweden. I met him once on the ferry between Horten and Moss, but that's all.'

He sat for a moment or two, lost in thought.

'Then all that stuff between their kids happened,' he added, moving his gaze to his lap.

Wisting got to his feet. He had the answers he needed.

Jonny Bakker pinched out his cigarette and dropped it on the ground. One thought still seemed to be bothering him.

'Where did you find the safe?' he asked. 'I mean, where exactly?'

'It was dumped just beyond the Yeller,' Wisting said. 'Where Reidar's son was found.'

'My goodness,' Jonny Bakker said again. 'That was . . . odd, wasn't it? The very same place.'

He went on sitting for a while before standing up.

'What was his name again?' he asked. 'The son?'

'Morten,' Wisting answered.

'He was a fine lad,' Jonny Bakker said. 'He probably wasn't more than ten or eleven the last time he was here with his father. He loved to see the various machines and all the other equipment here. Tragic what he got mixed up in.'

They moved towards Wisting's car while they chatted and arranged for him to come and pick up his belongings from the safe at the station.

Daniyal Rana had mostly listened intently to Wisting's questions. He sat in silence until the farm buildings disappeared in the rear-view mirror.

'Very strange that the son took his own life in the exact same spot where his father dumped the safe six years earlier,' he now said.

Wisting sat for a while without saying anything.

'You're going to experience a lot of unrelated coincidences in this line of work,' he said at last. 'Things that happen at the same time or place without any connection.'

The young police officer in the passenger seat glanced across at him as Wisting tightened his grip on the steering wheel.

'But this is not one of those times,' he added.

49

A bee perched on the rim of Evert Harting's glass of fruit squash, moving energetically. Its wings vibrated and became invisible when it flew around.

'Shall we take a wander up to Bratten?' Kjell-Tore suggested.

The bee flew off. Ella looked up from the magazine she was reading.

'You can't swim from there now, though,' she said.

'I'd just like to see how it all looks from that vantage,' Kjell-Tore said. 'It's unlikely we'll ever experience such low water levels again in our lifetime.'

Bratten was an outlook point over Lake Farris, seven or eight metres above the water surface. A narrow footpath made it easy to climb up from the lake so that they could also use it as a bathing spot. Isabell had jumped from the top for the first time when she was seven years old. Since then, it had become a daredevil stunt she and her father were obliged to perform every summer during her childhood. Evert had not been up there for several years now.

He stood up and lifted his mobile phone from the table.

'We should take some pictures before it's too late,' he said. 'After all, it's to rain for the rest of the weekend.'

Kjell-Tore glanced at his sister. 'Are you coming?'

She shook her head. 'My legs are so swollen in this heat,' she replied. 'It makes walking painful.'

Kjell-Tore disappeared into the motorhome and returned wearing a shirt. He sat down on the steps to tie his trainers.

Evert found his and put them on. Ella smiled as she watched them trudge towards the edge of the woods.

The path, in the shade beneath the deciduous trees, was more or less overgrown. Kjell-Tore walked in front, pushing aside branches as required. Evert studied his broad back. The contours of his muscles were visible through the flimsy fabric of his shirt. His sinuous neck was shining with sweat.

A dead tree blocked their path. The roots were partially pulled out of the ground and the bark had begun to peel off. Kjell-Tore walked around it and stood gazing at the way ahead.

'Long time since I was here,' he said.

'To the right,' Evert told him.

They rejoined the path. After a while, the terrain sloped slightly upwards. The forest opened out and they emerged on to the rough ground of the plateau. The air was still but clear. To the north they could see as far as the lake extended. In the south-west, dark clouds were piling up in the sky.

Evert peered over the edge. Now that the water was gone, there was a sheer drop of ten metres before the slope beyond that stretched out across an expanse of fallen rocks. The height made him feel unsteady on his feet, as if he was dizzy and faint.

Kjell-Tore stood immediately behind him. 'Have you seen anything like it?' he said, almost reverently.

Evert raised his head again. The lake lay shrivelled, its brown border snaking alongside the surrounding forest. In places where the water had been shallow, vast areas that looked like desert sand had appeared.

'Do you believe what they say – that climate change is man-made?' Kjell-Tore asked.

'I think it's important to listen to the scientists,' Evert

answered, taking a step back. 'It not something we can take a chance and gamble on.'

Kjell-Tore jiggled a stone, around the size of a handball, loose from the edge of the plateau.

'Weather and climate have always gone in cycles,' he said as he weighed the stone in his hand. 'They change from time to time. It's totally natural. We just have to accept it and learn to live with it.'

He lobbed the stone over the edge. It flew in an arc and the loud noise when it hit the scree below vibrated through the air.

Evert used his mobile to take some photos but could not seem to capture the overall impressions on the small screen.

'No matter what the cause, there's certainly reason for concern,' he said. 'Climate changes in the past had major, serious consequences.'

Kjell-Tore agreed. 'Some say the Gulf Stream may even collapse,' he said. 'Then heat and drought will no longer be the problem. Instead, we'll all freeze to death. Or become refugees and move to Africa.'

He picked up another stone and walked towards the precipice.

'In a way I'm glad I don't have anyone coming after me,' he said. 'No children to grow up. After all, it's not just the climate, but also wars and the whole global economy.'

Evert Harting felt his pulse accelerate, as if his body understood what he had to do before he had actually completed the thought. He would only get one opportunity. Kjell-Tore was more than fifteen years younger than him, bigger and stronger.

Before he had a chance to do anything, Kjell-Tore turned to face him.

'Don't you agree?' he asked, stepping back from the edge

again. 'Aren't you pleased you don't have grandchildren to grow up in this world?'

Evert met his eye, struggling to control the feelings his question unleashed. The muscles in his jaw tightened.

'It's something Ella misses,' he said. 'Me too, to be honest,' he added.

Kjell-Tore gave him a lingering look. 'Yes, yes,' he said. 'It's not too late, of course.'

He turned his back again and gazed out over the lake. 'Have you found anything else?' he asked.

'What do you mean?'

'You mentioned you'd found a gold necklace,' Kjell-Tore reminded him. 'Has anything else turned up?'

He waved his hand in a semicircle above the dry landscape below.

'Only old odds and ends,' Evert answered.

Kjell-Tore said nothing more. His question had seemed tentative, as if he wanted to kick off a conversation he was reluctant to initiate.

'I think I know who the necklace belongs to,' Evert said.

'Oh yes?' Kjell-Tore said, still with his back to him. One step from the edge.

Evert broke a twig off the nearest bush.

'I've realized how it ended up here too,' he said.

Kjell-Tore half-turned towards him. His eyes narrowed to shield them from the blazing sun.

'I see,' he said.

The narrowed gaze became evasive. His eyes flitted to the twig Evert held in his hand.

Evert tossed the twig over the edge. It spun through the air. Kjell-Tore leaned forward to watch it land. Evert felt his blood pressure soar, pressing on a nerve behind his eyes. He ran forward, taking two steps, using all his strength to plant his shoulder on Kjell-Tore's back and propel him forward, out into the void.

Before the free fall, he managed to twist his body around. Desperation flickered across his face. His arms flapped in the air. A scream was torn from his throat. It tapered off as he fell. Evert did not see the body land on the ground but heard the muffled thud as it hit the rocks below.

50

The wind was picking up. A breeze whipped off the top layer of dried mud and dragged it along the ground.

The georadar engineers had set up a tent with two side panels. It had no particular function now, except for providing shade from the sun, but if any finds were made, it could be easily moved to prevent unwelcome scrutiny.

The radar equipment was a robust unit on four wheels with solid handles. Usually, it was used for archaeological investigations. One of the men demonstrated how the machine worked. He pushed it a few metres forward and fine-tuned the sensitivity, depth and resolution. Wisting leaned forward and peered at the screen between the handgrips. It showed an intricate pattern of multicoloured graphs that represented the topography of the earth beneath their feet. Objects hidden by the dry lake-bed would register as deviations.

Nils Hammer instructed them to set to work. The inbuilt antenna emitted a rhythmic, pulsing signal as the radar unit trundled forward. They watched closely while Wisting brought him up to speed on what he had learned about the safe, lowering his voice so that no one around them could hear.

'What do you make of it?' Hammer asked. 'That Allan Broch-Hansen got rid of the body of his daughter's rapist in the exact same spot as he and Reidar Wendel dumped the safe six years earlier?'

Wisting raised his eyes and looked over towards the place where Morten Wendel and his motorbike had been found.

'His mother didn't understand why he chose this spot,' Wisting replied. 'He had never been on the roads over there and was not familiar with them.'

He turned and gazed towards the shore. Two police officers were stretching barrier tape between the tree trunks along the roadside. Ingrid Sandell stood beside the car talking on her phone. The news was out in the Swedish media. For the moment they had no rubberneckers, but given time, they would come.

'What do you think passed through Reidar Wendel's mind when he realized that his son had been found in the same location?' Hammer asked.

'I brought them with me to the discovery site,' Wisting said. 'Both him and his wife.'

'Did you notice any reaction from him?' Hammer asked.

Wisting mulled this over. Reidar Wendel had scrambled down the rocky bank and across to the spot where his son and the motorbike had been found. He had asked about the other objects that lay scattered there. In retrospect, his interest seemed conspicuous.

'Difficult to say,' he answered. 'They were suffering from shock and grief.'

The guys conducting the georadar survey had stopped. One of them placed a steel pin with a little flag on it before they moved on. Hammer grabbed a spade and strode towards the flag. Wisting once again looked up at Ingrid Sandell before he followed in his footsteps.

The blade of the spade slid easily into the dried earth. Hammer scooped it up without finding anything and took another portion. The base of a glass bottle appeared. Wisting pulled it out and placed it at the foot of the small flag.

'So what are you going to do?' Hammer queried.

'It's Maren who has responsibility for that case,' Wisting said. 'The result of the forensics tests will be available today. If they find injuries on the body, we'll have a bit more to go on. No matter what, I'll have to confront Allan Broch-Hansen with my suspicions.'

They walked back into the shade of the tent. Hammer picked up one of the bottles of water stored there, twisted off the cap and raised it to his mouth.

Ingrid Sandell had finished on the phone and came to join them.

'That was from our operations centre in Stockholm,' she said. 'The Solifer man is not in any of the photos from Bovikstrand.'

Wisting made no comment.

'That doesn't mean he wasn't there,' Sandell added, as if she could read his thoughts. 'Most of the images are family photos and don't include any strangers.'

'It was worth a try,' Wisting said.

They stood in silence watching the georadar activities.

'Annika's grandfather will be here soon,' Sandell said.

She had spoken to him on the first evening. He lived near Lysekil, only an hour beyond the Swedish border, and continually drove around with a spade in his car. Every time a new tip-off came in, he set off to search.

'He's dug on sandy beaches, in gravel pits and under bridges,' Sandell went on. 'I couldn't ask him to stay at home now.'

'Of course not,' was Wisting's response.

She moved slightly closer to him. The man driving the georadar unit stopped and laid out another marker flag between the wheel tracks. Then he walked on, stopped again and set out another flag a few metres further off.

Wisting cast a glance up to the road before they moved

towards the markers. Yet another patrol car arrived on the scene.

The first few spadesful were empty. Hammer had to dig deep before he lifted out a triangular object around the size of a dinner plate. Wisting picked it up and rubbed the soil off.

'Old ceramics,' he said. 'Maybe part of a serving dish. The man who found the initial necklace was here to search for surviving fragments from the ancient Fresjeborgen fortress.'

He turned to face Sandell and explained: 'It was destroyed by a flood and collapsed into the water four hundred years ago.'

She pointed at the ceramic plate. 'So that could be four hundred years old?'

Wisting handed her the fragment and peered into the hole it had come from. It had lain around forty centimetres beneath the surface.

'If the Swedish girl is buried here, she's unlikely to have sunk as deep as that,' Hammer said.

He walked on to the next flag.

Ingrid Sandell passed the ceramic fragment back to Wisting. He was not quite sure what to do with it and returned it to where it had been found.

One of the uniformed officers approached. Wisting nodded to him. It was Kittil Gram, one of the most experienced shift supervisors, who was often given responsibility for major operations.

'Found anything?' he asked.

'Nothing of any relevance to the case so far,' Wisting replied.

'I saw it's hit the news,' Gram commented. 'Do you want to handle things yourself when they turn up here?'

Wisting took out his mobile phone.

'I won't be staying here very long,' he answered, checking the online newspapers. Annika Bengt's face shone out at him from the screen.

'I can deal with it, then,' Gram said. 'Anyway, I don't know more than what the press release states, so I won't say anything untoward.'

Nils Hammer squatted down and pulled up another piece of ceramic, slightly smaller and rounder in shape than the previous one.

Kittil Gram gazed at the other marker flags that had been set out.

'You're going to be busy here for a while, I guess.'

His earpiece buzzed and he lifted the microphone from his lapel to answer. Wisting read one of the introductory paragraphs on his phone screen. Items had been found in Larvik that could belong to the missing Swedish fourteen-year-old. It was the middle of the night in Washington, he reckoned. Line would not have picked it up yet.

Kittil Gram had produced a notebook and was jotting down some keywords.

'Roger that,' he replied as he reattached the microphone.

He looked at Wisting. 'I have to go. There's been an accident near here, a fall.'

His hand pointed northwards along the lake.

'Serious?' Wisting asked.

'An ambulance is on its way,' Gram replied. 'But it's been reported as a fatality.'

'Who are we talking about?' Wisting asked.

'An adult male,' Gram replied, glancing at his notes. 'I don't have a name, but it's been reported by a cabin owner. Evert Harting.'

'Evert Harting?' Wisting repeated.

Kittil Gram confirmed the name.

'Does it mean anything to you?'

Wisting nodded. 'I'll come with you,' he said.

51

Wisting drove in front. He knew the way. As the gravel kicked up dust, the police car disappeared in the rear-view mirror. Where he had turned right the day before and followed the track to the turning place, now he turned left. Soon a red-painted cabin came into view, a motorhome parked beside the gable wall with its bonnet facing out. A Challenger. The sight of it reinforced something within him, like some sort of warning floating through his consciousness.

Evert Harting stood in the yard in front of the cabin, his T-shirt spattered with blood. A woman of around the same age struggled to get up from the steps. She covered her head with her hands, concealing her eyes.

Wisting parked, stepped out and looked back at the track he had driven along. Behind the patrol car came an ambulance, still with blue lights flashing.

'Where is he?' Wisting asked.

'It's too late,' Evert Harting replied.

He held out his empty hands, palms facing up.

'There's nothing more to be done.'

'All the same, you have to show us where he is,' Wisting insisted.

The woman was pacing around in circles. Evert Harting kept his eyes on her. Her face was contorted with grief and despair.

'It's her brother,' he explained.

'Someone will stay here with her,' Wisting said.

Three paramedics rushed up, one of them asking the same question as Wisting.

'Where is he?'

Evert Harting pointed towards the forest.

'You'll have to show us.'

One paramedic stayed behind while the other two accompanied him along the rugged path through the woods and up on to the plateau.

Wisting peered out over the edge, reckoning that it must be at least ten metres down. A man lay on his back on top of a pile of rocks. His limbs were twisted into unnatural positions and the stones were stained with dark, wet blood.

'I've been down to check on him,' Harting said, pointing at a path that sloped down to the shore. Kittil Gram and the paramedics followed it.

'What happened?' Wisting asked once he was left alone with Harting.

'We came to look at the view,' he explained, still out of breath. 'Because of the drought. The landscape . . . it was his suggestion. We used to swim from here. Jump from the edge.'

Wisting had taken out his notepad. 'What's his name?'

'Kjell-Tore Bonholt. He's my wife, Ella's, brother. I explained it all when I phoned. He's visiting us here. He does that every summer. He arrived yesterday.'

'Does he have any other family?'

Evert Harting shook his head.

'What about you?' Wisting probed. 'Do you and your wife have anyone who can be with you?'

'Just our daughter.'

Wisting made a note of the name, even though he would be able to find it in the population register.

'How did he come to fall?' he asked.

Evert Harting's breathing became laboured.

'I don't really know . . .' he began. 'He was careless, went too near the edge. I just heard some stones scraping and then I saw he'd lost his balance.'

Wisting looked across at the precipice. There were marks in the porous hillside where stones had slid out. He walked all the way across and looked down again. Kittil Gram and the others had reached the body.

He turned to face Evert Harting. 'Was it only the two of you up here?'

'Yes.'

'Your wife didn't come with you?'

'No. She stayed behind. Her legs swell up in the heat. It's painful for her to walk.'

Wisting nodded. 'Let's go back, then,' he said.

Evert Harting hesitated, looking up at the dark clouds drifting towards them.

'How will they be able to move him?' he asked.

'I think they'll arrange for an all-terrain vehicle that can drive where the water used to be,' Wisting answered. 'It's going to take some time. First, they'll have to take photos and carry out other investigations.'

They began to walk. The path was now well-trodden and easy to follow.

Wisting's mobile gave a silent signal. Taking it out of his pocket, he saw that it was a journalist trying to circumvent the usual communication channels. There were two similar unanswered calls. He let it ring and put the phone back.

At the tree that blocked the path, Harting stopped and leaned against the dark trunk.

'Will they manage it before the rain comes?' he asked, looking up through the canopy of foliage.

'I think so,' Wisting said. 'They'll transport him to hospital in Tønsberg and a doctor there will fill out the paperwork before the undertakers take charge.'

'Paperwork,' Harting repeated. 'You mean a death certificate?'

Wisting nodded. 'Is that Kjell-Tore's motorhome?' he asked.

It did not look as if Evert Harting intended to answer. He turned away and took a few steps before half-turning towards Wisting again.

'Yes,' he replied. 'He came from Denmark yesterday. He'd been to Germany and France. We'd arranged for Ella and me to borrow it and drive north while he stayed behind at the cabin. We usually do that every year.'

'I quite fancy a motorhome,' Wisting commented. 'It seems so free and easy.'

They walked on, over a rougher patch. Wisting kept his eyes down, watching where he put his feet.

His encounters with distressed relatives often went like this, he thought. He hit upon some everyday remark to make about the dead person and used it to fill the gaps in the conversation.

'Has he had it long?' Wisting asked.

'How long can it be?' Harting mused, pushing a branch aside. 'Three or four years, something like that. It wasn't new when he bought it.'

They continued in silence. Wisting considered telling him that the initial necklace he had found four days earlier had probably belonged to the missing Swedish girl, and that the news outlets would be full of the story in the next few days, but decided against it. They glimpsed the cabin and vehicles up ahead between the trees. Ella Harting had taken a seat on the verandah. She stood up when they arrived.

288

'What do we do now?' she asked, looking at Wisting.

He repeated what he had told her husband and explained that someone from the local authority's crisis team would soon come to support them. As for himself, he had to leave. He turned his car in the restricted space but stopped after a few metres and got out again. Evert and Ella were watching him from the verandah, but he could not leave without taking a look. He moved out of their field of vision, across to the motorhome and around to the back. It had a rear window on the right-hand side, with white net curtains drawn across it.

He lingered for a while before returning to his car, this time avoiding looking in the direction of Evert Harting and his wife. He thought of what he had said to the young police officer when they'd left the man whose old safe had been stolen: about pure coincidences that would crop up in the course of his work.

This was unlikely to be such an instance.

52

The journalists had arrived. They now stood in a scattered group immediately below the original shoreline, while other onlookers remained up on the track. Wisting called Ingrid Sandell as he drove past. He saw her take out her mobile and put it to her ear.

'I have to go to the station,' he said, dropping his speed.

She turned towards the track as if sensing he was there.

'Are you coming back?'

He raised a hand to the side window when she caught sight of him.

'Yes, I just have to check something.' It was too complicated to explain. 'It won't take long.'

'Then I'll stay here.'

The georadar unit was stationary and the men behind it seemed to be discussing something they could see on the screen.

'Have they found something?' Wisting asked.

'Nothing relevant.'

Wisting picked up the water bottle from the centre console. He gripped it between his legs and rounded off the conversation before twisting off the lid and taking a drink. The contents were lukewarm and stale.

Ten minutes later he was in his office. He riffled through his notes while his computer started up. In the interview with Evert Harting, he had asked specifically about motorhome traffic on the gravel track past the search area and towards their cabin. The answer had been non-committal. *The occasional one*, he had written in his notes.

The machine was ready. The accidental fall on the eastern side of Lake Farris was still listed as an active assignment in the operations log. The fire service had been called out to assist with removing the cadaver from the scene. The personal details of the fatality had been logged. Kjell-Tore Bonholt, forty-nine years old. Unmarried, no children.

Wisting filled in the date of birth on the motorhome register. The van was a Fiat Challenger Mageo, a 2008 model. In addition, he was listed as the owner of an old Toyota Hilux, a two-seater with a cargo bed. The motorhome had been registered in his name five years ago. *Three or four years* was what Evert Harting had told him.

Someone walked by in the corridor outside. Wisting stared at the screen, unsure whether what he had discovered meant anything. He wrote the date of birth and personal ID number down in his notebook and carried the search forward to the criminal records register. Kjell-Tore Bonholt had been fined twice for sexual harassment of youngsters under sixteen years of age. The first time had been sixteen years earlier, the second time eleven years ago. The earlier incident had taken place at Brynseng School in Oslo, while the other one had been in Lofoten in the far north of the country. Otherwise, the onscreen image did not provide much more information. He would have to get hold of the case files to find out what had in fact happened.

The damage in the corner of the computer screen broadened out while he was staring at it. His thoughts drifted without him really knowing what conclusion to draw. Kjell-Tore Bonholt was listed as the owner of one of 60,000 motorhomes in Norway, and he was one of a similar number of men who had been convicted of some kind of sexual violation. Sexual harassment was the lowest level of infringement. This represented cases in which the perpetrator had not been in physical contact with anyone and usually referred to indecent exposure, sending naked photos or using smutty language. It was a long distance from there to abduction, rape and murder, but there were several aspects that pointed in the same direction. The link to the discovery site, the vehicle, and a tendency to sexually deviant behaviour.

Ingrid Sandell had given him a memory stick containing the Swedish investigation material. He inserted it in his machine and opened a file in which all the reports and interviews were collected into a single document amounting to almost 7,000 pages. It took some time for it to download. As soon as he accessed it onscreen, he tapped in *Bonholt* in the search field. It brought zero results. He tried with the first name and numberplate of the motorhome, but that yielded no results either. In order to check that the search function was working as it should, he filled in the word *cat* and up came the statement given by the guest at the campsite who had lost a kitten. It was grey and white and was called Toots. He also tried to search for *Challenger* and obtained a few hits on the same type of motorhome as the one Kjell-Tore Bonholt drove, but with Swedish owners.

The fruitless search, however, did not exclude the possibility that he had been at Bovikstrand. The perpetrator was most likely not listed among the 1,843 registered guests at the campsite. If he had been, he would probably have been caught.

The digital gap in the screen was creeping downwards and the tiny pixels were flickering. The colours kept changing. Red turned to blue and green to purple. Soon it would be impossible to work on it.

He returned to the criminal records database and pulled up the photograph of Kjell-Tore Bonholt, taken in connection with the case in Lofoten. He had been thirty-eight at that time. Blond hair and blue, bewildered eyes.

Wisting saved it to allow Ingrid Sandell to search in the image database from Bovikstrand.

A marker down on the right alerted him to a follow-up message in the operations log, a text concerning Kicki Dalberg. He had not reported her name yet. All that had been logged was that Wisting had checked on a motorhome near Tveidalskrysset and that the vehicle could be linked to the vandalism at the golf course. The registration number of the vehicle had also been entered. It had been dealt with twice earlier in police records. One case had been a violation picked up by an automatic traffic management system on a major road near Halden, and the other was a case of indecent exposure in Stavanger six years ago.

Wisting followed the link to the case of indecent exposure. Two different teenage girls, one hour apart, had been offered money to masturbate a man who had exposed himself to them. Police patrol cars had searched the area but been unable to find anyone fitting the description. In connection with this report, the registration numbers of several vehicles parked in the vicinity had been recorded, but it did not look as if this had been followed up with any further investigation. One of these vehicles was a Peugeot Solifer 1996 model belonging to the Vestfold Caravan Centre in Larvik. A rental van, Kicki Dalberg had said.

His phone rang. A saved number for one of the forensics technicians examining the Solifer man's old motorhome.

'Are you anywhere nearby?' David Eikrot asked.

'In my office,' Wisting replied.

'We're almost finished down here,' Eikrot said. 'There's something you should come and take a look at.'

Wisting shifted the phone to his other ear. The computer screen was breaking up even more before his eyes, splintering in an assortment of colours before finally turning black.

'What is it?' he asked, as he pulled out the plug.

A moment's silence ensued, as if the experienced technician was hesitating before he answered.

'I believe someone's been held captive in this vehicle.'

53

The metal door slammed behind him as Wisting entered the inspection garage. The motorhome remained lit up by frame-mounted floodlights and all the doors were open. David Eikrot and Gina Lyng still wore their white overalls, but most of their forensics equipment had been packed away.

'What have you found?' Wisting asked.

'We can have a quick run-through,' Eikrot replied.

He took out a tablet computer and opened a folder of photographs.

'Hairs are always interesting when it comes to tracing people who've access to a vehicle,' he went on. 'We've secured strands of hair from several individuals, most of them in the sleeping alcove.' He showed Wisting a few images. 'But an animal has also been in the van,' he added.

'An animal?'

'We found a lot of animal hair,' Eikrot told him. 'Probably a dog since it's been clipped.'

He moved on to a new folder.

'There are a lot of fingerprints too,' he said without spending any more time on them before opening a third folder of photos.

These were pictures taken in ultraviolet light, showing small patches of varying sizes illuminated with a bluish glow.

'Semen stains,' Eikrot clarified.

He swiped through some of the images.

'On the floor, walls and textiles. Nothing unusual about that. It's a bit like a hotel room.'

Wisting looked up from the screen and across at the van.

'You said you thought someone had been held captive inside it,' he said.

'In the storage space,' Eikrot answered, pointing.

The hatch into the storage space was open. They moved towards it and Wisting crouched down. It was a large space beneath the actual living-room area, one metre in width and forty centimetres high.

The contents had been taken out and placed on a paper tablecloth – one set of camping chairs and a folding table, two badminton racquets and a transparent slipcover, a fire extinguisher, a thick blanket, a portable hotplate, empty water containers and various cleaning products. A coil of towing rope and a roll of canvas tape were stowed in two separate see-through evidence bags.

'We've found fingerprints inside there,' Eikrot explained. 'Under the roof.'

Wisting continued to crouch down, taking in this information and unable to make it add up. The motorhome had been brought in because a girl had been seen in the rear window.

'Could they have been left there in the normal run of things?' he asked. 'Someone could have crawled in to take out equipment kept inside here?'

He glanced over at the badminton racquets.

'That's not the way we read it,' Eikrot replied. 'There are repeated sets of prints, as if someone has been lying on their back trying to prise the roof up.'

Leaning back, he joined his hands as if they were bound together at the wrists and demonstrated how he thought the fingerprints had been left.

'They're small,' Gina Lyng pointed out.

She wrenched off her overalls and stepped out of them.

'From someone not fully grown or very small-built.'

Wisting peered into the storage space again. There was a lamp at the top of one of the side walls. The glass was stained black with fingerprint powder.

'I read about the Solifer man yesterday,' Lyng continued. 'No more than ten hours had gone by before he was stopped. At that point the abducted girl was in the bed, inside the van. This must have been a different girl.'

'Can you say anything about when the prints ended up there?' Wisting asked, even though he knew the answer.

'No,' was Eikrot's terse response.

He nodded in the direction of the open hatch.

'The space in there is a kind of protected environment. Little dust or any other kind of pollution. The prints could have been made last month or five years ago.'

Wisting's knees creaked as he stood up to his full height. What he had been told made sense, but it was difficult to reconcile it with the witnesses who had seen a girl in the van's back window.

'The girl he abducted three years ago had been drugged with diazepam,' Lyng said. 'He could have done the same with the girl from Sweden, but no one knows how long he drove around with her held captive. He could have kept her down here when necessary and taken her up into the van and drugged her again. Then she might have woken up while he was driving.'

Wisting agreed. Something like that could well have happened.

'What about DNA?' he asked.

'We've done some tests, but we're unlikely to get results on them until after the summer holidays. The simplest route would be if her fingerprints are available anywhere.'

'I'll have a word with the Swedes,' Wisting said.

David Eikrot hunched his shoulders to slip out of his overalls and pulled them down to his waist.

'You had cadaver dogs here yesterday, didn't you?' he asked.

Wisting turned to the open hatchway.

'Yes,' he replied. 'I'll arrange to get them back again.'

54

The sun disappeared while Wisting drove back to Lake Farris. He peered up through the side window. The banks of dark clouds had moved in overland.

He called Patrick Pape from the car.

'Concerning the Solifer vehicle we brought in,' he said. 'Have you managed to draw up a list of hirers?'

'Not quite there yet,' Pape replied. 'It's a time-consuming exercise, as I said. Kicki was to take care of it in between everything else, but she's not here now. I couldn't make her come to work today.'

'What protocols do you have when a van is returned?' Wisting asked.

'What sort of thing are you thinking of?'

'Cleaning and getting it ready to hire out again.'

'Well, they're washed down,' Pape replied, 'both inside and out.'

There was a brief silence.

'Have you found something in it?'

Wisting did not answer.

'How often is the luggage store cleaned?' he asked.

Patrick Pape had no good answer for this. 'As necessary,' he said. 'Previously, it was Roy's wife, the guy who works in the workshop, who cleaned them, but now I use an agency.'

'Is it possible to find out when the luggage store was last cleaned out?'

'Well, of course, I can ask,' Pape replied, 'but I doubt if that's ever been logged anywhere.'

Wisting had soon reached his destination.

'That's fine,' he said, rounding off the conversation. 'Phone me when you have a list of the hirers.'

There was no space for his car at the search area and he had to park beside the dog owners' club and walk from there. The number of journalists had swelled. Wisting ducked under the cordon tape, telling them he would be back in five minutes to give a statement.

Ingrid Sandell was standing beside the tent set up by the georadar team. A tall, burly man stood by her side. Wisting approached them both. The man was Stefan Lundgren, Annika's grandfather. His back was hunched, as if he was carrying a heavy burden of grief and anxiety.

'Thanks for doing this,' he said.

Wisting nodded, envisaging the sleepless nights this old man had endured. The endless hours of brooding and speculation.

'We're doing what we can,' he replied.

They went on gazing across the search area.

'Annika was so fond of water,' the grandfather said, as if there was some sort of comfort to be derived from that. 'She loved swimming and learned when she was only four years old. She spent more time under the water than above it.'

Nils Hammer arrived and ushered Wisting into the tent.

'We've found another shoe,' he said, his voice lowered. 'Exactly like the first one.'

He opened a cardboard box on the table and showed Wisting the contents. A black Converse shoe.

'It was situated almost in the centre of the search area.'

Wisting turned in the direction Hammer was pointing. The georadar machine was now close to the water's edge.

'What do we do when the search is over, if we still have nothing to show for it?' Hammer asked.

Wisting's eyes met Ingrid Sandell's gaze, and he moved his head to indicate that she should join them. Placing a hand on Annika's grandfather's shoulder, she excused herself and approached them.

'Do you have Annika's fingerprints?' Wisting asked her.

Sandell shook her head. 'Why do you ask?'

Wisting told her about the prints found in the storage space of the motorhome belonging to the Solifer man.

'What about the passport register?' Hammer asked. 'The fingerprints are probably stored there in the biometric data.'

'She didn't have a passport,' Sandell answered, glancing across at the grandfather. 'They'd never holidayed or travelled outside the Scandinavian countries. They only stayed at the campsite.'

'What about her mobile phone?' Hammer asked. 'Did she use her fingerprint to open it?'

'I don't know,' Sandell replied. 'Her phone is missing. It was an iPhone. It's possible that Apple holds information. I can get that checked out.'

'That'll take time, though,' Hammer said. 'We might as well wait for the DNA results.'

'What about something she's touched, where the fingerprints might still be present?' Wisting asked.

'I'd have to speak to her parents about that,' Sandell said. 'I can do it right now.'

Wisting asked her to wait.

'There's something else,' he said. 'I've sent you the name and picture of another possible perpetrator. Can you check to see if it comes up in the photos from Bovikstrand?'

'Who are we talking about now?' Hammer asked.

Wisting explained about the man who had died in the accidental fall. Hammer swore as if to say it would be too bad if the perpetrator had evaded them in that way.

Ingrid Sandell took out her mobile.

'I'll do that first,' she said. 'It will go faster now. The image base has already been built up.'

Out on the arid search area a new marker flag had been placed in the ground. Hammer moved forward to dig. Turning around, Wisting headed off to meet the press. They gathered in a semicircle in front of him. He had stood like this before, trying to maintain a secure façade of self-confidence, but doubt and disquiet gnawed at him now.

There were three camera teams among the journalists, and two of them appeared to be sending a live broadcast. He gave them time to prepare before delivering a brief, simple update on the case, but with slightly more comprehensive information than the previous press release had contained. His sentences were nevertheless short and formed in such a way that there was no room left for interpretation or speculation.

Even though the sun had gone, the air was still warm, but more humid. Wisting felt perspiration trickle down his neck as he spoke.

He stood with his back to the dried-out search area. On the road behind the reporters, one of the fire service vehicles passed by, towing an all-terrain vehicle on a trailer.

He rounded off his report with some words of encouragement to the general public about getting in touch if they had observed individuals or vehicles on that site in the days after 18 July four years earlier.

A young man with a *VG* logo on his microphone posed the first question: 'Do you have a suspect?'

Wisting met the journalist's eye. He had not been prepared

for such a direct question. There were two suspects. The Solifer man, Ove Rudi Werner, and the recent fatality, Kjell-Tore Bonholt. Two men who both had motorhomes and a back-story that meant they were of interest to the investigation. At first glance, an unrealistic coincidence, but not really. Recent research reports estimated that one in five men had committed some form of sexual assault during their lives. Statistically it was hardly noteworthy that two men with similar previous histories and backgrounds had been snarled up in the investigation. All the same, it was too early to mention it.

'This is a Swedish investigation of a Swedish missing person case,' he said, struggling to avoid the question. 'For practical purposes we've set up an investigation here. That means we don't yet have enough information to decide whether we're facing a situation that should be dealt with as a crime in Norway. Therefore, we don't have a suspect either.'

'Do the Swedish police have a suspect?'

This question came from a red-haired woman who spoke Swedish.

'I can't answer for the Swedish police, sorry,' was Wisting's response.

He was bombarded with more questions that challenged him to talk about what had happened to Annika Bengt and how she had been transported to this spot. Wisting answered mainly in the same vein, that they were now concentrating all their efforts on finding Annika Bengt.

'Are there any other locations where it might be a good idea to search?' was one question.

Wisting felt the drops of sweat move from his neck and run down his spine. If they failed to find Annika Bengt, it did not have to mean she was nowhere in this area. He had always thought that the initial necklace and fabric shoes were effects that the perpetrator had got rid of, and different means had been used to conceal Annika's body.

His gaze drifted northwards, in the direction of the old family cabin where Kjell-Tore Bonholt's motorhome was parked.

'It's possible,' he replied, avoiding mentioning that searches had already been undertaken with cadaver dogs.

Even more questions were rattled off before Wisting thanked them for their interest and returned to his colleagues. The georadar machine had run out of charge and it was driven into the tent to change the battery.

'How long do you have left?' Wisting asked.

The man who had explained the workings of the machine earlier cast a glance at the lake.

'Half an hour,' he estimated.

'There's another area I'd also like you to search,' Wisting said. 'Before the rain comes.'

With a nod, the man looked at his watch. 'Where?' he asked.

'Not far from here,' Wisting answered. 'A locus we've not searched with the dogs.'

55

Wisting drove on his own back to Evert and Ella Harting's cabin. When he had been there three hours earlier, it had been bathed in sunshine, but now the place looked dismal.

He parked where the ambulance had previously been. Evert and Ella Harting were sitting out on the verandah in front of the cabin. Evert rose from his seat when Wisting emerged from his car.

The sounds in the surrounding landscape had also changed since his last visit. The mixture of birdsong and buzzing insect life had been replaced by an oppressive silence.

'You've come back?' Evert asked from the top of the three steps leading up to the verandah.

'I wanted to talk to you both,' Wisting replied.

Evert made room and indicated that he should sit with them at the table.

'Kjell-Tore's been driven away,' Wisting said as he sat down. 'Maybe you've already had a message telling you that?'

They both nodded their heads.

'We've also spoken to the undertakers,' Evert Harting added.

Wisting put his notebook on the table in front of him and leafed through it to a blank page.

'We have freshly made coffee,' Evert said.

Ella got to her feet. 'I can bring some,' she said.

Wisting thanked her before asking his first question: 'You said that Kjell-Tore arrived yesterday?'

Evert Harting nodded.

'Where did he come from?'

'Denmark. That is, he'd gone home overnight before he came here.'

His wife returned with the coffee pot and placed a cup in front of Wisting.

'He'd been in France, the Netherlands and Germany before that,' she said.

Wisting poured himself some coffee.

'Does he go away every summer?'

'Usually for a fortnight or so.'

'To the same places?'

Ella Harting shook her head. 'Mainly different locations.'

Wisting had tried to steer the conversation in a direction that would answer whether her brother had been in Sweden the summer Annika Bengt had disappeared, but he was forced to ask the direct question.

The sound of a motor made him turn to face the track as the van with the geophysical search equipment drove over the crest of the hill.

'We're planning some investigations in the bay,' he explained.

A patrol car trailed behind the van with the georadar machine, followed by Ingrid Sandell in a car, accompanied by Nils Hammer.

Evert Harting put his hand reassuringly on his wife's shoulder.

'What kind of investigations?' he asked.

The vehicle convoy passed by and drove as far down to the lakeside as possible. Wisting waited until they had stopped.

'I don't know if you've seen or heard the news in the last few hours?' he asked.

The other two shook their heads in unison.

'It has to do with that necklace you found,' Wisting continued, glancing at Evert Harting.

'Have you discovered anything more?' he asked.

Wisting had the impression that the two of them had not spoken to each other about it. He did not answer, but instead thumbed through his notebook and pulled out a picture of Annika Bengt, a different photo from the one that had been publicized in connection with the case, but still showing the initial necklace hanging around her throat. As Evert and Ella Harting gazed down at it, Wisting saw it touched a nerve with both of them.

Ella Harting stood up.

'I . . .' she began, but her voice broke. She had to swallow hard and start again.

'I can't cope with this,' she said, looking across at her husband. 'You'll have to deal with it.'

Evert Harting got to his feet but stood watching as his spouse retreated into the cabin, her footsteps unsteady.

Wisting waited until he had sat down again.

'How much have you said about Annika Bengt?' he asked.

Evert Harting shook his head.

Wisting leaned forward a little. 'You were at my office two days ago,' he said. 'I told you that the initial necklace could have belonged to an abducted Swedish girl. Is that not something you and your wife have discussed?'

Evert Harting bowed his head and stared at the tabletop.

'I didn't get round to it,' he replied.

'Why not?' Wisting asked.

The only answer he received was a shake of the head.

'What about your brother-in-law?' Wisting pressed. 'Did you tell him about the necklace?'

'Yes.'

'And that it could have belonged to Annika Bengt?'

Evert Harting raised his head again and gave a deep sigh, the echo of an inner struggle.

'I don't remember,' he admitted. 'I don't think so. There was no more discussion about it.'

Down beside the vehicles, the small tent had been erected. The georadar machine had been lifted out and the operators were making their way with it to the present shoreline to begin the search at the furthest margin before the rain came and the waters rose.

'What thoughts have you had yourself since your visit to me?' Wisting forged on with his questions.

Evert Harting took a deep breath. 'I don't know what to think,' he said.

Wisting scrutinized the man facing him. Right at this moment his thoughts were too dreadful to share. He would have to wait until he was ready to put them into words.

It began to rain. At first, single fat drops that splashed on the ground around them, and then a sudden burst, in rapid succession, blanketing their surroundings in a grey mist. At the same time, the temperature dropped abruptly.

Ingrid Sandell came running up to them. Nils Hammer and the georadar operators were putting on rain jackets.

'Ingrid Sandell comes from Sweden,' Wisting explained. 'She's been working on the case for four years.'

Evert Harting reciprocated the introduction and Ingrid Sandell responded with a friendly handshake, before withdrawing her hand and wiping the rain from her forehead.

'Where were you during the summer of four years ago?' she asked.

'Here, I think,' Harting replied. 'Or somewhere further north. We're usually in both places. First here for a spell before we make a trip north. Ella has a book she writes things like that in. It's at home.'

They sat for a while in silence with the rain falling steadily on the roof above their heads. Down by the lake Hammer began to dig in the tracks left by the georadar machine. He waved to indicate that Wisting should join him.

Wisting stood up. He did not have any rainwear and was wearing light summer shoes. The police officer from the patrol car headed out with him.

The dry crust of earth had not yet absorbed the rain. The water ran down the cracks and lay like a glossy film on the surface.

'An oil drum,' Hammer said as Wisting approached.

The pale blue arch of the drum lay only a few centimetres beneath the ground, sunk into what had once been sludge. The metal clanged when Hammer tapped it with the edge of his spade.

'There's another spade in the car,' he said.

Wisting went to fetch it and was soaked through by the time he came back.

The earth around the drum crumbled and turned to thick mud. They dug on either side of it. With each turn of the spades, muddy water ran back down into the hole. At Wisting's end there was a dent in the side with a rusty gouge, shaped like an oblong crack. The narrow opening was filled with hard-packed soil, so that the contents were impossible to make out. At Hammer's end, there was a lid, tied down with steel tape and a looped clamp.

'Let's straighten it up,' Wisting suggested.

He dug out some more at his end before the other police-man helped them turn the drum over. There was a gurgling noise as it was released from the mud below. Hammer made sure it was standing steady before he flipped off the clamp. The lid was still stuck. He hit the steel tape with his spade to loosen it.

'Careful, now,' Wisting said.

The rain was bouncing off the ground around them.

Hammer lifted the lid. Wisting bent forward and smelled a slightly indefinable odour of rot or mould. Mud from the sludgy lake-bed had found its way inside and filled the drum. Several indistinct fibres protruded from the muck.

Wisting took hold of one and lifted it out carefully. Loose threads hung down from his hand.

'Fishing net,' Hammer decided.

He assisted with hauling out the tangled netting. At one end there was a rope, tied to a bed stone. It was tightly hooked on to another bundle of fishing net.

Wisting pivoted the drum over on its side again, pulling out the rest of the net and turning it upside down to make sure it was empty.

'Just fishing net,' he said, starting to stuff it back in again. 'Prepared and bundled up for winter storage. Must have ended up in the water and sunk to the bottom at some time or other.'

The policeman returned to his patrol car, hopping around the worst of the muddy puddles on his way.

The guys with the georadar machine had set out two new marker flags. Hammer approached them and dug up first one tin can and then another.

'He can't have been here with his metal detector,' Hammer commented.

'Not in this spot, at least,' Wisting agreed.

They walked in the tracks made by the georadar machine. Each step left a footprint that was soon filled with muddy water.

Hammer ran his hand through his wet hair and looked up at the cabin.

'Has he said anything about his brother-in-law?' he asked.

'Not yet,' Wisting replied. 'But he does have something weighing heavily on his mind.'

Hammer began to dig again. Wisting's phone vibrated in his pocket. He took it out and saw that it was Arne Steen calling, the man who ran the restaurant at the marina in Stavern, where he and Ingrid Sandell had eaten the previous day. He pressed the button to take the call.

'Arne here,' the restaurant owner said. 'I've seen the news and reckon it has something to do with the motorhome you asked about.'

'That may be so,' Wisting confirmed.

'My enquiry's been circulated,' Arne Steen went on. 'I just had a message from the Solplassen campsite. He checked in there an hour ago. Probably the weather has tempted him to pull in at a place with more formal facilities, where he can hook up to electric power and get some laundry done.'

Nils Hammer unearthed a bloated football from the mud.

'He's paid in advance for only one overnight stay,' Arne Steen added. 'Checkout is twelve noon at the latest, but now at least you know where to locate him until then.'

Wisting thanked him for his message and shared it with Hammer: 'The Solifer man has checked into Solplassen.'

Hammer leaned on his spade. 'Were you thinking of talking to him?'

'I should do that before he moves on,' Wisting answered. 'But we have to finish up here first.'

He looked around. 'I doubt we'll find anything. It seems illogical in relation to where the necklace and shoes were found, but it's work that has to be done.'

'We don't both need to be here, though,' Hammer pointed out. 'You go. Hear what he has to say.'

Wisting lingered for a few moments before nodding and heading back to shore. Rivulets of water were finding their way out to the lowest point.

Once back at his car, he stuck the spade in the ground and returned to the others. Ella Harting had emerged on to the verandah again to stand at the railings. In the far distance a crack of thunder resounded. Down in the bay, Hammer had begun to dig again. The older woman put her hands on the banister.

'They should search under the barbecue area,' she said, without turning round. 'He concreted that over when he got back from Sweden.'

56

Evert Harting had heard what his wife said. The breath stopped in his chest, and he scarcely dared to move a muscle.

'The barbecue area,' she said again, as if to make sure everyone had heard. 'That's the kind of work he does. He was apprenticed as an iron fitter, though he never achieved his craft certificate. But that's the sort of thing he's mostly worked on. Making casts and laying stones. He built the concrete platform while we were on a trip north in his motorhome, but he's never completed it. It still doesn't have the paving stones laid on top.'

Evert saw William Wisting and the Swedish investigator exchange looks.

'You said he came from Sweden?' Wisting asked.

'From the campsite where she went missing,' Ella replied. 'Bovikstrand. We talked about it when it came on the news. Joked about it, in fact.' She turned to face Evert. 'Don't you remember?'

She went on without giving Evert a chance to reply: 'We were here for a few days, all three of us, before Evert and I took over the motorhome. We drove through Gudbrandsdalen, round and about in Trøndelag and all the way up to Saltfjellet.'

Evert nodded. This was something he could confirm.

'When we got back, the concrete platform had been laid,' Ella concluded. 'It wasn't something we'd talked about in advance, or he'd even asked us about.'

She looked Wisting up and down before continuing: 'I'll go and get you a towel,' she said, heading indoors.

No one said anything while she was gone. When she returned, she had brought one of the floral-patterned towels with her. Wisting took it, ran it over his hair and used it to dry his neck. Ella crossed her arms. There was something upstanding about her, Evert thought. Something dynamic he had never seen before.

'I realize you're here because of K-T,' she said. 'You believe he's the one who took the Swedish girl?'

Evert Harting looked across at Wisting. Ella must have harboured this suspicion for a long time, longer even than he had. Maybe even since that summer four years ago, but she had never mentioned anything to him. Not even in her diaries had she written a single word about it. Or maybe that was exactly what she had done, when she always made a point of noting where K-T had been and when.

'We have reason to believe she was abducted in a motor-home,' Wisting said without really answering Ella's question.

Evert Harting was breathing with his mouth open. His chest felt tight and heavy. It was Ella who had decided that the initial necklace should be handed in to the police. She must have known what it could trigger.

He swallowed audibly.

Maybe that was exactly what she wanted. To initiate a confrontation with her brother that she had no need to be part of. To distance herself. Refuse to take the first step. That was what she was like, as well he knew. But now it was as if he no longer recognized her.

'Since it's your brother we're talking about, you don't need to tell us anything more,' Wisting informed her.

'There's not much to tell,' she said. 'After all, we don't know anything about it, but I understand that you do have questions. He can't answer for himself now, can he? We'll have to do the best we can.'

The downpipe from the gutters on the roof gurgled loudly, an irregular, burbling sound.

'Are you sure about this stay at Bovikstrand?' the Swedish detective asked. 'He's not mentioned on the guest list there. Nor is his motorhome registered.'

'That was what he told us,' Ella replied. 'He came to Sweden by ferry from Poland and called me from the campsite. It was a Saturday, two days before the girl went missing. He stayed there that weekend. Then he arrived here on the Tuesday evening.'

She described it in a way that made it sound as if this was a timeline she had gone through countless times.

'And it was that motorhome?' Wisting asked, pointing at Kjell-Tore's van.

Ella nodded.

'He cleaned it right away when he came here,' Ella added. 'Inside and out. Very thoroughly.'

She glanced across at her husband, as if seeking support.

'He'd brought a kitten with him from Sweden,' Evert forced himself to say. 'He called it Tuffy. Its faeces were all over the van.'

He saw that Wisting was taking notes. A half-page in the stiff notebook was already full. Mostly keywords, apparently. It was upside down and too small to make out.

'We're going to bring in the motorhome for inspection,' he said, looking down at it. 'Does he have any belongings any-where else?'

'No,' Ella replied.

'He had his mobile with him when he fell,' Evert said. 'We took some photos.'

'I have photographs from that summer,' Ella volunteered.

Her phone was on the table. She picked it up, skimmed

through the images and showed some to Wisting and the Swedish detective. Evert heard Ella say something. She was talking in a matter-of-fact tone about what Kjell-Tore had been accused of when he had worked at Brynseng, and what had happened in Lofoten, but her words became fragmented in his mind. If Ella had carried all this within her, she too must have had a few thoughts about why Isabell wanted nothing to do with her uncle.

A gust of wind sent a sheet of rain in under the verandah and made Evert Harting shiver. His thoughts piled up and made him dizzy, but all Ella was speaking about were things the police probably already knew or would find out regardless. She was simply playing on their team. Slowly it dawned on him what Ella was doing. Without necessarily being aware of it, she was constructing some kind of alibi for him. She let him sit there like an unwitting husband who had no reason to push Kjell-Tore off the cliff edge, if anything of the sort should ever occur to the police.

She stood there as if she had full control over the whole situation. Evert realized that watching her behave like that made him feel inspired. They would get through this. Nothing would ever be the same again, but then that was not something to aspire to anyway.

'What happened to the cat?' the Swedish investigator asked.

'It disappeared,' Ella answered. 'When we got back with the motorhome, it was gone.'

Another clap of thunder rang out, slightly closer this time. Ella turned and looked down at the men who were busy with the georadar machine.

'They should search at the barbecue area,' she said once again.

57

The water poured down into a crack in the middle of the concrete platform. Wisting carried one of the chairs out on to the grass while Nils Hammer and the officer from the patrol car lifted off the table.

'The ground conditions here are a bit more challenging,' said the man standing beside the georadar machine, but at the same time he assured them that a cavity or any other kind of anomaly under the concrete would be revealed.

Wisting cleared away the last chair. The platform was around twenty square metres in area and the search would not take long.

They lifted up the equipment – the machine was now caked in mud and the undercarriage was clogged with wet, sticky sludge. The operator picked off most of it with his hands and pushed the machine back and forth a few times to check that the wheels were turning freely. Then he adjusted a few settings on the user panel before he set to work.

Wisting stepped down from the platform. Hammer stood by his side.

'Is there anything to suggest that Kjell-Tore Bonholt and the Solifer man knew each other?' he asked. 'I mean, it looks as if they had shared interests and lifestyle.'

'There's nothing to indicate that,' Wisting replied.

'I just can't get it all to add up,' Hammer said. 'How do you explain the fingerprints in the luggage space on the Solifer van?'

'I can't explain it,' was Wisting's response. 'Not yet at least.'

The man with the georadar equipment stopped and studied the screen image but decided to move on. Hammer turned and looked up at the verandah, where Ella and Evert Harting still sat. Ingrid Sandell had gone to shelter in the car.

'Do you think she knows more than she's already told us?' he asked.

'They have a grown-up daughter,' Wisting said. 'She left before her uncle arrived. There could be more to it.'

Hammer removed a nicotine pouch from under his lip and put it back in the tin.

'Why on earth start talking . . .' he said. 'After all, her brother's dead. Those were suspicions she could have let him carry to the grave or shared only with her husband.'

He spat on the ground.

'But then they'd always have thought about Annika Bengt while they sat here eating, I suppose,' he answered his own question.

Half the platform was soon surveyed. This would be a good hiding place, but at the same time there was something implausible about it.

'If she's buried here, he must have first hidden her somewhere and then brought her here after his sister and brother-in-law had left in the motorhome,' Wisting said.

'He could have decided on reflection that the first place wasn't good enough,' Hammer pointed out. 'That kind of thing has happened before.'

Wisting agreed he was right but said that bringing a dead body almost all the way home was nevertheless irrational.

'What do we do if we find her here?' Hammer went on. 'There would be several implications. He's travelled through-out Europe in that motorhome over a period of years. There could be other girls, other cases.'

'Let's cross that bridge when we come to it,' Wisting replied.

A car door slammed, and Ingrid Sandell arrived to join them.

'I've had a response from NOA,' she said. 'Kjell-Tore Bonholt isn't in the photo database from Bovikstrand.'

'That was quick,' Hammer commented.

'Artificial intelligence,' Sandell answered. 'Once the image database is built up, the search doesn't take long. The principle's the same as searching for a fingerprint. The fact that we haven't found it doesn't prove anything, but it would have reinforced our suspicions if we'd confirmed he was there.'

The georadar operator pivoted at the end of the platform and embarked on the final round. Wisting turned to gaze up at the verandah. Evert Harting had put on a rain jacket and was on his way down to them.

'Nothing?' he asked, pulling the jacket up at the neck.

'Doesn't look like it,' Wisting replied.

They stood in silence. Evert Harting followed the georadar machine with a steely gaze.

'Something else crossed our minds,' he said.

Wisting nodded, encouraging him to say more.

'Until two years ago, we only had an outside toilet here,' he said, pointing to the edge of the forest. 'Kjell-Tore was the one who emptied it out. He dug a hole in the hillside further back in the woods up there and filled it with the contents of the toilet. There are five or six of those dumps in among the trees.'

Everyone present knew what he meant.

'I can show you,' Evert Harting added.

Wisting glanced at his watch. 'Go ahead, then,' he said.

He issued instructions to the georadar team before they walked up to the woods. Some of the rain turned into steam when it struck the warm, dry ground. Veils of white mist swirled around them as they walked through the grass.

The places Evert Harting was referring to were easy to spot, situated one after the other like little burial mounds.

The georadar operator followed in their wake.

'Twenty minutes left, then we'll run out of charge,' he warned as his eyes scanned the area. 'We should just about manage it.'

He fine-tuned the settings before pushing the machine forward across the long grass and over one of the mounds before pulling it back again in a parallel line.

Wisting cleared his throat before speaking to Harting.

'What were you talking about, up there at the viewpoint?'

Evert Harting thrust his shoulders forward in a shrug. 'Nothing in particular. The view. The weather. The lake. He was talking about scientific facts. About the volume of water in the world being constant and wondering where the water went to when it wasn't here. That kind of thing.'

'Do you recall the last thing he said?'

The rain pattered on the foliage around them.

'I really should remember that, of course,' Harting replied, 'but I honestly can't.'

Wisting nodded to show he understood. From a purely theoretical position, there were three possibilities for what had happened up there at the lookout point. One was that it had been an accident, just as Evert Harting had explained. A second possibility was that Kjell-Tore Bonholt had decided to jump. Or else he had been pushed over the edge.

'I gained the impression that it's been on Ella's mind for a long time that her brother might have had something to do with this,' Wisting said. 'Could Kjell-Tore have realized that?'

'Maybe,' Harting answered after a lengthy pause. 'I didn't

notice anything like that about Ella, but he could have per-
ceived her differently from me.'

It seemed as if Evert Harting also envisaged the possibility
that it could have been suicide.

'He was the one who suggested we go up there,' he said.
'None of us had been there for years.'

The georadar team had now covered two of the mounds
and were embarking on the third.

'Have you told your daughter what's happened?' Wisting
asked.

'Ella phoned her.'

'Is she coming here?'

'No, we're going home tomorrow.'

Wisting weighed up the third possibility, that the death had
been neither accident nor suicide.

'What sort of relationship did she have with her uncle?'
he asked.

Evert Harting crouched down and picked up a branch from
the ground.

'They didn't talk to each other much,' he replied, starting
to peel off the bark.

'She left before he arrived?'

'Yes,' Harting answered. 'That's how it is in summer. Short
and sweet – there's so much going on. We're just pleased she
managed to fit in a visit to us.'

'She's not married? No partner?' Wisting asked. 'No grandchildren?'

'No.'

Evert Harting wheeled around to look back along the path
they had walked.

'I should go back to Ella,' he said. 'I guess you'll let us know
if you find anything.'

Wisting nodded and watched as he left.

'Very odd for it to have been an accident, with all the other stuff that's going on just now,' Hammer mused once Harting had gone so far that he wouldn't be able to hear. 'A bit like Morten Wendel and his motorbike on the other side of the lake. That wasn't an accident either, but we'll probably never find out what happened.'

Wisting picked up the branch that Evert Harting had tossed aside. He could live with both those scenarios, if only they could find out what had happened to Annika Bengt.

The rain was still falling steadily, but it seemed colder now. From time to time a gust of wind shook the water from the surrounding trees.

They were reaching the end of their search. The guy behind the georadar machine swung the apparatus around one final time before trundling it towards them, shaking his head. He was confirming what they had already grasped: 'She's not here.'

58

It was late now, almost 9 p.m. Wisting drove along one of the narrow lanes, between rows of caravans. The rain lay in puddles on the asphalt and patches of mist slithered along the ground.

'Next on the right.' Hammer barked directions from the passenger seat.

The touring pitches were situated at the far end of the campsite, furthest away from the beach, the shower block and all the other facilities.

They encountered a boy on a bike in shorts and a rain jacket. Water splashed up from his rear wheel.

'There!' Hammer said, pointing.

The word *SOLIFER* was emblazoned in large letters on the cover over the front windscreen. Blue light from a TV set glowed at the windows.

Turning one pair of wheels on to the grass, Wisting switched off the ignition and climbed out. The air was cold and raw, filled with the tang of salty sea.

The curtains twitched at the window of the nearest caravan as they slammed the car doors shut. Wisting took his police ID from his jacket pocket and hung it around his neck. Hammer walked ahead and rapped on the side door. They could hear movement from inside the van.

'Who is it?' a man asked, a hint of caution in his voice.

'Police,' replied Wisting.

It took a moment or two for the Solifer man to show

himself in the doorway, wearing a loose-fitting pair of joggers and a crumpled T-shirt. His hairline had crept further back than in the pictures taken at his arrest three years earlier.

'Yes?' he asked.

'Can we come in?' Wisting requested.

Ove Rudi Werner looked from him to Hammer and back again.

'Why's that?'

'We need to talk to you,' Wisting replied, with a rapid glance up at the rain. 'Either here in your van or else in our car.'

The Solifer man withdrew from the doorway and Wisting squeezed his way in. The bed at the back of the van was unmade, but they found somewhere to sit at a seating area beside the kitchenette near the front.

'Have you been following the news?' Wisting asked.

'I don't have anything to do with that sort of thing,' the Solifer man was quick to say.

'We're talking to several folk in your situation,' Hammer said, shifting into a more comfortable sitting position.

'It was all a misunderstanding,' the Solifer man protested, referring to the time when he had been arrested. 'I didn't touch that girl. She just came with me in the van.'

'We've a few questions about the motorhome you drove at that time,' Wisting said.

'I told you everything then.'

'There are still a few outstanding questions, though,' Wisting said, taking out a pen and paper. 'Has anyone other than yourself used it?'

The Solifer man seemed confused. 'No . . . but I bought it used . . .'

'You'd had it for six years when you were arrested?'

'Something like that.'

'Did you lend it or hire it out to anyone during that period?'

'No.'

'So it was always you who drove it?'

'Yes.'

'Did you ever have a companion with you on these trips?'

'What are you getting at?'

Hammer leaned forward. 'Did you have anyone with you in the van?' he clarified. 'Passengers?'

The Solifer man hesitated. 'My mother came with me once,' he said, seeming pleased to be able to give a positive answer. 'She didn't stay the night – it was just a test drive.'

'No one else?'

He shook his head.

Wisting made some notes. They had no information to use to check his answers, and this procedure was mainly to exclude the possibility of him later coming out with explanations for the fingerprints and DNA found in his vehicle.

'What about visitors, such as us?' Hammer ploughed on. 'Folk who just popped in?'

'No. Who would that have been? Is somebody claiming that?'

'Do you know Kjell-Tore Bonholt?' Wisting broke in.

'Don't think so,' the Solifer man replied. 'Doesn't sound familiar.'

Wisting took out his phone and showed him a picture of Bonholt. The Solifer man gnawed at his lower lip before shaking his head.

'Who is he?' he asked.

'He drives a Challenger,' Wisting elaborated, showing him a photo he had taken of the motorhome parked along the gable wall of the cabin.

'I don't think I've ever seen it,' the Solifer man replied.

Wisting left that subject in abeyance.

'Where have you been for the past few days?' he asked.

Ove Rudi Werner seemed uncertain. 'Just round and about,' he answered.

'Here in this area?'

'Yes.'

'Where exactly?'

The Solifer man did not seem keen to answer.

'Roppestad,' was his eventual response.

This was a naturist beach situated further north beside Lake Farris. Wisting should almost have anticipated that.

He looked across at Hammer, letting him understand that he had no further questions.

'Where do you live when you're not out driving?' Hammer asked.

'I haven't really got anything sorted out yet,' the Solifer man replied. 'For the moment I'm living in the van. Just taking it one day at a time.'

Hammer pushed himself halfway out of the cramped space and crashed his forefinger down on top of the table.

'Stay right here,' he said. 'Don't move on without letting us know.'

59

The phone rang just after 3 a.m. The screen shone brightly on the bedside table as Wisting reached out for it. The day had been a chain reaction, one incident after another. He had deactivated the 'do not disturb' function, almost anticipating that there was more to come.

The number was not among his stored contacts.

'Yes, this is Wisting,' he said, sitting up in bed.

The woman at the other end apologized for calling but said she did not know what else to do.

It was Irene Broch-Hansen.

Wisting immediately thought it had something to do with her daughter.

'It's Allan,' she said. 'He's gone.'

The rain outside was lashing down, drumming loudly on the window ledge.

'What do you mean?' Wisting asked.

'He hasn't come home,' Irene Broch-Hansen explained. 'I went to bed but he's still not back. He's not answering his mobile either.'

Wisting did not like what he was hearing. His instincts told him that something serious had occurred.

'When did he go out?' he asked.

'Early this morning, as usual.'

'With his lorry?'

Irene Broch-Hansen confirmed this.

'He's usually home by six, but sometimes he has a long trip . . .'

There was a momentary silence.

'We haven't . . . He normally lets me know if he's going far, but we haven't talked very much since this business with the Wendel boy. I wondered if there had been an accident, or something.'

Wisting had got up and was standing with his trousers in one hand. He didn't need this now, in the midst of everything else that was going on.

'I'll investigate,' he said.

'He's not answering his mobile,' Irene Broch-Hansen repeated. 'It seems to be switched off.'

'I see,' Wisting said. 'I'll phone you as soon as I know something.'

She thanked him.

Wisting pulled on his trousers once he had both hands free and paid a brief visit to the bathroom before putting on the rest of his clothes.

He called the police switchboard from his car. Neither Allan Broch-Hansen nor his vehicle had been logged in any messages in the last twenty-four hours.

'Send out an all-points bulletin,' Wisting instructed, 'for both him and his vehicle.'

The operator read back the name and personal ID number and Wisting confirmed them.

'Do you have any patrols I can requisition?'

'Two,' replied the operator, seemingly studying the staffing rotas as he spoke. 'Fox 2-o and Fox 3-o. Officers Evanger and Boger. Jansen and Rana.'

'Send Fox 2-o to look for the vehicle,' Wisting said. 'Car parks and streets, in every direction. Then I want 3-o to meet me at the Yeller,' he added, explaining that the case most likely had something to do with the dead boy who had been found with his motorbike at the start of the week.

'You don't want Evanger and Boger with you?' the operator queried. 'Jansen and Rana in Fox 3-0 are summer temps.'

'I want Daniyal Rana,' Wisting answered. 'He knows the place and was there when the boy was found.'

'Fine.'

'Then you'll have to wake Maren Dokken,' Wisting continued. 'She's the senior investigating officer on the case. Send her to the Broch-Hansens' home.'

'Anything else?' the operator asked.

'Just get cracking,' Wisting replied.

The roads were deserted. The wipers spread thin, glistening layers of rainwater mixed with old dust kicked up from the asphalt. It clung to the windscreen like an impermanent film. Each time he passed a streetlamp, a flicker of light and shade crossed the glass.

As he approached town, he swung up the steep hillside at Langestrand. He drove slowly past the house where Reidar and Gunn Hilde Wendel lived. Both cars were parked outside. There was a faint glow from a couple of the windows, including from what had been their son's bedroom, but it was not easy to tell if anyone was awake.

A cat was wandering along the pavement as he drove on. This was the third time since Monday that he had turned into this narrow street along the western fringe of Lake Farris. At the turn-off leading to the Yeller, a patrol car was parked and waiting. Rana was behind the wheel with a young, fair-haired woman in the passenger seat beside him. Wisting had seen her in the corridors at the police station and thought her first name was Ada. Ada Jansen.

She indicated that Wisting should lead the way. He waved his hand at the windscreen in acknowledgement and turned in ahead of them.

Light mist crept up from the ground and swirled in the headlights' beam. Rainwater had collected in small puddles, and it was impossible to see if any other vehicles had been on the track before them.

Wisting drove all the way up to the wooden fence. Rana parked beside him. The open expanse of Lake Farris spread out in front of them like a vast darkness.

Daniyal Rana put on his uniform cap. The brim kept the rain off his face.

'What are we doing here?' he asked.

Wisting was not keen to say that he was following his intuition, but this was precisely why they were here. Some kind of instinct that arose without any conscious thought process, perhaps the essence of all the component parts, large and small, in a case.

'This is a pivotal point,' he said, zipping up his jacket. 'In the past few days everything has circled around this spot. Both for Allan Broch-Hansen and for Reidar Wendel.'

The wind picked up, shaking the trees around them. Rain dripped steadily from the leaves.

'Do you have flashlights?' Wisting asked, glancing back at the police car.

Ada Jansen went to find them and brought back one for each of them.

'But his vehicle's not here,' she pointed out, looking back along the track at the way they had come.

Wisting did not answer. They climbed over the fence, moving to the edge and playing the light beams from their torches over the lake-bed. They could see how the water level had risen, maybe by as much as ten centimetres.

Wisting let the light slide across the rubbish piled up there. Old kitchen equipment and garden machinery. Soon it would all be hidden beneath the water again. Nothing of what he could see caught his attention.

'What made you think he was here?' Rana asked.

The rain trickled down the back of Wisting's neck.

'What do *you* think has happened?' he asked, instead of answering.

'I've no idea,' Rana replied.

'But what do you *know*?' Wisting pressed him. 'What do you know about Allan Broch-Hansen?'

Daniyal Rana seemed confused but launched into a summary all the same.

'His daughter was raped, and the rapist disappeared,' he said. 'He was found here.'

'Go further back,' Wisting insisted. 'You were the one who discovered the connections.'

'Allan Broch-Hansen and Reidar Wendel stole a safe together,' Rana went on. 'They emptied it and dumped it here.'

Water was dripping from the brim of his skip cap. Wisting saw the deep concentration on his face as he gave this some thought.

'Morten Wendel may have been murdered,' he said tentatively.

He saw that Wisting was nodding his head.

'Allan Broch-Hansen may have done it, because of the rape,' Rana continued. 'In revenge. Reidar Wendel may have realized that, when his son was found in the same place where they dumped the safe.'

Daniyal Rana was warming to his subject now.

'He may have met Allan Broch-Hansen somewhere,' he said. 'Struck him down and taped him tightly to something, just as his son was taped to the motorbike. Brought him here and thrown him over the edge. Waited for the water level to rise and finish off the job.'

His police radio crackled. A call-out for the other patrol.

'Drive to Tveidalskrysset,' was the order issued. *'Report of a motorhome on fire. Fire engine and ambulance already on their way.'*

'Roger that.'

Rana walked all the way to the edge to light up the innermost stretch. His foot slid on the wet ground, but he managed to stay upright.

'We can't get down there,' he said.

He pointed with the beam. Just ahead of them, a cataract of water was gushing along the dry stream-bed they had scrambled down a few days earlier. Wisting raised his torch and illuminated the downward flow of the stream. The water was pouring out of a pipe that ran underneath the track.

The police radio crackled into life again. Rana turned down the volume.

'What were they saying?' Wisting asked.

'It had to do with the vehicle fire,' Rana told him. 'Fox 2-0 asked if there was anybody inside the motorhome.'

'No confirmation that anyone has come out,' the switchboard operator at headquarters reported.

Wisting produced his mobile phone, walked a few steps away from the precipice and rang the switchboard. It took a while before he received a response.

'About the fire in the motorhome,' he explained. 'I've an outstanding inquiry in the log, made around twenty-four hours ago. Checking out an old Solifer. It had been left there. I assume it's the same vehicle, since it was abandoned.'

The operator called up the message. 'Belongs to the Vestfold Caravan Centre,' he read aloud.

Wisting confirmed this was correct, but did not spend time explaining any further about Kicki Dalberg or anything else beyond what the operator could read for himself on the computer screen.

'Thanks,' he said. 'Then we can tone down the response and resources.'

They rounded off their conversation and soon afterwards the conclusion was repeated over the radio.

'Probably an abandoned motorhome. Apparently, no one aboard.'

Wisting wondered whether he should call back and request a patrol car to check whether Kicki Dalberg was at home. There was no reason for the motorhome to suddenly catch fire. She had pretty much admitted the vandalism and criminal damage, but the evidence was now going up in flames.

Ada Jansen interrupted his train of thought. 'Did you hear that?' she asked.

Rana looked at her enquiringly.

'Shh,' she said, even though no one had said anything.

Now Wisting heard it for himself too. A rhythmic tapping sound, though it seemed impossible to localize.

'Switch off the engine,' he said.

He strode to his own car and turned off the ignition. Rana did the same on the police car but left the headlights on. Rain slashed across the harsh light.

The weather made it difficult to hear anything, but this was a metallic sound. Ada Jansen moved in the direction she thought it was coming from, further along the track. Rana and Wisting trailed behind her.

'Hello!' Jansen called out. 'It's the police!'

The sound grew louder. It seemed to originate from the top of the track.

'Over here!'

Jansen slid down towards the stream. Wisting could make out the outline of a human being. He trudged down after her, now up to his knees in water.

'He's stuck!' Jansen shouted.

Allan Broch-Hansen was sitting with his back pressed against the grating that prevented large twigs from ending up in the pipe beneath the track. Blood was seeping from the back of his head. In the torchlight glow, he appeared absolutely exhausted, his face pale and expressionless, apart from the bewilderment in his eyes.

The water reached up to his chest. Broad gaffer tape was wrapped around his head and across his mouth.

Wisting tossed aside twigs and other brash that had been carried by the surging water and now lay packed around him. Jansen tore off the tape, reassuring him by saying he was safe and that he would be OK. A gurgling noise came from his chest when he took the first deep breaths.

Rana had produced a pocket knife and began to slice through the straps used to tie him firmly to the grating. Once he had been released, they dragged him up to the track, his hands and feet still taped together. Rana cut through the tape with his knife.

Wisting knelt down and bent over the man they had rescued. 'Talk!' he demanded.

Allan Broch-Hansen coughed and shook his head.

Ada Jansen used the police radio to report their discovery and request an ambulance.

'You have to tell us,' Wisting said.

The man in front of him coughed again. A few fragmented words issued from him, but they made no sense.

Rana got to his feet. 'There's a car coming,' he said.

336

A pair of headlights glimmered through the trees. When the light fell on the patrol car, the vehicle drew to a halt. Wisting saw the reversing lights flash on.

'Stop that car!' he shrieked, clambering up.

Rana leapt behind the steering wheel of the patrol vehicle and moved it round in a swift reversing manoeuvre. Wisting jumped into the passenger seat. The car in front wobbled. It was down at the very edge of the track but managed to right itself again.

Wisting located the switch for the extra lights on the dashboard panel and flicked it on. The interior of the other car was bathed in floodlight. Reidar Wendel sat with his arm behind the backrest of the passenger seat and his head turned round. The car struck a stone at the verge, swerved across the gravel and had the wing mirror torn off as it scraped along a tree trunk. It continued along the edge of the ditch, skidding further and further off the track, ploughing through vegetation until it came to an involuntary stop.

Reidar Wendel lifted his hands from the wheel. The windscreen wipers slid from side to side.

Wisting stepped forward and yanked the car door open. 'Out,' he ordered.

Wendel did as he was told.

'You don't understand . . .' he said. 'I can explain.'

'Later,' Wisting said, turning to face Rana. 'You've got handcuffs?'

Nodding, Rana produced them at once.

'Put him in the back of the car,' Wisting said.

He returned along the track while Rana took care of the arrest formalities.

'The ambulance is five minutes away,' Jansen told him.

Allan Broch-Hansen had struggled into a seated position.

Wisting glanced down at him. He saw that the flashlight was blinding him.

'Talk,' he said once again.

The man in front of him tried to struggle to his feet, but Ada Jansen held him down.

'Sit quietly,' she said.

Broch-Hansen spoke in single syllables.

'He thinks I took his son,' he said, gazing past Wisting towards where Reidar Wendel had arrived in his car. 'He thinks I killed him.'

He was gasping for breath and shaking his head.

'I didn't . . . I swear to you . . . He wanted me to confess. Wanted me to sit here and drown if I didn't admit it, but I didn't do it.'

Wisting stared at him. 'Where were you that night?' he insisted.

Allan Broch-Hansen was blinking in the light from the torch.

'You've asked me that before,' he said, swallowing uneasily. 'My head was full of what had happened to Adine. With Morten being released from custody. I was wandering about aimlessly, driving around. Into the Bøkeskogen woods or along the quaysides. That went on every night for weeks on end. Sometimes it's like that still.'

Wisting did not say a word.

'That's all I can say,' Allan Broch-Hansen continued. 'I don't know anything more. I've told you all of it, exactly as it happened.'

Wisting looked at Ada Jansen as if to see whether she had any opinion to contribute.

'Maybe we should wait . . .' she said.

'OK, then,' Wisting said. 'That's enough for me.'

Allan Broch-Hansen shot a glance at Wisting. He coughed up some phlegm and asked what Wisting meant.

'That you've told us everything, exactly as it happened,' Wisting repeated. 'Let's just say that I believe you.'

Then he switched off the flashlight and headed back to his car.

60

Wisting sat opposite Irene Broch-Hansen at the kitchen table, drying his face with the towel she had given him. She followed his every movement. The inflamed circles around her eyes told of more than one sleepless night.

Maren Dokken had been with her for the past two hours. She now stood silently beside the kitchen worktop with her arms crossed.

'Allan has told us everything, exactly as it happened,' Wisting said, laying the towel aside.

Irene Broch-Hansen sat immobile. All Wisting noticed was a faint trembling of her lower lip. He let his words sink in before he started once again.

'We found him at the Yeller,' he said. 'His vehicle was parked nearby at Farriseidet. Reidar Wendel had arranged to meet him there, but instead attacked him and dragged him to the spot where his son had been found. He left him there but was coming back to check before the water rose above his head.'

He reiterated the facts that her husband had sustained only minor injuries and that Reidar Wendel had been arrested.

'I have Allan's account of the evening Morten Wendel disappeared,' he went on. 'He's told me everything. Now I want to hear it from you.'

The way he said this could make Irene Broch-Hansen believe that her husband had given a full confession. His choice of words was on the margins of what he could allow himself. It was not a matter of enticing Irene Broch-Hansen to say something she would not otherwise have volunteered, but of reaching out for a final answer. He had prised an opening into the old missing person case. He had waited for such an opportunity ever since Morten Wendel's disappearance.

He heard the kitchen tap dripping behind his back.

Maren Dokken took a couple of steps forward and placed a recorder on the table between them.

'You're not obliged to tell us anything that might implicate Allan or yourself in the commission of a crime,' Wisting advised her. 'But if you have something to tell us, then the time for that is now.'

Irene Broch-Hansen continued to sit for a while longer without speaking, but then it was as if something loosened within her and everything she had carried close for so long was released in a flood of words.

'That boy destroyed our daughter's life,' she said before her voice broke. 'Our life,' she continued after a pause. 'Then he came to the door here and wanted to ask for forgiveness, as if it was something it was even possible to beg forgiveness for.'

Wisting sat without moving a muscle, paying close attention to every syllable she uttered. Irene Broch-Hansen blinked away tears.

'He followed me into the house,' she said. 'With his motorbike helmet under his arm, as if he was just running a routine errand before going out for a bike ride.'

She gasped for breath.

'The knife lay there,' she said. 'I'd been cutting up vegetables. I put it down when the doorbell rang.'

Her confession was delivered succinctly, as if Wisting already knew how it had all happened. Despite that, the details were overwhelming. Irene Broch-Hansen had grabbed the kitchen knife. Brandished it and stabbed Morten Wendel in the face and throat. He had died on the floor in front of her.

'Allan sorted everything out afterwards.' Her voice was now subdued. 'Drove him away, both him and the motorbike.'

Wisting nodded slowly. The fire had removed all other evidence, but he decided not to question her about that. Instead, he reached forward and switched off the recorder. The timer stopped at just under fifteen minutes. Every vibration in Irene Broch-Hansen's voice had been caught. Every sob and sigh from the desperation of her inner conflict.

It felt exhausting. Listening to someone confess to murder was more than simply hearing them recount a chain of events. It was accompanying that person down into the darkest recesses of a human soul, where deep emotions, pain and despair were rooted.

'You shouldn't say anything further, not until you've spoken to a lawyer,' he said.

Maren Dokken turned her head abruptly towards the doorway that led into the living room. Wisting swivelled round in his seat. The daughter had appeared from within the dimly lit room.

'Adine . . .' her mother said.

'It's my fault,' the daughter said. 'If I hadn't sat out there sunbathing . . .'

Wisting got to his feet. The frail young woman was already carrying a burden that was too heavy, too much.

'No,' he said firmly. 'Nothing is your fault.'

He did not know what else he could say. The mother's confession had not been meant for her daughter's ears, but perhaps it was something she needed to hear. At least he liked to think that the truth was never destructive, but always healing. That in time, blame and shame would be replaced by relief and inner peace.

Irene Broch-Hansen had risen from her chair. She walked across the room and held her daughter close. Wisting averted his eyes. Outside, a new day was dawning.

61

Wisting stood bare-chested, relishing the cool air from the air conditioning on his skin. The atmosphere in the changing room was clammy, a mixture of unwashed sportswear, soap and the detergents used to clean the room.

The only dry clothing Wisting possessed was his uniform. He stood with his back to the wall, buttoning up his shirt.

His mobile phone rang inside his locker, lighting up and vibrating on the shelf where he had laid it down.

David Eikrot, Forensics.

'Did I wake you?' he asked.

Wisting had been awake for almost five hours now.

'No, not at all,' he replied, fastening the last button with his free hand.

'I've just forwarded an email to you,' Eikrot said. 'It's to do with the fingerprints in the storage space of the motorhome. I wanted to call you to make sure you'd received it.'

Wisting glanced across at the massive mirror on the other side of the room, showing his messy hair and his shirt tail hanging outside his trousers.

'The results arrived faster than I'd expected,' the crime scene technician continued. 'It must have been one of the last things they sent out yesterday, but I've only just sat down at my computer.'

A rapid response usually meant that a search had come up with an immediate result.

'What did they find?' Wisting asked.

'The fingerprints matched a print taken from the Aliens Register in connection with a missing person case,' Eikrot explained. 'A thirteen-year-old Afghan girl who disappeared from a care facility in Halden last summer.'

The door to the cloakroom opened and one of the officers about to start a shift in the patrol section entered in cycling gear. One of the young, fit members of staff. His shoes clicked on the tiled floor.

'Last summer?' Wisting repeated. 'Are you sure?'

'Marwa Armini,' Eikrot replied. 'You've been provided with her full personal details and the case number in the email I forwarded. She went missing on the thirteenth of August. The prints were less than a year old. That's why they were so intact.'

Wisting stood in silence for a moment or two. This was brand-new information being thrown at him. His thoughts turned back to Annika Bengt. He struggled to see the connection and place it in some sort of timeline, but he was still reeling after his recent experiences.

'Thanks,' he said, as he began to tuck his shirt tail into his trousers with one hand.

'Let me know if there's anything else I can do for you,' Eikrot said, seemingly energized by the surprising information about the Afghan girl. 'You'll receive a final report from us by the end of the week.'

Wisting thanked him again as he snatched up his car keys and other bits and pieces from the pockets of his wet clothes. The guy who had cycled to work walked past, naked, heading into the communal showers. In the corridor outside he met another two men on their way in to get changed.

En route to his own office it dawned on him that his computer screen was no longer functional. Turning on his heel at the door, he went instead to Hammer's office.

'Looks as if I missed out on all the fun last night,' he said, looking up as Wisting entered.

Wisting made no reply. 'I need to use your computer,' he said. 'Mine's broken.'

Hammer rolled his chair aside and made room for Wisting. He logged Hammer out and keyed in his own user ID and password while recounting what he had learned in the phone call.

'That excludes the Solifer man, then,' Hammer answered. 'He didn't get his provisional release until Christmas.'

Getting up, he pushed his chair back to let Wisting sit down. He stood behind him, propped up against the window ledge.

'Well, it is a hire van, of course,' Hammer went on. 'It should be easy to find out who was in Halden with it in August of last year.'

'I've already chased up Patrick Pape about that list of all the hirers I asked for,' Wisting said. 'Three years back in time.'

He had opened the email and brought the documentation up on the screen. The case of the Afghan girl had been shelved between Christmas and New Year, in that quiet week when the top brass in the prosecuting authority prepared their annual statistics. In one document it was assumed that she had been collected by family in Sweden and was now living in Malmø, but no action seemed to have been taken to verify this.

'Haven't you received it yet?' Hammer asked, referring to the list of hirers of the Solifer man's old motorhome.

Wisting shook his head and checked the time. The caravan centre would be open in quarter of an hour.

'Come with me. Let's chase it up,' he said.

62

A man with an umbrella crossed the road in front of the car. Wisting swerved to avoid him, without braking. The rain fell steadily, obscuring their surroundings.

In the course of a few morning hours, the case had veered sharply in a direction Wisting had not anticipated. His obsessive thoughts had failed to consider any possibilities other than the Solifer man before the metal detector man's brother-in-law had turned up. He should have known that the horizon was even broader.

Water splashed up at the side of his car as he swung into the caravan centre. He parked in an empty space immediately beside the entrance. Faint radio music could be heard from somewhere within the premises. An elderly man and his wife were testing out a camping chair.

Kicki Dalberg rose from her seat behind the counter.

'Is Pape in?' Wisting asked.

'He just drove off,' she replied.

'Will he be away long?'

The girl seemed worried. 'I don't know,' she said. 'He was going to Tveidalen to look at a motorhome that went on fire last night.'

Wisting nodded to show he was aware of what had happened.

'Do you know anything about it?' he asked, mainly to test her reactions and hear what she had to say.

Kicki Dalberg merely shook her head.

'Maybe you can help us,' Hammer said. 'We need a list of all the hirers of that Solifer vehicle we picked up on Wednesday.'

She seemed relieved to hear the question, as if this was something she could handle. She sat down again and drew the keyboard towards her.

'Do you have the reg number?'

Wisting did not have it to hand. 'Didn't Pape ask you about it earlier?' he queried.

She shook her head. 'No, but I can find it here.'

Her fingers raced across the keys. There were still speckles of orange spray paint on her right index finger.

Pape's dog was stretched out on the floor beside her. Now it got up and moved to its water bowl as Wisting watched.

'Is he an old dog?' he asked as he waited for the result of the computer search.

'About ten, I think,' Kicki answered, her eyes fixed on the screen.

The dog slurped the water.

'What's its name?' Hammer asked.

'Camper,' Kicki replied. 'Old Camper. He had another dog before, and it was also called Camper.'

Nils Hammer laughed. 'So he called the new dog *old*?'

Kicki Dalberg began to smile.

'He just calls it Camp, anyway,' she said, her focus still on the screen.

'I'd really have to print out each individual hire agreement,' she said. 'Is there any particular date you're after?'

Wisting was unwilling to share any specific information.

'We need all of it, actually,' he replied. 'For the past three years.'

Kicki Dalberg reached out to switch on the printer. Her sweater sleeve rode up, exposing some of the scars on her arm that Wisting had noticed when he had found her in the motorhome. He had wondered what had upset her so much, had been so painful, that she had had to resort to inflicting more pain on herself.

Clenching his jaw, he felt the muscles in his neck contract.

'Can you look up a date for me?' he asked, changing his mind.

'When?'

'The thirteenth of August last year.'

Kicki Dalberg's fingers darted across the keyboard. 'It wasn't hired out then,' she replied.

'No?'

'No. It says it was booked for a demo trip.'

'What does that mean?'

'That someone has tried it out with a view to buying it.'

Wisting looked across at the computer screen. 'Can you see who it was?'

She switched between different screen images.

'No,' she said. 'But it's been blocked out for five days. I'll bet he was using it himself.'

'What do you mean?'

'That Pape has gone on a trip with it,' Kicki explained. 'He does that two or three times a year. Different vans each time. He's never away very long.'

When she straightened up the papers spilling out of the printer, her sleeve slid up again. An inkling of what could lie behind the scars began to cross Wisting's mind. Something that allowed her to come and go at work more or less as she pleased and ensured that her uncle had no objections to her taking off on a whim in a motorhome.

'Does he usually have Camp with him on these trips?' he asked.

'Yes, of course. He's had all the vaccinations. Goes with him everywhere, but he's rarely been further than Sweden or Denmark.'

Nils Hammer broke in with a question: 'Is your uncle a member of the dog owners' club, the one up beside Lake Farris?'

'Yes.'

The elderly couple who had been looking at camping chairs now approached the counter. The woman held a small solar-powered garden lamp in her hand. Turning towards her, Hammer whipped out his police ID and took the lamp from her.

'It's closed here now,' he said. 'Sorry.'

The woman began to protest, but Hammer ushered them to the door, pushed it open and locked it behind them.

Wisting went round to the other side of the counter. 'Can you check another date?' he asked.

Kicki Dalberg was again wearing a slightly worried expression.

'How do you mean?' she asked.

'Which vehicles were hired out in the middle of July four years ago?'

She sat listlessly in front of the computer screen, rubbing her right hand anxiously up and down her left forearm.

'I'm not quite sure how to do that,' she said. 'Without a particular van to search for.'

The printer was still working, churning out a fresh sheet of paper in response to the previous question.

'Start with the Solifer van that went on fire last night,' Wisting prompted. 'Check who was driving that one.'

Kicki fumbled for her water bottle, but did not manage to drink much from it. It looked as if she was having difficulty swallowing the water she had gulped down, but eventually succeeded.

Wisting and Hammer exchanged glances. Something was wrong. The girl's hard outer shell was fracturing.

'Do you need the vehicle number?' Hammer asked.

Kicki Dalberg cleared her throat and shifted position in her seat.

'No, thanks,' she said.

The dog returned and lay down again in the same spot. Outside, a car drove slowly past the glass façade. The computer screen changed and scrolled through different images.

'It was him,' she said, nodding at the screen.

Wisting was not quite sure what he was looking at.

'Pape?' he asked, seeking confirmation.

The answer came almost in a sob.

'Was that when she went missing?' she asked. 'The Swedish girl.'

There were people at the door, rapping on the glass when they could not get in.

'It was on the news all day yesterday,' Kicki Dalberg continued, paying no attention to the customers. 'This is what you're really working on.'

Wisting looked at her.

'Is there anything about your uncle that makes you think he might have something to do with it?' he asked.

She had turned pale. Her breathing was laboured. Wisting regretted asking the direct question. He was ill prepared to guide her through the heavy burden she carried.

'He's coming,' Hammer warned, heading for the door. 'Pape is here.'

63

Patrick Pape was making his way into the new building on the other side of the concourse. He cast half a glance over his shoulder as Wisting and Hammer emerged from the customer service centre. Wisting realized that Pape had seen them, but he did not stop. Instead, he veered to one side and moved across, in between the rows of used motorhomes.

Hammer shouted his name.

Breaking into a run, Pape disappeared out of sight. Wisting set off after him. Hammer darted in a different direction to cut him off.

The rows of parked motorhomes stretched out in both directions to form a labyrinth of narrow passageways and possible hiding places.

Wisting reached the other side without catching sight of the man he was pursuing. He turned first one way, then another, until he was left standing on the wet asphalt. The rain drummed on the vehicles around him, creating a monotonous rhythm that filled the air.

Hammer reappeared. He flung out his hands in frustration and angled them on his hips in despair. Wisting wheeled around for a third time in the hope of spotting something he had missed.

The area was fenced off and there was no exit route to allow Patrick Pape to escape.

Wisting hunkered down and peered under the nearby motorhomes without glimpsing anything noteworthy. He walked along the rows and squinted underneath again. Hammer did likewise.

'The fact that he's scarpered is surely an indication of guilt,' Hammer commented. 'He must have realized we're breathing down his neck.'

'Seems that way,' replied Wisting.

He looked through the windows of the nearest motorhome. Condensation on the Plexiglas made it difficult to see anything.

'That's the reason he never handed over the list of who had hired the old Solifer,' Hammer added. 'The information wasn't difficult to find at all. Kicki printed it out right away.'

'He must have gone into one of the vans,' Wisting said.

He tried the nearest doors. All locked.

'I suspect he set fire to the motorhome in Tveidalskrysset last night,' he went on, trying the next door. 'For fear that we might find traces of Annika Bengt. He knew we'd examine it in connection with his niece's environmental protest.'

Hammer swore under his breath.

'We need help,' he said, taking out his phone. 'I'll call HQ and get some patrol cars out here.'

As he made the call, Wisting moved on along the parked motorhomes, trying doors and peering in through windows.

His own phone rang – Ingrid Sandell calling. He had not spoken to her since the previous day. Today the status of the investigation had totally changed.

She began talking about searches in the Swedish records and said something about Kjell-Tore Bonholt's motorhome having crossed the Øresund bridge from Denmark. Wisting interrupted her.

'It's Patrick Pape,' he said softly, looking around the corner at the nearest motorhome. 'We're at his caravan centre now. He's done a runner.'

He told her about the Afghan girl, about her fingerprints being found in the storage space of the van Pape had used when she vanished, about the dog hairs, and about his trip four years earlier that corresponded with the time Annika Bengt had gone missing. Now the motorhome used at that time had been set on fire.

Hammer had finished his phone call.

'I have to go,' Wisting said, without giving Ingrid Sandell a chance to quiz him.

'The dog patrol is coming,' Hammer told him. 'They're not far off.'

Wisting did not answer. His thoughts had been racing while he was speaking to Sandell.

'How long has the caravan centre been here?' he asked.

'A long time,' Hammer replied. 'Why do you ask?'

A train was approaching from the east. Wisting waited until it had passed on the other side of the fence.

'They call that the new building, though,' he said, pointing at the location of Patrick Pape's office.

'Looks more like an extension to me,' Hammer replied.

He was right. The new building had been constructed beside a workshop with high vehicle entrance doors.

'Stay here,' Wisting told him. 'I'll have a word with Kicki.'

He returned to the customer reception area, where Kicki Dalberg stood at the window watching them.

'The new building,' Wisting said, pointing across the yard. 'When was it completed?'

The young woman seemed mystified.

'Six months ago, something like that,' she replied, scratching her arm.

'Before or after Pape went on the trip in the Solifer?'

'After,' she answered. 'I was working here last summer.

357

They hadn't made a proper start on it yet. They'd just excavated the site.'

'What about the workshop?' Wisting asked.

Kicki shrugged uneasily. 'That was longer ago.'

'Four years?' Wisting suggested.

'Probably,' Kicki replied. 'I wasn't here then.'

Wisting briefly nodded his thanks. They were going to need the georadar team once again.

'What's going on?' Kicki asked. 'Where's Pape?'

'I've no idea,' Wisting said.

He pushed open the door and moved out into the rain just as the dog patrol van drove into the yard.

Hammer waved them over. The two officers were given a brief explanation before releasing the dogs from their cage at the rear of the van and sending them off to search.

The dogs followed the route Wisting and Hammer had taken, zigzagging between the vans and back again, following their tracks.

'Can't find any real way out,' one of the dog handlers declared.

'He can't possibly have gone far,' Hammer insisted.

Yet another police patrol arrived.

'We should search the buildings,' the dog handler advised.

Hammer shook his head, as if ruling out that Patrick Pape could have gone indoors.

Wisting looked around. The closest motorhome had a rear-fitted bicycle rack and an accessible ladder. Wiping the rain from his face, he approached it, took hold of the ladder and hoisted himself up on to the first rung before climbing further up. The rungs were cold and slippery.

He stood balancing on the top rung. On the roof of a van at the end of the row he spied Pape, lying flat on the chassis.

The owner of the caravan centre lifted his head, realizing he had been discovered, and got to his feet.

'Over there!' Wisting shouted and pointed.

Pape heard the dogs down below. He slid on the roof, slick with rain, clambered across to the ladder and disappeared out of sight.

Wisting dropped behind as the others spread out. He cut across to the new building in case Pape decided to run in that direction. Through the heavy rain and clamour of dogs barking, he heard an engine start up.

An old motorhome with an orange stripe along the sides shot round the corner of the workshop, rocking from side to side. The revs increased and the driver changed gear as the vehicle approached the exit gates at breakneck speed.

Dashing to his car, Wisting threw himself into the driver's seat and followed. He sounded his horn to warn the others. In the rear-view mirror, he spotted Hammer and one of the dog handlers running forward from the row of parked vehicles.

They rapidly picked up speed along the wet, slippery road through the surrounding industrial area. Wisting kept a tight grip of the steering wheel, his eyes locked on the vehicle in front. Behind him he heard the blare of sirens.

At the T-junction leading to the main road, the motorhome swung to the left, still driving at excessive speed. It tipped over on two wheels and wobbled on for a few metres until it canted over on one side. As it smashed on to the asphalt, it slid onwards with a loud grinding, forcing oncoming traffic to swerve aside. The body of the van tore open and the contents spilled out. Smoke belched from the engine when it finally came to a halt in the middle of the carriageway.

Wisting leapt out, scooted around the motorhome and leaned in through the smashed front windscreen. Patrick Pape was slumped across the passenger seat, surrounded by debris, his face covered in blood. A sliver of splintered fibreglass protruded from his arm. His mouth hung open, but he could not utter more than a gasp, as if pain muffled any other sound.

Wisting scanned the area while the smell of diesel hung in the air. Two police officers came running. He stepped aside and left the first-aid routines to them.

Ingrid Sandell arrived on the scene, sprinting from a taxi at the back of the growing queue of stationary traffic. Wisting lifted his face to the rain and closed his eyes as he felt her touch on his arm.

'You got him,' she said.

Wisting merely nodded.

64

The jackhammer broke up the concrete floor piece by piece, as if a jigsaw puzzle was being torn apart. Each blow sent vibrations through the entire workshop.

Wisting stood, wearing ear defenders. The noise from the compressor made it impossible to hold a conversation. From time to time a workman with an angle grinder stepped forward and sliced through the iron reinforcement bars.

The sun had returned, and light flooded in through the open garage doors. Fine concrete dust hovered in the air, settling on Ingrid Sandell's hair, tinting it grey.

The georadar team had discovered two discrepancies. One beneath the concrete flooring in the workshop and another in the centre of the new extension. They made a start in the workshop. The building contractor had explained that the cement was poured the week after Annika Bengt had disappeared.

They broke up a circular-shaped cavity, about a metre in length from one side to the other. Severed plastic cables from the underfloor heating system hung down at the edges. Fragments of concrete were heaped up further inside the empty premises.

The man wielding the jackhammer gave a signal and the compressor was switched off. Wisting moved forward to the edge. They had reached the gravel foundation.

The next stage of work was left to the crime scene technicians. The loose gravel was collected in basins and lifted out. According to the geologists' calculations, they were less than half a metre away from a find. In the course of the next half-hour, they might discover the final answer.

Pape had been discharged from hospital and transferred to a remand cell to await interview. His credit cards had been traced to Sweden the summer Annika Bengt had gone missing. In his home office, drugs had been found, suitable for sedating someone. His computer contained illegally downloaded pornographic material of rape and sexual abuse. In the DNA register, a match was found for an unsolved sexual assault and rape in the Vestland area in 2014.

Under the top layer of gravel, there was another layer of coarse aggregate. The technicians took it apart stone by stone, working their way further down.

Ingrid Sandell, sipping water from a bottle, offered some to Wisting. He accepted – the dust in the air had made his throat parched and dry.

'Find!' one of the technicians called out.

At the end where he was working, a flap of faded fabric jutted out. He picked off a few more stones before stepping back to avoid obstructing the photographic documentation. It was a plain-coloured blanket with a fringed border.

Wisting could hear that Sandell's breathing had become shallower.

Soon the whole blanket was uncovered. Badly creased, it gave no indication of what lay beneath.

Moving to either end, the two technicians took a firm hold and unfolded it.

Wrapped in the faded fabric was a shape, a figure reduced to bones, dust and earth.

Brown, shrivelled skin covered the delicate bones. Tangled hair was still attached to the skull and the mouth gaped half-open.

There were no remnants of clothing, and no shoes.

Wisting turned on his heel and strode out. Ingrid Sandell followed him. The sun was high in the sky above them. A gentle breeze meant the air around them was only warm rather than scorching.

They found the Afghan girl the next day, four hours prior to the prearranged press conference. Marwa Armini, born in Bagram, a town situated north of Kabul. Her mother had been twenty-one when she gave birth to her and already had a two-year-old son. Her father worked as an interpreter for the NATO forces. He had taught his children English as well as some of the German and Norwegian he himself had picked up. In the chaos that ensued when the allied forces pulled out, the family was split up. Marwa was the only one who could be said with any certainty to have succeeded in leaving the country.

Ingrid Sandell thought Marwa was an Arabian word for a sweetly scented plant. The girl was wrapped in a discoloured quilt. Her body lay in a shallow grave in the gravel layer approximately in the centre of the new building. It had been there for no more than eleven months. The moisture had been drawn from her body and turned it into a weather-beaten sculpture. Her naked flesh was stiff, as if dried by the searing desert sun of her homeland, but her facial features were still recognizable.

Ingrid Sandell put her foot on one of the fragments of concrete and rocked it to and fro. The brittle cement scraped on the floor.

'I spoke to Samuel Bengt at length yesterday,' she said. 'Annika's grandfather.'

Wisting looked at her.

'He said something I felt I could relate to,' she added.

'What was that?'

'That solving the crime doesn't mean very much when push comes to shove. It doesn't lift the burden of lies and secrets and pain from someone's soul.'

'There's certainly something in that,' Wisting replied. 'But the alternative is worse. Then you can't reproach anyone except yourself.'

He took the car keys from his pocket.

'I need to go somewhere,' he said. 'There's someone else I should speak to, before we discuss the case at the press conference.'

She nodded. 'I'll see you there, then,' she said.

Wisting strolled to his car. He got in, flipped down the sun visor and managed to catch a fleeting glimpse of his own eyes in the little mirror before driving off.

65

Evert Harting put the metal detector on the back seat before returning to collect the basket of dirty laundry and the bag Ella had filled with food from the fridge.

'I think we should sell up,' she said to his retreating back.

Evert turned around and looked up at the red-painted cabin they had inherited from her parents. Despite its being a simple, off-grid dwelling with no running water or proper sewage facilities, he had seen other similar cabins sell for around a million kroner. Though many had also languished on the market for a long time before a sale was announced.

'We're getting old,' Ella went on. 'And we can no longer rely on help from Kjell-Tore.'

'We won't get much for it,' Evert said, stowing their bags in the car boot.

'It's worth something,' Ella insisted. 'Isabell can have the money as a down payment on her inheritance. We don't need it.'

He nodded. He had already thought along these lines himself.

They did not have a chance to discuss it any further. A car appeared, driving over the brow of the hill and down towards them.

'It's the police,' Ella said. 'Maybe they're going to collect the motorhome. It's odd they haven't done that already.'

'He's on his own, though,' Evert said as the car approached.

William Wisting was in the driver's seat. He drew to a halt and stepped out.

'Glad I caught you here,' he said. 'I wanted to talk to you and didn't want to do it over the phone.'

'We've already been home,' Ella said. 'We just popped back to pack things up and close the cabin. We're going to put it on the market.'

Evert was really not keen to ask, but thought he had to say something.

'What was it you wanted to talk to us about?'

'Kjell-Tore,' Wisting replied. 'He's not under any suspicion as far as we're concerned. All charges dropped. Completely exonerated. I apologize for the additional stress all of this must have caused.'

'Oh,' was all Evert managed to say.

He began to feel light-headed, the sense of wooziness that crept over him every time his thoughts turned to his brother-in-law. He had to fix his eyes on a point on the ground and concentrate hard so that the policeman would not notice anything was amiss.

'Now I don't understand . . .' Ella said.

'Maybe we can sit down,' Wisting suggested, pointing at the table on the verandah.

Evert's hand had been gripping the open boot lid for support. He slammed it shut and followed on their heels.

The outdoor furniture had not yet been taken inside. That was usually one of the last tasks to be done.

They sat down at the table, though Ella could not offer any refreshment.

'We've charged a man with the abduction and murder of Annika Bengt,' Wisting clarified. 'That frees Kjell-Tore of all suspicion.'

Evert could not understand. His breathing grew laboured, and he felt stabs of pain in his chest. Kjell-Tore had virtually admitted it, just before he had gone out to the cliff edge. '*I see,*' had been the last thing he said. As if they had some kind of shared understanding, that they both knew what he had done.

He managed to gather his wits sufficiently to ask a question.

'Who's the man you've arrested?'

'I can't give you his name, but I can say that he was arrested in a motorhome.'

The chief inspector glanced in the direction of Kjell-Tore's vehicle.

'He's also charged with murdering a girl who went missing from a care facility for underage asylum seekers,' Wisting continued. 'Both bodies have been recovered. We intend to give a full account of it at a press conference later today.'

'So there's no doubt at all?' Ella asked.

Her voice was listless, with no trace of enthusiasm or relief.

'No,' Wisting answered. 'The circumstances are so unique that I don't believe there will be any suggestion of other suspects being involved.'

Evert Harting struggled to force a smile.

'That's some consolation,' he said, looking across at his wife.

She returned his smile, but he had to avert his eyes, afraid he would give away the burden of his hidden secret.

The police officer provided more details of the case. Something about the dog owners' club and how they thought the killer had got rid of Annika's belongings, but the words were lost on him. He thought of all the mistakes he had made in his life. The one detail that occasionally bothered him was his blunder with the confidential documents he had sent to the wrong recipient. That had almost cost him his job in the Department, and the very thought of it even now could still bring a knot to his stomach. But that had been a mistake he could rectify. Death was not like that. Taking someone's life meant taking everything from them. It could not be reversed. You could regret it and wish it undone, but it could never be put right. Not even if he came out with an admission and begged for forgiveness.

William Wisting asked them about the motorhome and whether they planned to do more travelling in it once they sold the cabin.

'We're going to sell that too,' he heard Ella reply. 'I expect we'll get around the same for it as for the cabin.'

She chuckled softly. Wisting smiled and got to his feet. Evert pushed himself up from his chair and followed him down to the car.

The policeman lingered for a moment at the car door. It looked as if he was going to say something or ask a question, but he changed his mind. Instead, he simply thanked him, sat behind the steering wheel and drove off.

66

Two months had passed and most questions had now been answered. Gaps in the investigation had been filled, explanations had fallen into place, and several jigsaw pieces had settled into the spaces where they belonged. But not all of them.

Wisting glanced across at Evert Harting. The metal detector emitted a signal, the sound oscillating in tone and frequency. Evert Harting pushed aside withered autumn leaves with the search probe and pointed out the exact discovery site. Wisting squatted down and dug with the small spade. Very soon he struck something, some kind of curved piece of metal. He tugged it out with his fingers and turned it this way and that. It reminded him of the handle of a bucket. Anyway, it was of no interest. He dropped it into the bag along with the other scrap metal they had unearthed.

'I didn't know who else I could ask,' Wisting said. 'I don't know anyone who has a metal detector.'

Strictly speaking, this was not true. There were ten names listed by the police of people who were able to assist with searches for buried objects.

Evert Harting walked on, swinging the detector from side to side.

'My pleasure,' he said.

A lorry passed out on the road. Wisting pulled his jacket shut at the neck.

They had been walking together for nearly half an hour,

but he had not been able to initiate a genuine conversation. Wisting had told him how Irene Broch-Hansen had stabbed her daughter's assailant to death in a fit of rage, and how her husband had transported the dead body and dumped it in Lake Farris. He had thrown the murder weapon out of the side window of his van as he turned out on to the main road on the way back. The knife must be somewhere along the verge, no more than five or six metres in, according to Allan Broch-Hansen in his confession.

Wisting had related how they had both felt an overwhelming sense of relief by being released from the constant battle with their own consciences. Evert Harting had concentrated all his attention on the search. The time was not yet ripe to ask him what had really happened when his brother-in-law had fallen off the cliff.

'I was once interviewed for a school magazine,' Wisting said. 'It was at a senior high school, and the student journalist was sixteen or seventeen years old. She asked me if I thought anyone could become a murderer.'

Evert Harting glanced across at him, squinting in the low autumn sunshine.

'What do you think?' Wisting asked.

'It would probably take some degree of provocation,' Harting said, continuing the search.

The uneven terrain was difficult to navigate. Trees and bushes made it tricky for the detector to reach every nook and cranny.

'I think everyone has the potential within them,' Wisting ventured. 'A psychologist I know was of the opinion that when we don't understand what it is that makes people commit murder, it's more a matter of us not having ever been placed in a similar situation.'

The metal detector gave off another signal. Wisting waited until Harting had marked the spot before he continued.

'I'm a father myself,' he said. 'As a parent you're torn apart if anyone does anything to your children.'

He began to dig. 'It triggers intense emotions,' he went on.

In the top layer of turf, he found a misaligned iron bolt coated in verdigris. It looked like the bolts used by the roads authority when erecting crash barriers.

'I do think anyone is capable of murder,' Wisting said, standing up to his full height. 'As long as it's someone who threatens our own domain.'

Evert Harting did not say anything as Wisting rounded off his argument.

'I understand what Irene Broch-Hansen did,' he said. 'It was an emotional reaction. The justice system has a certain acceptance of that sort of thing. She'll be dealt with by the most lenient means possible.'

Another signal came from the detector, louder this time. They heard a metallic scraping noise as Harting pushed leaves and other withered vegetation away from the search probe.

'There you have it, I think,' he said.

Wisting had not really had much faith that they would find it, but there was the knife, covered in leaf litter left by the changing seasons. The plastic handle was black, just as described. The dull blade was coated in rust that had eaten into the metal.

Wisting used his phone to take a photograph before tugging on a pair of latex gloves. He lifted the knife carefully from the ground. It felt heavy in his hand, almost as a reminder of the dreadful damage it had done.

'Are there any traces left on it?' Harting asked.

'Hardly,' Wisting replied. 'But the fact that we've found it supports the statements given by Allan and Irene. It makes it easier to believe their story.'

They walked together back to their cars. Harting put the metal detector on the rear seat of his. Wisting took out a plastic container he had brought with him and dropped the knife into it.

'Would you like to come for a coffee?' he invited him. 'I think I may have some cake as well.'

Harting was changing from his boots into a pair of shoes. He hesitated.

'I don't think so,' he said. 'I need to get home to Ella.'

Wisting did not feel quite finished with their conversation as yet but could not think of any other way to prolong it.

'Thanks for your help, then,' he said, holding out his hand to Evert Harting.

'I'm not sure we'll see each other again,' Harting said, shaking his hand. 'We've had an offer on the cabin. We're going to sell.'

'Take all the good memories with you, then,' Wisting commented.

He stood waiting until Evert Harting had driven off. Autumn leaves in every hue swirled around in circles behind his car. They would meet again, Wisting felt sure of that.

67

The smell of freshly baked apple cake wafted out when Wisting arrived home. Ingrid Sandell had stayed at his house for two days while in town for another coordination meeting connected with the investigation into Patrick Pape.

It felt good to have someone waiting for him, as if his life had taken a new direction after meeting the Swedish detective.

'We found the knife!' he shouted to her from the doorway.

Ingrid Sandell came out into the hall, something else clearly on her mind.

'Did he say anything?' she asked.

Wisting shook his head.

'There are two things you can never take back,' he said. 'Things you have done, and things you have said.'

Ingrid Sandell smiled as if she'd had similar thoughts herself.

'If you've done something that can't be put right, you face a long road ahead before you're able to admit it,' he concluded.

They moved into the kitchen. Sandell dried her hands on a towel.

'The mills of justice grind exceedingly slowly, as my first boss used to say. But they grind.' She smiled. 'It took eight years for Morten Wendel.'

Wisting returned her smile.

'He would still have been lying there if it hadn't been for the dry summer,' he said.

'The mills of God, that was what he was talking about,'

Sandell corrected herself. 'It's his mills that grind slowly. It took four years for Annika Bengt.'

They ate in the living room. Warm apple cake with cream.

Ingrid Sandell pointed to the round table by the window.

'What's that you have there?' she asked.

'An LP,' Wisting told her. 'It also came from the bottom of Lake Farris.'

He told her the whole story of the stolen safe.

'It contained signed records by Frank Sinatra, Louis Armstrong, Bing Crosby and Dean Martin.'

'Have you tried playing it?' Sandell asked.

There was a smudge of cream in the corner of her mouth.

Wisting stood up. He had a turntable at the far end of the room.

'Not yet,' he said.

There was a stack of records on the lid of the turntable. He cleared them away and inserted the plug in the socket. The loudspeakers crackled slightly as the power came through.

Ingrid handed him the disc.

'It's pretty unique to hold the same record that Louis Armstrong may have held,' she said. 'After all, he must have done when he signed it, don't you think?'

Wisting agreed with her as he took the record, even though it had been a more momentous sensation to hold the chain necklace that Annika Bengt had worn round her neck when she was killed, or the knife that had deprived Morten Wendel of his life.

He wiped the disc with the dust brush that had come with the record player, placed it on the platter and lifted the stylus arm into place. The turntable began to revolve automatically. To begin with, there was a faint crackle, and then the first notes drifted out into the room.

'It's Frank Sinatra,' Ingrid said enthusiastically as they heard the charismatic voice, singing about the warm summer wind.

Wisting tentatively held out his hand. She took it and moved closer to him. They swayed slowly across the floor, as if they had danced together for years.

'Do you know what I like best of all about sailing?' She spoke softly in his ear.

He waited for her to tell him.

'That moment when the sail fills with the strong breeze and sweeps you away,' she said. 'Sometimes that's all you need, to go wherever the wind takes you.'

The stylus hit a scratch on the record. The music stuck, stuttering on the same groove.

Ingrid Sandell pulled Wisting into an embrace and whispered: 'I think a fair wind brought me here.'